SHIELD
OF THE
KING

ELOWEN BOOK 1

Yorkshire Publishing
TULSA

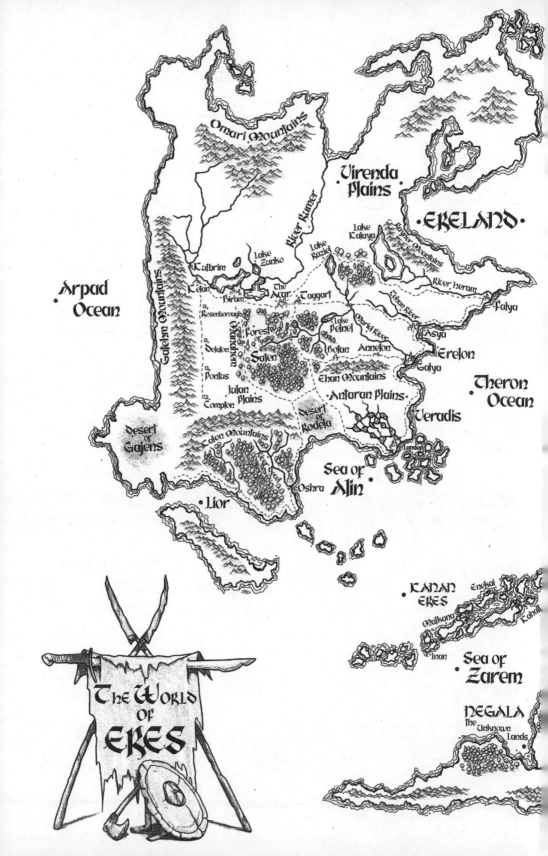

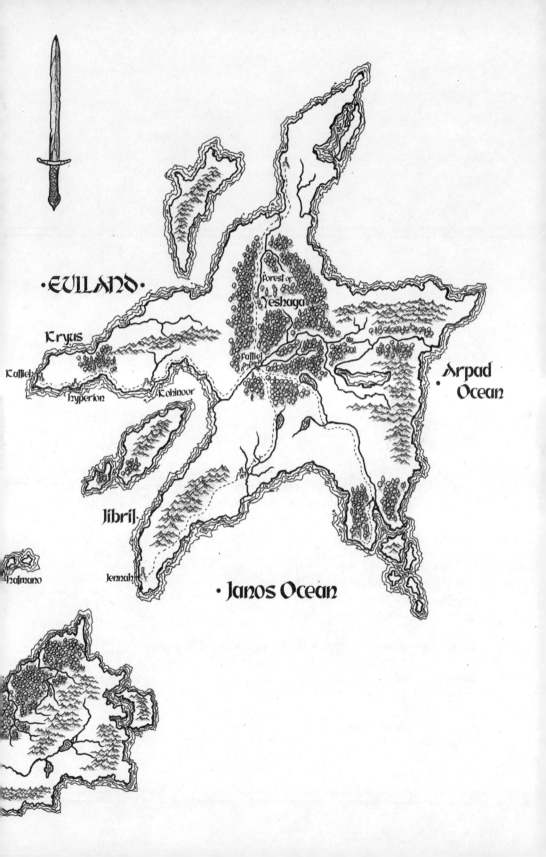

ISBN: 978-1-957262-74-1
Shield of the King

MB Mooney
authormbmooney@gmail.com / 678-943-3804
www.mbmooney.com
Agent: Cyle Young – cyle@cyleyoung.com

For permission requests, write to the publisher at the address below.

Yorkshire Publishing
1425 E 41st Pl
Tulsa, OK 74105
www.YorkshirePublishing.com
918.394.2665

Printed in Canada

Shield

OF THE

King

ELOWEN BOOK 1

MB Mooney

To all the misfit heroes of the world – past, present, and future.

CHAPTER

My father glared down at me while we walked along the street underneath the hot afternoon sun.

I swallowed. "I'm sorry, Father. But the Keeper was wrong."

Father strode with such ferocity, and I struggled to keep up with him, even with his slight limp. The scars on the dark skin of his face deepened when he frowned. "He expelled you from the school, Elowen."

I lowered my head. When he pulled me close to him on the bench at home and told stories of the old wars with elven and dwarven kingdoms, he called me Wen. He used my full name when angry. "I know. But he didn't quote it right."

The grunt transformed into a growl. "You aren't allowed to speak during the lessons. You know this."

They didn't allow elfdaughters to speak. Only the sons. I nodded, my fists clenching.

"The Keeper allowed you in the class as a favor to me," Father continued. "He risked his reputation by including you at all. This was the only way for you to get an education."

"What kind of education keeps half the population silent?"

He shook his head. "We can't change everything all at once. He allowed you in his classes. It was a great opportunity."

"What opportunity?" I said. "I would learn the parchments, but I can read those on my own. Complicated mathematics and science were interesting, even though I had to hear him preach about how everyone but the perfect is cursed. But where would I go from there? Would they let me in the university in Jennah? Even your reputation wouldn't get me that far."

Father's brow furrowed. An average height for an elf, he had started showing signs of the age the last few years, of the epochs and battles he fought over the centuries. Being a retired General of the Desert Corps, he had many friends and admirers in our small town near the coast. But he knew I was right. His influence and favor could only reach so far.

If I had been a son, it would have all been different. He never said that. Never once showed an ounce of regret or treated me as less. But the world around us did.

We hurried along past the shops and canopy-covered booths. The scent of a flat, sweet biscuit wafted over and called to me, but Father wouldn't slow down, not in a mood like this. I had to straighten my head covering when it flapped in the dusty wind.

He waved his hands to the sky like a prayer to the Onamaker. "You don't want me to approach any of the males in town for court-ship, don't want the life of a housewife. I don't know what else you want."

It wasn't that I lacked interest in marriage. However, the idea of settling down, taking care of a house, and popping out little elves for a husband made me feel trapped.

My voice was low, but he heard me. "You know what I want."

He rolled his eyes.

I spent my life with a father who told stories of faraway lands, armies, and battles. I never knew my mother, so my days were with a hero of our kingdom, Jibryl. All the legends shaped my imagination.

"You can't be in the Desert Corps, Elowen." His voice was a low rumble. "I've told you a thousand times. They will not allow it."

"I know." And he had. Thousands of times wasn't even an exaggeration. It had probably been a million. We didn't need to have the conversation again. Even though he trained me in weapons and I was as good as I could ever be with a sword, they would never allow it.

Father skidded to a halt and turned on me. "Hold on. Did you get kicked out on purpose?"

I blinked and stumbled before recovering. "No. I didn't."

Those dark eyes pierced me, and I forced my back straight under his stare. "You swear?"

"By the Great Ona, yes. I just can't stand when the Keeper rails against the cursed. And misquotes the parchments. Makes me angry. Don't you want to know what he said?"

His jaw tightened. "I don't."

The sigh he released sounded tired, filled with the years behind him. "Perhaps this is my fault," he said. "If I had married when you were young, you wouldn't have been stuck with an old soldier and his rambling. Maybe you would have known another life. Maybe …"

He never spoke of my mother. I always suspected he never remarried because of his love for her. But he wouldn't talk about it. She had died the day I was born.

Grabbing his arm, I stepped closer. "Don't say that. It's not your fault. It's mine. You should have had a daughter who wanted to do all the elfdaughter things, someone who could be satisfied with all that."

"It is not wrong to want more," he said. "But an education would have afforded you the opportunity to go work for an elf of business. That's not unheard of for a capable elfess. But now that you've been expelled, I don't know."

"You're right." My fists clenched again at the thought of another limited path. "I'm sorry."

"Perhaps he'll allow you back next season," Father mused. "If I talk to him."

I suppressed a cringe. I didn't want to deal with that class or that Keeper again. But if it was the best I could do, I should endure it. "Thank you."

"It may be too late. But we will try next season." Without another word, he faced toward home again and began walking. I straightened my shoulders and rushed to catch up to him.

After a few moments of silence, he glanced over at me. "How did the Keeper misquote the parchments?"

I turned away while I grinned, then faced him to provide an answer. "He said that the Onamaker didn't really praise Selina the Brave for the battle of the Eastern Front. Even though she saved the elves of Jibryl singlehandedly, he said the original verb there didn't mean *praise* but *to mock*. He said the Onamaker mocked Selina!"

Father's brow creased. "He said that the Onamaker mocked her? She's one of our greatest saints."

"Exactly. What was I supposed to do? She was a mighty warrior, an elf of faith, and he was tearing her down in front of everyone just because she wasn't an elfson. She's one of my heroes. I'm sorry. I couldn't keep quiet."

His gait evened out. Between the afternoon sun and the long walk, beads of sweat gathered underneath my long robe.

"Remember the lesson on control," he said.

The corners of my mouth turned down. "Control is the difference between victory and defeat."

"The Keeper was wrong, but you cannot allow others and their actions to control you. You must rule your own heart and mind. Otherwise, they will win."

"Yes, Father."

"This is important." One side of his mouth twitched in a smirk. "Because the world is full of stupid, wrong people."

I breathed a chuckle. "I will remember."

"That's what you said last time, Wen."

My grin turned into a smile. He called me Wen. Everything would be okay now.

CHAPTER

W e approached our property at the far edge of town, and the two sahala battle lizards lumbered to the wooden fence of the pen behind the house, lifting their long snouts in the air. I separated from Father and ran toward them. Sliding to a halt at the fence, I reached out and brushed my knuckles along Laila's leathery jaw. She made a rumbling, cooing sound in her throat. Zaran, the grumpier of the two, growled.

I turned to Zaran. "Don't be jealous, you old war beast." I stretched out my left hand to stroke his long neck. Both lizards stood almost a mitre over me.

Zaran opened his jaw to show long, pointed teeth, pawed at the ground with his thick hind leg, and clawed at me with the much shorter front leg, a show of affection. Trained battle lizards could show restraint, but if they sniffed any threat when protecting their lair, the sahala would attack. Our property was their lair.

We didn't get many visitors.

Father had passed me and almost entered the house. "Wen, come help with dinner."

With a final pat on the neck of each lizard, I gave them kissing noises and ran inside.

Father already had the flat, round bread out of the pantry and placed two on the counter. "Let's have snake tonight."

Opening the cabinets, I took out two bundles of snake jerky, breathing in the spicy aroma, and I turned, unwrapping and spreading them evenly on the bread.

"One time," Father said, "I led a corps detachment to the east of the mountains." He liked to tell stories during dinner or really any time we did chores together. Father grabbed a jar of delan sauce and poured the chunky mixture of flour paste and tomberries over the top of the bread and jerky.

"Uh-huh." I unsealed another glass jar of white bosaur cheese and sprinkled it over the top.

"There were only thirty of us," Father continued. "We came across a Kryan division that had made its way into our territory. A raiding party."

Father lit the coals on the stove. We each took one of the dressed flatbreads and transferred them to the iron grill over the coals.

"A hundred of them. They outnumbered us." He watched the bread warming, the cheese melting on the stove. "But we couldn't allow them to continue raiding."

The heat of the stove filled the room, and I was thankful for the large open windows that gave a breeze across the kitchen.

Kryan divisions were well disciplined and organized, adding to their threat. "What did you do?" I asked. Father often required an encouraging question, or the story would drag out.

"We tracked them, difficult to hide in the open ground of dunes and brush, and we waited until we found the right spot, a narrow ravine. I separated my elves – ten ahead and twenty behind."

The delan bread was done. We used wooden spatulas to remove them from the stove.

"We waited until they emerged from the ravine," Father said, "and allowed them to see the ten ahead of them."

"You distracted while the others came from behind."

"Yes." Father waved his calloused hands over his delan to cool it. "Their attention was on us. Confident in their numbers. They were soon surrounded. Their Captain hesitated. I killed him first."

I blew on my delan bread. "Leaderless."

He nodded. "With their leader gone, it took them time to regroup and adjust to counter our attack."

"That hesitation nullified their advantage."

"It did," Father said.

"And you killed them all."

Father hesitated. "We did. Confusion is a powerful weapon, more powerful than a sword or bow. Even outnumbered, remaining focused while others freeze in battle determines the destiny of the day."

He often used ancient sayings like he had heard them a thousand times. And said them a thousand more.

The meal cooled enough to begin eating at the counter in the kitchen. The walls and rooms of the house lacked any real decoration or character. From his minimalist military days, Father liked to keep his life simple and clean. His only reminders of the old life were the weapons in the sparring room out back, many of them souvenirs from the countless battles.

Nothing of my mother. Nothing to remind him. Also, nothing to tell me of her.

I knew the old stories meant something to him, and I know he used them to teach me lessons. I wasn't that light in the head. But it seemed cruel to use stories of a life I would never have.

I frowned. "Like today. I didn't stay focused."

"You're learning more than you think, Wen." He grinned. "Come. Let's clean up and get to the forms."

Finishing my delan within three large bites, I wiped down the counter, placed the jars back in the cabinet, and met him in the sparring room.

CHAPTER

No one knew he taught me. A daughter seeking an education turned enough heads in our town, the town of Rami. It was about a two-day ride north of the capital, Jennah. Teaching weapons to an elfess would be even more controversial. No law existed to keep him from doing it, but sword skill was the realm of elfmen. Unheard of for someone like me.

However, it was the only place I felt truly alive. All my frustrations and fears left me when I found the calm of the discipline, the freedom and strength of my body in the mastery of martial arts from long before me, an art that would exist long after I was gone.

The forms Father taught me were creative and structured all at once. Where others may only see a way to inflict damage, pain, or death, it was truly an art. In those hours every night, my mind, body, and soul aligned completely.

I could imagine I was Selina the Brave, fighting to save the kingdom from the horde of enemies arrayed before her.

While she battled and slew thousands of barbarian elves, I had to fight my father. It might have been better to trade with Selina.

After dinner, we entered the room twenty mitres square and bare except for the weapons and banners hung on the wall. Banners from a dozen different detachments over the centuries in the Desert Corps. Every weapon one could imagine.

Father lit the lamps, the setting sun streaming orange through the high windows.

I always began with the sword. Mine hung hear the door, and I lifted it from the wall. I moved to the center of the room.

My father walked with a stiff gait to the far end of the room, his limp more pronounced. His hand hesitated and hovered over the hilt of his sword, Qatal, featured among the weapons. I raised a brow. He hadn't touched it in years. A golden amulet – the championship prize of the Kaila Tournament—hung across the pommel.

He grunted, reached beyond Qatal, and chose a long spear. Twirling it in his hands, he rolled his shoulders and shook each leg.

Then he pounced.

In one motion, he vaulted and turned, the spear coming down toward my head with a whistle through the air. The blade of the spear flashed when it caught a weak ray of sun.

I was ready. He began this way every time. No warning. He had taught me that warnings were rare or nonexistent in battle.

I blocked high, and my slash met empty space since he could attack at a distance with the spear. He whipped it back and forth at blinding speed, and I deflected each strike so fast it went beyond conscious thought, only pure reaction.

Redirecting the spear to my left, I spun and shot forward to close the distance, but he swung the blunt end of the weapon toward my head, which I ducked. I fell to my knees. Father stepped further away – not a retreat, an adjustment for a better angle – and stabbed, ripping a tear in my robe near the ribs. I grunted and swung down on the spear, connecting with a clang, allowing me time to take a step back.

He struck again. I met the shaft with my blade. I slid forward and grabbed the wood of the spear, and pulled him toward me, hoping to catch him off balance. He leaned forward. I slashed at him with the sword.

Changing direction, my father slipped back to the side, at the same time wrenching the staff in my hand. I had to let go to stay on my feet, and he used that opportunity to swipe the staff in a wide arc at my calves.

Upending me.

My feet shot forward, my body hanging helpless in the air for a moment before hitting the hard, stone floor on my arse and back. The breath left me in a whoosh. When I caught oxygen again, I gasped and cursed. The point of his spear rested on my neck.

"Good try." Father wasn't even breathing hard. "Remember to think through your attacks. Always be two or three moves ahead. They could be used against you. Reversed." He removed the blade from my neck.

I grunted. "What if they're thinking four or five moves ahead?"

"Then you lose." He turned and walked back to the far end of the room, placing the spear back on the wall.

I rose to a sitting position. "And how often will I fight someone as good as the Champion of Kaila?"

He didn't turn to look at me. "Hopefully never."

"Why never?"

He scanned the weapons along the wall. "You are skilled. However, that doesn't always determine the winner. Battles are often games of chance as much skill."

"Even a novice can beat a master on the right day," I spoke the lesson he often taught.

"If the Onamaker wills it."

I got to my feet and stretched my back. "And yet, after all these years, I've never bested you."

"Neither luck nor the Onamaker has given you the day." Father smiled. "Yet."

Growls and snarls met our ears from outside, the war lizards in the pen were reacting to a person approaching the house. My head cocked to the side and turned toward the window. Father's head did not move, but he heard it, too. Hooves clopped on the rocky sand on the path to our home.

Father nodded to my sword. "Let us meet our visitor. Get your covering."

I sighed, put my sword back on the wall near the door, and walked out of the back room into the house. My father followed and went to the front door while I stopped to pick up my shawl.

Father stood at the open door when I arrived. I waited behind him.

The rider halted his horse two paces from Father, who stepped forward and grabbed the reins. The animal flashed wide eyes at the snarling sahala war lizards.

The elf on the horse sat tall and regal, the patch on his tunic – a hand with a flame in the palm – signifying his position as a Royal Courier. The sun had set only moments before, the sky a gray haze behind the Courier.

"Good evening," the elf said. "May the Ona bless you."

"And to you." Father nodded at the patch. "How may we be of service to you?"

"Not to me," the Courier said. "To the King."

Father didn't speak for a moment. I knew that quiet pause, one of silent anger, and my eyes narrowed. "How may I serve the King?" Father's voice was low and dangerous.

The Courier shifted in his saddle. "I am searching for General Natanel, son of Wahid, Champion of Kaila." The Courier hesitated and bowed. "The Shield of the King."

I made an embarrassing gurgle sound in my throat. "What? Shield of the King?"

Father glared at me. My mouth snapped shut.

The Courier threw a reproving frown at my father like it was his fault I wouldn't keep quiet.

Shield of the King. Elven warriors who protected the Royal Family, carried out the King's most important assignments and answered directly to him. The Shields were legendary, nigh invincible, almost immortal in the myths. When children in Jibryl pretended to be god-like, they imagined they were a Shield of the King, vanquishing monsters and villains for our people.

Even I had done it as a child.

I had been living with one my whole life and never knew.

"I am Natanel, son of Wahid," Father said.

The Courier sat straight. "It is an honor, sir. I am Baruch, son of Mendel. King Yacob, First Lord of Jibryl, Light of Jennah, requires your presence at the Kaila Festival." The Courier pulled a rolled-up parchment from his coat and handed it to Father.

Father's brow creased. He took the letter and unrolled it. "He wants me to compete again?" Father had retired from the Kaila Competition decades before I was born.

"No," the Courier said. "He calls you as his trusted friend and needs your service as Shield."

Lifting the parchment to get a better view in the waning light, he read the missive and studied the bottom. I glanced over his shoulder. There it was. The King's Royal Seal.

"I retired from service years ago," Father said. "And he has a Shield."

"He calls for you, specifically," the Courier said.

Father groaned. "The Kaila is in less than a ninedays."

"Yes," Baruch the Courier said. "And we leave for Jennah as soon as you are able."

Like a statue at our door, Father stood motionless. The ticks of time passed. He took a deep breath and nodded. "The hour is late. You are welcome to stay with us tonight, and we will leave in the morning."

While the horse stamped and snorted, the Courier's eyes glanced back at the sahala. The war lizards no longer snarled, but their quiet, piercing stare promised even more threat.

"I have a room at the hostel in town," Baruch said. "Please meet me there when you are ready in the morning."

"That is well," Father said.

Baruch bowed once more. "It is an honor to meet you, General." An emphasis on the title.

"And you," Father said. "May the Ona give you rest."

The Courier swung the horse around and left without acknowledging me at all.

The hoofbeats grew faint, the Courier out of earshot, when I jumped to Father's side and caught his eye. "Why did you never tell me?"

He blinked from staring at the dark, distant figure of the Courier and horse, like from a dream. Then his dark eyes met mine. "It is not the way." He spun on his heel and went back into the house.

"Not the way?" I followed him. "You tell me everything else. Every battle, every campaign, all the stories."

Reaching the kitchen, he stopped and faced me. He straightened, and in the dim lamplight of the kitchen, he transformed. Not my father. A killer. A warrior. Cold and hard. "Not all of them."

My chest heaved with a short breath, but I pressed him. "It is also not the way to educate your daughter. Definitely not the way to teach her weapons and battle strategy. Why is this different?"

Father sighed and turned away from me, his voice so low I strained to hear him. "Every Shield is sworn to secrecy. About what we do. What I did." His shoulders slumped. "As an officer in the

Corps, I was a hero, fighting against enemies I could see. I was an elf of honor, my opponents standing before me. Even as champion of Kaila, I worked hard, and earned that. But as a Shield … I did things that needed to be done. Dark things. To protect the King, yes, but things no one could know. Not even you."

So much pain in his voice. I took another step toward him. "Why does he want you now? The King?"

His lips became a line. "I do not know."

Not to compete, Baruch had said. "He called you as Shield. That means something for the King, something personal."

"The Kaila is a time when elves, humans, and dwarves from across Eres come to celebrate and compete in peace. There are also opportunities for those who seek to do evil. The peace of the festival is more fragile than most realize."

"But why you? He has another Shield now. You've retired. You …" My mouth hung open for a moment. "You said sworn to secrecy. This is about a mission from your past, information only you would know. Something about the goblain rebellion?"

Father gazed out of the kitchen window, open to the night. "It doesn't matter. The King calls. I will answer. I leave in the morning."

"You mean *we* leave in the morning."

His brow furrowed. "No. You will stay here."

"Stay here? No. I'm going with you."

Rubbing his jaw, he scanned the kitchen. "I'll leave you some coin for supplies while I'm gone. Enough for two or three months … maybe more."

"You're not listening. I'm going with you."

He stood tall. "You can't come with me. This is for me alone."

I paused, searching his face, the strength within it, and the pain behind his stare. "Why did you train me? Why teach me the sword and spear?"

"For a day like today. To protect yourself if one day I had to return to that old life."

Waving my arms, I acted like I searched the room around us. "Protect myself? From who? We live in the middle of nowhere."

"There is evil in the world. People willing to kill and do whatever they can to get or maintain power. As Shield of the King, I made enemies. Many of them. I retired here, far away from that world, so you would never have to know it. I trained you so you could survive without me."

"Without you?" My voice cracked. "I have nothing here. The elf-sons don't want to court a strong wife. The elfdaughters want to talk about cooking, keeping house, and having a family one day. I just got expelled from school." I moved within a pace of him, breathing in his scent of leather and worn cloth, studying the handful of scars on his face. "You're all I have."

"Wen ..." he said.

"Can you promise me that you'll return?" I said. "Will you swear it?"

His jaw tightened. He said nothing.

"You taught me to fight, not to run, not to hide," I said. "And I'm glad that you did. How can I stay here when all I have goes into danger? Maybe to never return. Would you allow me to go into danger alone?"

"I would not."

I sniffed. "Then don't ask me to. Please. I know you trained me to keep me safe. What if the Onamaker had other plans? What if you trained me so I could save your life? Protect you? Fight with you?"

His jaw tightened. "I did not train you for this. Not for what is ahead, what I may have to do. There will be enemies on every side."

"Then train me for that. Sounds like you will need someone you can trust."

"This is not the life I wanted for you."

I took a deep breath. "Will you refuse the King? Stay here with me?"

"I can't."

"Then I'm coming with you."

"You don't know what you ask. I can't allow it."

I set my shoulders. "I'm not asking. You will have to break my legs and arms to keep me here. Even then, I will try and follow."

His face fell. His eyes brimmed with tears. "Don't do this. I beg you. I know you dream of being a warrior like the legends, but this will not end the way you think. When this is all done, there will be no heroes, nothing of honor, only sorrow and heartache. No one will sing songs about you or tell your story. The world will not change. It will continue to be evil and corrupt, shrouded in darkness. But you will change. You will never be the same. There will be a stain on your soul no laundry could ever remove. Please. I don't know if I can endure that."

I couldn't speak for a few ticks. My face blank, I stared at him for that space of time. I shook my head and then leaned in closer, touching my forehead to his. I put my arms around his neck.

"Listen to me," I whispered. "Even if you went into the Four Hells, I would go with you. I wouldn't let you go alone."

We stood like that in the dim light for a long time. Finally, he said, "Very well."

My father pulled away enough to place his lips on my forehead. Then he removed himself from my embrace. There were wet streaks down his dark cheeks. He turned and went further into the house without another word to me.

Alone in the dim kitchen, I stared into the empty space where he had just stood.

The Onamaker had given me the day where I bested the master, my father. Why didn't it feel like a victory?

I was going with him, but it was like he had just told me goodbye.

CHAPTER

4

Father woke me before the sunrise. "Gather the weapons."
Rolling over, I caught his blurry shadow. It took all my effort
to speak coherently. "What weapons?"

"All that you can carry." His dark figure disappeared.

I was surprised he woke me at all. I laid awake for an hour the
night before, thinking he might leave without me and make me race
to catch up with him. But he didn't.

Lighting my lamp, I dressed for travel in baggy trousers under a
long tunic. Leather boots covered my feet, and I chose a light wrap
for my head covering. I made my way to the sparring room with
some extra underclothes stuffed in a bag over my shoulder.

The first hint of light crept through the window and gave the
space a warm, hazy glow. My father wore his own tunic and trousers
with leather boots and belt, and he stood at the far end near the
ancient sword.

Qatal. Made by the mystical elves of Faltiel, the name meant
death-bringer. He lifted the golden amulet and set it aside on a hook
on the wall. His breathing was heavy and sad. He touched the sword

lightly on the pommel. In one swift motion, he tied the sword and scabbard to his waist, like it was a part of him and always had been.

"Take your sword, the bow, the quiver, all the arrows, two spears, two shields, the daggers, knives, and both short swords." He spoke with his back to me.

"The daggers *and* the knives?" Ten battle daggers. Thirty throwing knives.

"Yes."

I scoffed. "What are you carrying?"

He gazed down at the sword on his hip. "Too much already." Father glanced over his shoulder. "Or you can always stay here." He turned and strode past me into the house.

So it's going to be like that. I faced the wall of weapons, my eye hesitating on the Kaila amulet. "Well, break me."

Ten minutes later, I lumbered out the back door, bent over from the weight of the daggers, knives, the quiver of arrows, and more. I dragged both spears behind me.

Father had saddled Laila. He left me Zaran, who actually sneered at me when I picked up a saddle and approached him.

"Shut it," I snapped, and he hissed. Zaran kicked at me twice while I saddled him, making it near impossible with the load of weapons hanging off of me. But I got the saddle on, and he growled when I lashed the weapons to it. I climbed up on Zaran's back. Zaran shifted beneath me, settling in with my weight.

Father sat atop Laila by the road. The cloth bag on his shoulder smelled of jerky and bread. Another bag behind him held his personal items. "You ready?"

I glared. "Are you?"

The war lizards always caused a commotion in town, the rare times we took them. The baker set out his pastries but froze for a tick when he caught sight of them. Other merchants moved behind their wares like a stack of hats would protect them from the claws and jaws of a sahala.

Despite the legendary tales of their acts in battle, the war lizards were better trained than horses. Due to their potential for violence, they had to be. Corps trainers had mastered the process, becoming the best in the world of Eres. The sahala walking and snarling through town were safer than the horses tethered at the hostel.

Father never announced those facts. He found it amusing to allow people to have their fear. He didn't grin today.

Baruch stood next to his horse, tightening leather pouches on his saddle. His uniform was clean and wrinkle-free. His eyes narrowed at me. "The King didn't request your daughter."

"She has a name," Father said. "Elowen. She is my weapons-master."

It took effort to keep my jaw from dropping like the Courier's did. Weapons-masters were usually old elves past their prime, in the last of age. They served officers in the Corps. Or a competitor at the competition during the Kaila Festival.

The Courier recovered and laughed. "She's an elfdaughter. And too young."

"And yet I chose her," Father said. "I trained her myself from the day she could walk. She knows more than any young officer in the Corps."

Baruch shook his head. "You're not coming to Jennah to compete. I thought I made that clear."

"Whether I compete or not is yet to be seen," Father said. "I am well known at the capital and will return as General of the Corps. And Elowen will come with us as my weapons-master. I trust no one more."

Trust no one more? Not going to cry. Nope. Keep it together. I shut my mouth and held my breath.

"I read the King's missive," Baruch said. "It is for you alone."

Father bared his teeth and turned the war lizard under him to face the Courier. "You may try to stop me if you wish. Or try to stop Elowen. I don't think you'll enjoy either of those options."

Laila growled. I smirked.

"The King was specific." The Courier heaved himself onto his horse.

"I will deal with the King," Father said.

The way he said it, I would not have wanted to be the King.

We left the town and rode in silence, the heat of the day bearing down on us hours later. We neared the next village after midday. Baruch had ridden ahead, just out of hearing.

I spoke under my breath. "A weapons-master? Seriously? While I appreciate the confidence, you're really going to make me spend time with old elves that tell longer stories than you?"

His face remained blank. "This gives you more freedom. Simple attendants or elfdaughters cannot even enter the inner palace. A weapons-master must be allowed everywhere I go."

"Ah, a loophole."

"Watching our own gruts," he corrected. "Those old elves with stories know more than anyone in the kingdom. Keep your ears up."

"Then a game."

"At court, they play this like a game. But it isn't one we can win."

I frowned. "What does that mean?"

"You've been to the city before but not at court." His voice was a low rumble. "In competition or battle, the enemies are clear. In politics, they act as friends, but everyone is an enemy. There are no friends, no honor. Remember that, and we may survive."

Ten daggers and thirty throwing knives.

"Survive?" The second time he'd used that word.

"The King would not have called me unless ..." His jaw clenched. "We cannot win, but we might make it out alive. This is your first lesson at court – remember that no matter what you may think or what people say, you can't trust anyone."

No one? The scars on his face deepened. He rode ahead to join the Courier.

Within the hour, we passed the village. Baruch slowed his horse and glanced up with a squint at the afternoon sun. "We can bed here for the night."

Father didn't slow his lizard. "We can make another five kilomitres before dusk. Maybe more."

"But this village has a hostel," the Courier said.

"You are welcome to stay there." Father's voice rose to cover the increasing distance to Baruch. "I have slept in the sands before. We will be fine."

Riding next to my father, I peeked back at Baruch, who looked from us to the village nestled near a large pond with trees and grasses amongst the buildings and houses. The land ahead appeared dry with sparse vegetation.

"I already paid for the night on my way through the first time," Baruch called. "And a room for you."

Father kept riding without a word.

I leaned closer to him, my voice low. "I have to admit, a bed sounds nice. If it's an option."

"We will be in palaces soon enough," he said.

Hooves pounded on the road behind us, and the Courier reached us. His face locked in a frown, and sweat poured from his brow and hair. He kept his gaze forward and shifted in the saddle like his underclothes bunched in his arse.

We made it almost ten kilomitres before Father pointed to a high hill to stop for the night. Tying the horse to shrubs at the bottom, we only took the bridles off Laila and Zaran, letting them roam or hunt. The sahala would return before sunrise, maybe with some leftover dirtdog or sanddragon for us for breakfast. They could be nice like that. Sometimes.

Father took dry branches from the shrubs and cut thicker branches from a small tree nearby with his sword. I hefted the weapons and our bags – his and mine – up the hill, sliding in the sand. I dropped a spear twice, had to regather the weapons, and made it up the hill by the time Father returned with wood for a fire.

Baruch waited for me at the top, and his look of derision was constant. "Some weapons-master."

I set our things to the side while Father built a fire and had it cackling by sunset. We set in for the night. An hour passed, and the air grew cool. I pulled a cloak over my head as the wind started to pick up, and I shuffled closer to the fire.

Father and I had a dinner of flat biscuits, jerky, and water from our skins. Baruch stared at us with only his water skin, pointedly taking a sip and exhaling.

I rolled my eyes, and Father took a biscuit and two strips of jerky and tossed them across the fire. The Courier bobbled them, catching the biscuit but dropping the jerky into the sand. He grabbed the strips, hesitated, shook them, and ate. "Thank you."

Father nodded.

On the rare occasion we went to Jennah, or anywhere, Father was more comfortable sleeping on open plains or dunes, outside underneath the stars. Not happy but more at ease.

"Baruch," Father said. "You are the son of Mendel?"

The Courier swallowed. "Yes."

"What family?"

Baruch sat up straight. "The Calnari."

"Ah," Father said. "From the northern lands. I know them. Your father, Mendel, fought in the Corps as a captain, I believe."

Baruch chewed on a biscuit. "Yes, a captain."

"He served in the Nine-Year War, in the 22nd division."

"I believe so," Baruch said. "Although long before I was born."

"A long time ago." Father nodded. "I drank Tamba tea with him many a cold night in the northern forests. He was strong enough to wrestle a hornoth. How is Mendel? Last I heard, he retired. Enjoying it?"

"Definitely," Baruch said.

"Where is his home now?"

Baruch paused. "He lives in an apartment in Seniah. A nice place."

"Seniah is a good town. Far from the capital. Sounds nice." Father took another bite of jerky.

We ate in silence for another few moments.

Father finished the last of his food and clapped his hands free of any crumbs. Then he said to Baruch, "How many of your friends were waiting for us back at the hostel in the village?"

Baruch coughed and covered his mouth. "I'm sorry, sir. What?"

My eyes widened. *What?*

"You heard me," Father said. "What were their orders if we didn't show up in the village?"

The Courier stammered. "Orders?"

"Their orders." Father sat still and peered over the fire. "If we didn't show up at the hostel, were they to follow? Ambush us on the road? Wait until the next town?"

I scanned the dark horizon. No shadows moved. My hand drifted to the sword at my side and found the hilt.

Baruch's eyes flitted from me back to Father, whose face was unreadable. "Ambush? What are you talking about?"

"You are not Baruch, son of Mendel."

"Of course I am. I am the Royal Courier. I gave you the missive. You saw the King's Seal."

"That is the King's Seal and likely his missive. But you aren't the son of Mendel." Father's eyes narrowed. "Mendel served as a *Major* in the Corps, and he never fought in the Nine-Year War. He fought in the 3rd Kryan. And the 4th."

Baruch froze for a moment. "Yes, yes. I got the details wrong. As I said, it was all before I was born."

"The son of Mendel would not get the details wrong. He would be proud of his father's service. It would be the reason he had a superior position as Royal Courier. Mendel of the Calnari also died in the second battle of the 4th Kryan Conflict." Father let some time pass, Baruch and I motionless, before continuing. "I don't know who lives in that apartment in Seniah, but it is not Mendel of the Calnari."

Baruch's confused face melted to a frown.

My whole body tensed, my hand gripping the hilt of the sword next to me. I breathed in the cold air through my nose, ready for anything.

Father said, "Do you remember lesson one, Wen?"

I licked my lips. "Trust no one."

He nodded. "This is lesson two." Father nodded toward Baruch or whoever he was. "That is the Royal Courier's uniform, but that is not the elf sent by the King. The Courier's uniform is custom-tailored. His presence and bearing reflect upon the Sovereign. That uniform doesn't fully fit our assassin friend here, which is why he's been shifting and squirming most of the trip."

Father was right. The elf's shoulders were too broad for the tunic. His waist too narrow for the belt. The trousers bunched at the bottom, made for a taller elf. The not-Baruch had been acting like a sanddraggon lived in his pants.

The elf hadn't flinched at the term assassin, either.

"That began my suspicion," Father said. "And since he knew little to nothing of the heroic elf that was supposedly his father, he has confirmed it."

The elf assassin's brow lowered, and he glared.

"I ask you again," Father said. "How many should we expect, and what were their orders if we didn't arrive at the hostel?"

The wind blew cold across my face and stirred up sand along the top of the hill.

Not-Baruch squared his shoulders and blinked in the wind. "You will never reach Jennah. The Knights of Truth will have their revenge on Natanel, the Shield of the King, and the Tyrant King will fall soon after. You cannot stop ..."

In a tick, Father leaped to his feet, and his sword flashed in the light of the moon and then the fire. I only registered the slash of the blade after it ended, Qatal back at his side in less than a heartbeat.

The assassin's head lolled to one side, then fell off the neck, blood spurting from the wound, and the rest of the body followed. I gasped – which was a mistake, blood landing on my cheek could have been my mouth – and I scrambled backward. I was on my feet with my sword out in a front guard, not near as smooth as Father, sand flying everywhere.

"Crit of the gods!" I said.

Father frowned down at the dead body.

Wiping the blood from my cheek, I looked down and saw a little more on my tunic. "I can't believe you knew Mendel. What are the odds?"

"I didn't know Mendel." His voice was so calm. He took a rag and wiped Qatal.

"Um, what? How did you know he was lying?"

"As I said, I knew his uniform was not his own," Father said. "Could have been a number of reasons, but I doubted Yacob would send a shabby courier to me. Since I have long learned lesson one, I asked questions. There are times one lie will uncover others. Lies are like magnets to one another."

"Lesson two?" I said.

He nodded. "I also suspected that the King called me regarding the rebels among the Ruchali people. I have had … experience with them."

The Knights of Truth will have their revenge against Natanel, the Shield of the King …

"You mean the goblain?" I used the ethnic slur for the rebels of the Ruchali.

"They are zealots, and zealots are always ready to spout their beliefs unless they are well-trained," Father said. "This one was not well-trained."

Feint. Distraction. Strike. Just like he taught me in the sparring room, only now with words.

I had never seen a dead body before, and it transfixed me. Not horrified, although the sight was gruesome enough. As someone who had trained with weapons and ways to kill, the reality of death sobered and fascinated me. The finality. How quickly life could turn to death, from one tick to the next.

"You just killed him," I said. "You didn't wait to see if he would give more information."

"Once zealots begin their preaching, there is no more conversation. And zealots take time and torture to give more information. Time we don't have. Lesson three, I guess."

"But how …" I swallowed. Torture? "Where is the real Baruch?"

"Dead, I'm sure," Father said. "My guess is goblain waylaid Baruch on his way out of the palace or Jennah. He then discovered my name in the missive and developed a plan. Unless the King has a spy in his Royal Trust." He rubbed his jaw. "That might be why he called me. If he knows."

I had heard of the rebellion. Not an official war with armies but an underground movement of the Ruchali, the northern elves who questioned the royal authority in Jibryl. I had never heard them called Knights of Truth, though. Only the goblain.

"Spies in the Trust?" I said. "Assassins? Rebels? What in the Four Hells is going on?"

"I don't know." Father lifted his sword. "But get ready. Here they come."

CHAPTER

ere they come?
"Who?" I crouched low and surveyed the darkness and shadows.

Now some of the shadows moved. Several. Father heard or saw them before I did. The assassin's friends. More goblain.

"Get behind me," was his answer. "Back to back." He lifted a spear in his hand. "You are better with the shield."

"Yeah, yeah," I mumbled, leaning down and grabbing a shield, the round one with a hornoth painted on the front, a fierce pachyderm with a trunk, tusks, and curved horns on its thick forehead. I turned to stand behind my father, facing the other way, the fire to my left.

This is why he wanted the high ground. But who am I kidding? He always wants the high ground.

My breathing quickened, and my whole body went rigid. I sucked air deep into my lungs and focused. Our survival depended on my strength and skill.

Survival. *We can't win, but we might make it out alive.*

Figures approached all around us. One flew at me to the right. I raised the shield to block, which almost knocked me down, so I crouched lower and stabbed through the middle of the shadow with my sword. The blade punctured cloth, skin, and slid easily into flesh.

The figure made a desperate, pained sound, but I had no time with two more figures on my left, jumping over the fire and yelling. They wore dark clothing, had hooded and covered faces, and carried short swords. I slashed through the closest, using the shield to block the other. A limb holding a sword, unattached to a body, hit the sand in front of me. I used the momentum of my blade to stab through the upper body of the second elf, killing him, pulling the blade out again, and ending the screams of the first while he held his stump.

"Elowen!" Father called. "Rotate left."

Turning, I shifted my feet in the sand and felt something pass millimeters from my head. In a split moment, I caught an image of my father, sword in his right and spear in his left, moving and slashing with blades. No figure from the dark came close.

I had sparred with Father but never saw him fight before. Not really. It was a thing of beauty. And death.

The tick passed, and I looked to the left and slammed the shield into the face of one elf, blocked another with the sword, and kicked back at the first, shattering his knee. I ducked and crossed arms, stabbing the goblain with the shattered knee through the chest and blocking the other with the shield.

The remaining elf swung with short, quick attacks, but he was too slow. Or I was too fast. I easily blocked with the shield and ended him with my blade at the first opening.

The fire blazed before me now, everything past it pitch black, and I cried out when two figures jumped out of the darkness. A third came from the right so fast all I could do was lift the shield and take the body blow.

He knocked me off balance. I staggered and blocked another strike from the left with my sword, but the first and second elves stood before the fire and attacked at once. I went small behind the shield to block a blade, but a kick struck my knee. I tried to recover but couldn't.

I went down. The last place I wanted to be. I didn't panic, but I wanted to.

Get up get up get up …

A sword slashed down at me, glowing yellow from the nearby flame. I grabbed his legs with my own and dumped him into the fire. He squealed and yelped, his clothes catching flame. I turned and blocked another with the shield, which drove me into the sand. The two elves above me were joined by another, ready to kill. I couldn't fend them off, not from this position …

Then a deafening snarl came, and a giant creature sailed over me and swept all three of them away. White teeth flashed. Elves screamed in horror, one silenced with slashing black claws, another's head ripped from his body by powerful jaws. The third elf screeched and tried to run, but that was a mistake.

Sahala are born to hunt, and it jumped more than five mitres to land on the elf's back and ripped him to shreds, black cloth and blood sailing into the air.

"Zaran," I whispered. The war lizard raised his head and looked at me; the flames reflected in his wild and feral eyes, his teeth red with blood.

His jaws snapped, and he went back to his meal.

I scrambled to my feet, dirt and sand flying around me.

"Elowen." My father's voice.

With wide eyes, I held the shield close to my chest and the sword out before me.

He took a step toward me. "Elowen."

I blinked at him.

He stood near me. "It's over."

I panted like I had run to Jennah and back, my head swerving back and forth. I lowered the weapons. "It ... it's over?"

"Yes." Father glanced at the bodies around me. "You did well. Let me check you." He leaned over and patted me down. "No wounds. You're okay."

I dropped to my knees with a wave of exhaustion. "There were so many. In the end, if not for Zaran ..." Why was my mouth so dry?

Father kneeled before me. "It's your first battle. I know you're tired, but we must move."

Tired? That didn't begin to describe it. I could fall asleep right here. Dead bodies stretched out before me. No longer fascinating. Now I knew horror. "I killed them. I ..."

"Stand up."

This was not like sparring at all. Not art. Not creative. Just death.

"Elowen. You must stand up."

A father's voice has a power like no other. Not pleading. Firm. I stood. And then vomited out the night's dinner into the sand. "Oh, Ona. I'm sorry, Father. I don't know what to do."

"I'm telling you what to do. Don't worry about throwing up. We've all done it."

"You're not."

He hesitated, not looking at me. "It is not my first battle. Now gather the weapons and put out the fire. We are moving."

"Moving?" It came out like a pitiful whine. I hated that sound. But the last thing I desired was to move.

"Further toward Jennah," he said. "There may be more close by or in the next village. We will ride through the wilderness, off the road. Make better time."

"More?"

"Possibly. Now gather the weapons."

The weapons. I could do that. I turned around to face the weapons but also the elves my father had killed. I killed a handful. Zaran three. There were far more on his side. A dozen? Hard to tell in the dark.

Laila prowled just out of sight.

I groaned. "So many. For us?"

"For me," he corrected. "They should have sent more."

I counted almost twenty, including the headless Courier-pretender. More than twenty for one elf?

Then I remembered the sight of him fighting and moving. Yeah, maybe they should have sent more.

Father moved some bodies down the hill, out of sight from the road. Then he jogged down the hill to release the not-Baruch's horse, which ran off into the night.

The sahala didn't chase it; they had plenty to occupy them. Zaran and Laila fed on dead elves for a few minutes. Then they stopped. Full? My stomach lurched again.

I gathered the weapons, wiping blood off of blades at Father's insistence, using some of not-Baruch's extra clothes from his bag. After adding our food, cloaks, and clothes to the pile, I whistled for Zaran, and he plodded over obediently. Was he docile now that he had hunted and eaten? I shook my head of the thoughts and lashed what we had to the saddle, and climbed up on his back. He settled.

Father sat astride Laila by then. "Follow me."

Zaran and I ran with Father across the dunes and through the underbrush. I kept in the saddle, though, for what may have been an hour or ten, I don't know. Most of my energy was focused on staying awake and upright.

We reached a stream with trees and grasses along the bank. Father brought us to a stop and climbed down. He helped me me unpack Zaran. He laid out a blanket and cloak. "Here. Sleep."

I was suddenly thirsty, and I took a few gulps from the water skin.

"Careful," Father said. "Not too much."

I set the water skin nearby and curled up on the blanket, pulling the cloak over me. My eyes were heavy when Father sat and rested against a tree. Qatal and a spear leaned next to him. He draped his cloak over his shoulders.

"Father?"

"Yes?"

I licked my lips. "You said you got sick after your first battle?"

"I did."

"What about the second battle?"

He shook his head.

I cleared my throat and coughed. The back of my throat was raw. "It gets better? Easier?"

He paused. "It gets easier to kill. But that's not necessarily better."

I squirmed to meet his sad eyes.

"Go to sleep, Wen. It will be a hard day tomorrow."

I didn't think I would sleep, the images of carnage revisiting my mind unbidden. Carnage we created. How I had been a split tick away from dying. I wanted to ask Father if he would sleep. Didn't he need it, too?

With Zaran and Laila resting on either side of me and the sounds of the thin brook in my ear, I did find sleep. It wasn't a restful one.

CHAPTER

I wasn't wounded, but everything hurt.

The land grew flatter and greener while we neared the capital city, riding through ranches and farms the next morning. The sahala bounded across the vast plains and hills of southern Jibryl. We kept a good pace but not too fast, saving the strength and stamina of the lizards.

Muscles ached, even ones I didn't know I had, and my left arm and knee hurt every time I moved them. Father examined both of my areas of pain and determined that they were sprains. He wrapped them with extra cloth.

The sun was hot, making for a miserable day, but Father pushed forward, wanting to arrive at the walls of Jennah before nightfall. With no one else around, I still wore my head covering, partly for shade from the sun. Another part of me wanted to hide. From what, I didn't know.

Around mid-day, we retrieved some food from our bags. Father slowed the pace so we could eat while we were in the saddle.

Chewing on jerky, I said, "I heard of the rebellion, but not calling them Knights of Truth."

Father swallowed and took a breath. He didn't look up, Laila moving steadily beneath him. "That is what the Ruchali people of the mountains call their warriors, who we call the goblain."

"But goblain aren't knights," I said. "They're cowards, right? Hiding and killing the innocent in the name of their rebellion."

"True. That is why the Ruchali are contained in the northern part of the city. But the goblain have found ways to survive for hundreds of years. They are dangerous, as you saw. Such enemies aren't easy to detect or notice."

"Which is why you want to enter the city before it gets dark."

"Correct."

I gazed at him. "These Knights of Truth, or whatever, don't they believe in the Onamaker? Or do they believe in the Kryan gods?"

"They believe in Ona," he said. "But not as we do."

"How are they different?"

"The Ruchali believe and use magic," he said. "While our Keepers call those magicians cursed."

"They call a lot of people cursed," I muttered.

Father shrugged. "I'm not a Keeper. It is all beyond me."

I shifted in the saddle. "But I thought the wizards were all dead. I thought the King purged them all a long time ago."

"He tried. A few may still exist."

"Is that why they are rebelling? A different name or a different god?"

Father frowned. "That is one aspect. It is about religion and ancient conflicts that have taken root deep in our being. Their leaders talk about what the King and people of Jibryl have taken from them. But the rebels know only violence and anger."

"You've dealt with them before. The goblain. When you were a Shield."

He grew quiet for a moment, staring down at the reins in his hand. "Yes."

I drew in a breath through my nose. "You think that is why the King has called on you?"

Father hesitated so long that I thought he wouldn't answer. "We will know tonight when we see the King. Come. Let's pick up the pace again."

He kicked Laila with his heels, and the lizard lurched to a brisk walk. I stuffed the last of the jerky in my mouth and drove Zaran to follow at a high enough pace that it made conversation difficult.

The landscape became steadily greener and lusher the closer we came to the capital city, with more villages and buildings. Late afternoon, while my stomach rumbled in hunger and my body begged to be horizontal for sleep, the walls and towers of Jenna rose over the trees.

Despite what the goblain assassin said, we did make it to the city of Jennah.

More people milled about in the waning light, and I made sure my head was covered. Elves took notice of the war lizards, usually seen when divisions of the Corps made their way from the capital in a parade of force.

That morning, Father had changed into his Corps uniform, a fine blue and gray tunic over white trousers. Generals usually rode horses, not sahala, and not with an elfdaughter weapons-master along with them. Thus, further reason for the frozen stares and wide eyes.

Wanting to avoid the Ruchali area of the northern part of the city, we rode on the street along the wall to arrive at the Southern Gate. The Palace and Great Ona Temple were closer to the southern gate anyway.

Soldiers on the wall called down to my father. "Hail, General!"

A platoon of soldiers waited for us at the Southern Gate, also known as the Heart of Ona, all of them in dark tan uniforms and standing at attention. An officer rode toward us through the gate on a horse. "General. Ona's peace. I am Lieutenant Pincas." He gave a slight bow.

"Ona's greetings," Father said. "I am General Natanel."

Pincas had short, cropped hair. Twenty elf soldiers stood behind him in formation. "Peace to you. I have heard of your exploits in the Kryan Conflicts with the Hornoth Legion."

"We lost a number of elfsons braver and stronger than me," Father said. "The Great Ona remembers them well."

"Yes, sir," Pincas said. "The King has been waiting for you. Shall we escort you to the Palace?"

Father gestured through the gate. "Lead the way."

Lt. Pincas narrowed his eyes for a tick but recovered to smile. "Of course." He spun his horse and entered the gate, barking orders to the twenty corpselves. They organized in two lines and marched behind the horse.

Father whispered to me. "Keep your ears up and eyes open."

The lesson again. *Trust no one.*

I nodded. With the attack on the dune fresh on my mind, I would have kept focus whether he reminded me or not.

We rode together past the gate guard, bringing up the rear of the procession. I adjusted the shield to sit on my right side and placed my hand on the hilt of the sword at my hip.

So many people. Jennah was not a small city, and as the center of trade, religion, and government, it bustled with elves from the other kingdoms. Even the occasional human and dwarf would make an appearance, as well, more than usual, with the Kaila Festival coming up.

Pincas led us down the main street toward the palace. The crowd parted at the sight of the Corps platoon and sahala war lizards. I tried to keep my eyes from bulging at each person and shadow. Expecting an assassin's knife or arrow at any point, my head stayed on a swivel.

Scents and sounds from merchants and booths overwhelmed me. Any other time I would have enjoyed it all, the faint drum and lyre music from the alley to the right, all of it. But not today.

I tugged on my head covering, making sure it was proper. I rode with my father, and we were going to see the King.

The Ona Temple emerged as the first large building on our right – a massive white, box-shaped structure with pillars and a wide stair-case at the front that led to golden doors. Keepers in their long robes traveled in pairs in the street. Other priests sat in groups on the stairs, talking or arguing or both. A few sat alone reading a parchment.

I said a quick prayer to Ona, hoping to come back to worship at the great Temple.

Zaran snapped his jaws, and after patting his head, I turned to the left. A lone Keeper watched me, his dark eyes following us as we moved. My heart rose in my chest. My shoulders tensed. Could that be a goblain? How could one infiltrate the Temple? But an assassin pretended to be a Courier, so why not a priest?

It was also possible the Keeper didn't appreciate an elfess weap-ons-master riding a Corps war lizard. My back straightened, and I glared back.

Now in the thick of the city, I continued scanning the crowd. I tried to calm my breathing.

More than a kilomitre from the Ona Temple, the street opened up to a massive square, the central area of the Southern District of Jennah. Merchant booths lined the outside of the square, all differ-ent sizes and colors selling whatever they could – vegetables, meats, robes, jewelry, and more. Other booths clustered in the middle but made space for people to move through.

"Make way!" Pincas cried from the front of our column, and the platoon tightened up, lifting their small shields and placing hands on the curved swords at their side. However, when elves saw Laila and Zaran, they gave us a wide berth without any command.

Zaran snarled at an elf woman and her daughter. They squealed, the mother pulling the girl close.

"Stop that." I smacked the tough hide of his neck to get his attention. I called to the quickly retreating mother and girl. "Sorry!"

Turning to the left, I lifted my head, and the palace rose before us.

A curse escaped my lips. The fortifications blocked out the setting sun to the west. Six squared towers at regular intervals surrounded the main building with a high wall connecting them.

The formidable walls of Jennah had stood for two thousand years, and the palace was a fortress within, built another millennium before the walls around the city by master architects and crafts-elves. The palace shone white across the people below.

Lt. Pincas led us to the space between gathered merchants and pointed the procession at the main entrance to the palace – tall, rectangular doors. Elves atop the wall of the palace called down inside when we approached. We neared the fortress of the King, and I had to crane my neck up to admire the height and strength of the walls and towers, the possible assassins all but forgotten.

We had visited the capital before but had never gone to the palace. The royal family and system was as much of a hidden mystery to me as it was to all the citizens of Jibryl.

My father sat calmly on Laila, moving with the gentle sway of the war lizard. His hand rested on his sword, his shoulders square.

I squared my own.

The golden palace doors possessed intricate designs of palm trees, fruit, and warriors carved within them. They opened enough for our group. Elven guards with arrows nocked in bows appeared on either side of us and scanned the crowd.

Marble covered the path from the doors to the palace proper. The hooves of the Lieutenant's horse clopped and echoed through the open space. Statues of former kings and warriors, a mixture of real people and myths, glared at us from either side. They each stood in an intimidating or active pose, depending on their legend. Not an elfess among the statues. Selina the Brave didn't even stand among them.

The golden doors slammed shut behind us with a boom that shook my gruts. I relaxed a bit, though, safe within the palace walls now and under the King's protection.

Trust no one. Were we really safe?

The platoon separated and hung back, standing at attention. We followed Lt. Pincas to the foot of the stairs that led up to the spacious palace entry.

Mitres away, another dozen guard dressed in silken robes filed out of the entrance. Long, curved swords hung at their hips.

Then the King appeared.

He was a tall elf with a graying beard clipped short. His own silken robe was embroidered with detailed designs in gold along the sleeves, waist, and hem. A small golden crown sat atop his graying hair. When he saw Father, he smiled.

Then he noticed me sitting atop the battle lizard, and the King's smile faltered. King Yacob recovered his smile and opened his arms. "Natanel. My friend. Thank you for coming."

Father swung a leg and dismounted the war lizard. He took a step forward without bowing. "My King called, and I answered," Father spoke over his shoulder. "Elowen, gather our things."

I slid off Zaran and first made sure I bowed low when facing King Yacob. Then I began to untie the lashes that held the myriad of weapons and bags to the beast. Servants came and took the reins of our sahala.

Father took his bag from Laila and addressed the servant closest to him. "Treat them well, and they will not rip out your heart. I will check on them in the morning."

The servant gave a wary glance to both of the lizards and then looked up at the King, who nodded. The servant gulped and moved to obey, leading the sahala away.

Father faced the King. He took a deep breath before walking up the stairs. I followed. The clattering and clomping sounds I made when I did lessened the effect, however. At least I didn't curse in front of the King.

King Yacob scanned the area behind us. "Where is my Courier?"

"He is dead, I assume," Father said. "Although I do know the goblain assassin that took his place is dead."

The King frowned. "Assassin?"

Father reached the top of the stairs, halting a few paces away from the King. He didn't acknowledge the guard. "We need to talk."

No *sir* or *your majesty* coming from my father, and I froze a step from the top, wincing when the spear smacked on the stair and made a loud, awkward noise.

The King's face went blank. "I believe we do." He lowered his voice but not low enough. "You brought *her*?"

"She is my weapons master," Father said like that was sufficient explanation.

Yacob snorted. "Then come." He turned and led the way into the palace, the guard following behind.

CHAPTER

We walked down a wide hall with plush red carpet and engraved panels in silver and gold on the walls, many of them scenes from battles and heroic figures. Others were pictures of lush vegetation and abundant harvests.

With a glance behind me, the guard possessed stoic faces and stepped in unison.

A breeze brushed past us through the hall, like the palace had been designed to include the wind.

Yacob led us to another staircase, this one wide and curved. It ascended to a second level, where the passageway was also decorated with more engraved panels. The hallway ended at a set of doors that a pair of servants opened up for us – the King, mostly – to walk through. The guard remained outside while Yacob, my father, and I entered the spacious room that contained a long table and luxurious chairs around it and against the wall.

The servants closed the door behind us. We were alone.

Father crossed his arms and scowled at the King. "What kind of crit show are you running here, Yacob?"

My jaw dropped, and I tightened my eyes to keep them from popping out of my head.

The King's dark features twisted. "Natanel, remember who you are speaking to."

"I know who I'm speaking to," Father said. "And you should have remembered I retired. You gave me your word."

"Kings are allowed to change their minds," Yacob said. "And speaking of my word, I didn't ask for her. Only you."

I sniffed. *I'm standing right here.*

Father lowered his arms and stepped around the table, continuing to face Yacob. "She's the reason I retired. If it's me you want, you get Elowen in the deal. I needed someone I trust."

My chest pushed out in pride.

Yacob's brow furrowed. "You don't trust me?"

"I assume whatever duties you have for me aren't to lounge around this palace," Father said. "Will you go out in the streets to the Northern city and watch my back? You lost one Courier to the goblain, and we were attacked by twenty or more on the road here. She's with me."

"As your weapons master?" The King pointed at me. "She's in the palace with enough weapons to kill half my guard. What are you doing?"

"However much I don't want it, this is what must be if you want my help," Father said. "If you have a problem with Elowen being here, you can find someone else to help you with whatever mess you're in."

The King glanced over at me before looking at Father again. "You know why I had to call you."

Father's shoulders sagged for a moment before he answered. "I suspected."

Yacob's gaze narrowed. "You've told her?"

"I have kept your secrets, as you commanded," Father said.

Those words hung in the air for long ticks, the room silent but filled with tension.

"You are prepared to tell her?" the King said. "Everything?"

What are you talking about? I wanted to scream at them, but I couldn't move – much less speak – for fear of interrupting whatever was going on between my father and the King of Jibryl. The most powerful elf in the kingdom. My arms and back grew sore from holding all our stuff.

Father said, "I will do what I must."

King Yacob looked from me back to my father. "Very well. If that is your wish. But you play a dangerous game, Natanel."

Father sighed. "It is not a game. Now, tell me what is going on."

"Over the last few years," the King said, "the goblain have been gathering their strength."

"In the mountains?" Father said.

"Yes." Yacob met Father's hard stare. "But the greater threat is the violence in the northern district."

"Here in Jennah?" Father's lips became a line. "They haven't made a push here in decades."

The King nodded. "Not since you were Shield, no."

Father rubbed his chin. "What has emboldened them?"

"Two things, we believe," the King said. "As you know, the goblain are notoriously divided and difficult to unite. But they have been working together under new leadership."

Father lowered his stare. "Who?"

"We only have a title. He calls himself the Hateph."

"And you have sent your soldiers into the Northern District?" Father said.

Yacob huffed. "Not my first round of Tablets, Natanel. We round up elves, capture a few, and question them. But they will only call on Hateph to come and rescue them. They give no information. We don't even think they've seen this character. They will die for him, though."

"I see," Father said.

"There have been three assassination attempts on my life in the last two years," the King continued. "They have been closer to success than the public knows."

"And one of your royal couriers was killed and replaced," Father said. "Close enough that you don't trust those in your inner circle."

Yacob blew air through his nostrils. "I can't accuse anyone specific, but yes. It must be someone within the King's Trust or connected to them. And with the Kaila Festival opening tomorrow ..."

"There will be even more opportunity to cause violence and sneak assassins into the city," Father finished.

The King now took a step toward Father. "You have experience and more success with the goblain than any in the last five centuries. You are separate and independent from anyone in my Trust. And as a former champion of the Kaila Tournament, you know the ins and outs of the Festival better than anyone. I am sorry to order you out of retirement, but I need you. There is no one else."

Father paused, his face unreadable. "I understand. When is the next time your Trust meets?"

"Tomorrow afternoon," Yacob said. "Final details about the Kaila."

Father nodded. "We have had a hard road. We will rest tonight but meet with your Shield first thing in the morning. Then we will attend the meeting with the Trust."

The King said, "Very well. The servant outside will show you to your room."

Father turned to leave. "Come, Elowen."

The weapons made a racket when I bowed to the King before following Father from the room.

A servant in a fine coat waited beyond the guards, and he inclined his head when we entered the hallway. He offered to take the weapons or our bags, but Father didn't answer him.

We followed the servant back down the hall and took a separate staircase up and around to another floor of the palace, less ornate but still decorated with finery I had never seen in our little town. We seemed to be in another world. And that statement may not have been far from the truth.

The servant opened the doors to a spacious apartment of rooms halfway down the hall. Filled with couches covered in silk and two bedrooms and a sitting area with real books, the apartment sprawled like a palace unto itself.

Once we were inside, Father didn't speak to the servant; he only glared at him. The servant got the hint and left, closing the doors behind him.

Father took his bags from me and set them in one bedroom. I arranged the weapons as well as I could in the sitting area and carried my own into the other.

When I emerged from the bedroom, Father had opened the glass doors to the balcony and stood at the edge, staring out into the night.

The night had cooled, and the air refreshed me after a hard ride and the tense moment with the King. I strode out to the balcony, taking the breeze through my nostrils, and I leaned against the railing next to my Father.

We stood high enough to see over the taller buildings of the city. The Ona Temple rose to my right.

Exhaustion hit me in that moment, and while the air kept my eyes open, they began to feel heavy. I stretched the soreness in my back and shoulders, even my legs and knees.

"We should rest," I said. "Sounds like a big day tomorrow." I had met the King today. Tomorrow I would be in the company of the current Shield and then the Royal Trust. I faced him for a moment when I said, "Good night."

But while I turned, I heard Father's low voice. "Elowen."

My full name. Not a command, but I knew his meaning. He had something to say.

I rocked on my feet and stood back at the railing, waiting.

Father stared out over the city. "The King spoke of secrets kept, information he forced me to keep over these years. I have kept them as I swore I would."

The air felt colder suddenly.

"But now that he has called me to return, I am not bound by those vows, especially now that you are here. There is a secret that you must hear. It belongs to you, as well."

I shivered. He didn't look at me.

"It is time I tell you about your mother."

CHAPTER

I don't know if I could have moved if I wanted to.

This was it. This was the moment I longed for my whole life. To know of my mother. Who was she? What had she been like? What had happened? A part of me had been missing, due to her absence, and I had no memory of her. And my father had never shared his own with me. It may not have filled that absence, but it might have given me something. A dying elf in the dry desert finds the smallest amount of water to be a salvation.

My eyelids no longer felt heavy. My breathing came short. I gripped the railing.

"Her name was Talia," Father said. "We met in the years I was the Shield.

"I was a soldier, highly decorated as a general. I won many battles. I believed that being Shield would be the pinnacle of my career. Of my life. That is not odd. Many believe that about the position of Shield.

"I had … relationships over the centuries, all of them short. None of them serious. My commitment to the Corps was absolute. I didn't have time to be married, to raise a family, not if I wanted to fight for the kingdom. Not if I wanted to be Shield.

"As Shield, part of protecting the King is gathering information. It is easy to think that it is simply being a better swordmaster, fighting off the random assassin. But if an enemy's plan gets that far, I failed as a protector. It is far preferable to end a rebellion at the outset, at its inception, rather than the alternative, which can lead to civil war and the death of thousands of innocents.

"To better find the sanddragons in the brush, I needed other agents, informants that would infiltrate certain groups and report back to me. Talia was one such agent."

Father lowered his head, but he smiled for a moment. Not one of joy.

"You are much like her. She was a gifted warrior. But what place could she have in the Corps? None. She had a Ruchali background and could pass as one with her darker skin and features. Her mother was a trusted servant in the palace. And Talia was brilliant.

"While you may bristle at the limits to elfwomen, it also makes them unseen in certain situations. Easily overlooked. Not someone to be taken seriously, especially as an agent of the King. She was a perfect choice. Together, we ended many attempts by the goblain to bring violence into the city or to the King.

"Despite my years of discipline, despite my absolute duty, there is one thing no one plans for. Love.

"Over time, we grew close. Like I said, I had other relationships, but I had never met an elfess like her. And even though I was older, we became very close. In secret."

He was quiet for a few ticks, staring out over the city. Then he shook his head, like waking from a dream.

"I started getting reports from other agents about the goblain gathering an army in a Ruchali village north of the city, a half day's ride. The goblain did not gather an army traditionally. They were too smart for that. They hid much and had thousands of years of experience adapting and adjusting. I sent my best agent to investigate. Talia.

"Then she became pregnant. With you, of course. And I was the father.

"I pulled her from the investigation. To protect her. She disagreed and continued to work with the goblain to bring me information.

"Or so I thought.

"Other trusted agents brought me rumors and reports that Talia was a member of the goblain, that she was a double agent. At first, I denied it. Refused to believe it. But those other agents gathered more and more evidence that the village was harboring a rebel army. Talia's reports conflicted with the others. She found things, but it was inconclusive.

"And you were about to be born.

"I knew better than to get emotionally involved with one of my agents. I knew how she could manipulate me, all the more because she carried our child. At some point, I had to know. It tortured me that she could be a traitor and that my failure contributed to it.

"I went to confront her, but she had escaped. Disappeared.

"In my failure, I went to the King and confessed everything. Yacob did what I knew he would. He sent a Corps legion against the village.

"Anything can happen in a battle. Violence is difficult to control, especially in a situation when a village has been hiding rebels. My concern was for you. Had you been born? The night before the attack, I snuck into the village to find you. House by house, I was a shadow. In a home in the center of the town, I found Talia, your mother, and you, a newborn, in a basket nearby. A daughter.

"I did confront her then, and she pleaded with me to understand. But I couldn't. She had betrayed me. She had betrayed the King and kingdom. I moved to take you with me.

"She tried to stop me. We fought. As I said, she was a great warrior. I was stronger, however, more experienced, and she had just given birth."

My mouth was dry. I licked my lips. Blinking, I found that tears had fallen from my eyes.

Father lowered his head like a prayer. His words barely carried through the night air on the balcony.

"I struck her down, a killing blow. Others heard our voices and came to her aid. I took you in my arms and fought through them like a blade through sand. They couldn't stop me.

"I escaped into the night.

"To this day, I can still hear her weak, plaintive cry when I close my eyes. Not for me but for you. Before she died.

"*Elowen. Elowen.*

"That is how I learned your name."

In the pause, he raised his head to gaze over the city. Tiny points of light in the darkness spread before us. So close, yet so far.

"Not an hour later, before the sun rose, the Corps attacked the village. Elfwomen, elfmen, children. All of them awoke to violence. Many of them were killed in their bed. I could hear the screams from a kilomitre away.

"The General had given the order. Everyone in the village was killed. Every soul. Then the village was burned to the ground. No one escaped.

"Yacob approved of the action but knew the word of the complete destruction of a village would strengthen the rebel cause among the Ruchali. He came up with another story: the village had been a rebel military installation, not civilians, and they had attacked the Corps, and our army had only acted in self-defense.

"A thin story, but thin stories are often easily believed.

"Due to my failure and now having a daughter to raise, I asked to retire from service as Shield. A Shield cannot simply retire. The King must release him. Yacob allowed me to retire only if I never told you of your mother, never told anyone about Talia, never told anyone the truth about the village. A daughter of a traitor, you would have been considered cursed. It would look bad for the King to allow you to live and for his Shield to have been so compromised.

"I could not imagine raising you in the shadow of this place, this palace, and the King who would always see you as the daughter of a traitor. I retired, took you far away, and raised you on my own."

Father shook his head and chucked. "I couldn't get far enough away, no matter where we went." He did look at me, then. "You look so much like her. Every morning I saw Talia greeting me. When you expressed interest in learning weapons, that didn't surprise me. Every evening I sparred with her once more. Your mother is gone. But she has never left me.

"I should have known that Ona would lead me back here once more. That I couldn't escape facing the past."

Silence reigned. And once it became clear he was done talking, I spoke. "She ... she is dead?"

Father nodded.

"You are sure?"

"It was a fatal blow. I've given many in my day. I saw the light fade from her eyes. And the Corps is well versed in surrounding and taking a village, making sure no one escapes. No one did. The charred bodies were buried in a mass grave outside the village."

I pursed my lips. "You killed her."

He turned from me again. "Yes. That is true. I killed her. I killed your mother."

I stared at him.

I wiped tears from my cheeks. Then I turned and went into the bedroom, where I laid my things. Grabbing my bag and my sword, I left the apartment.

CHAPTER

O nce in the hallway, the servant from earlier waited at the end of the hall, standing straight when I approached. "Can I help you?"

"The stables. Where are they?"

"The stables?" he repeated. "Why do you ...?"

"I want to go to the stables. Am I not allowed?"

The servant eyed my bag. "It's not that. Only that it grows late, and you must be tired from your journey."

I put my hand on the hilt of my sword. "I am tired. I'm also not in the mood to try to find them myself. Will you help me or not?"

He nodded. "Of course."

The servant led me down the stairs and then another set. He didn't lead me out the front of the palace, however, which was the way we went in. Instead, he took me through a side entrance that opened to another courtyard. The stables waited at the other end.

"The sahala we came with," I said. "Take me to them."

"Very well." The stables were dark, only the moonlight giving any light through windows and doors. The servant took a lamp from the courtyard, and we entered the stables. Their growls led me to them.

We grew near Zaran and Laila, and I stopped, addressing the servant, "You can go."

He stammered. "But wouldn't you like to return to the apartment after seeing the lizards?"

"No. I'm staying here."

I entered the stall in the stables that held both war lizards. Laila nuzzled me.

"Would you like for me to leave the lamp?" the servant asked.

"I would prefer it dark."

He nodded and left.

Over the years, I had wondered what happened to my mother, and a child's imagination can run to faraway lands and fantasies, both ridiculous and boring. From the simple possibility that she died in childbirth, common to many, to heroic acts like Selina the Brave.

Not that she was a traitor. And killed by my father.

I was the daughter of a traitor and a murderer.

I sat down in the straw of the stall, my back against the wooden wall. Laila curled up on my right. Then Zaran on my left.

I bent my head, and something broke within me. I wept as I had never wept before. Never knew a person could break so deep within them. But I knew now.

CHAPTER

I woke lying in the straw, curled in a ball, the sahala snoring on either side of me. The predawn light announced that the sun would be rising soon. For a moment, my mind still slept, so I remained ignorant of how I arrived at the stall. Was I in the stable at home? What had happened last night? Then my brain caught up with my body, and I remembered. Like a shock, it exploded in my mind.

At the palace. We saw the King. My mother was a traitor, and my father killed her.

Moaning from the accompanying pain, I moved to rise, and a blanket fell away from my shoulders. Looking down, a small pillow nestled underneath my head. Someone had given these to me in the middle of the night. The servant? My father?

My father.

What was I going to do? I didn't want to see him. Didn't want to look at him.

I also couldn't lay there all day, although the thought tempted me. Wiping my eyes, I took a deep breath and stood in the grey light.

Zaran's head perked up with a snarl, looking around the stall, his nostrils flaring. Laila stirred.

"It's okay," I mumbled to them.

Had it been my father? Had he tracked me down, found me last night, and given me the pillow and blanket? Was he being kind? Manipulative?

A part of me was glad for the kindness, but another part sneered at the comfort. I brushed off the straw and dirt from my clothes, and ran a hand through my hair. Should I go back up to the room? My father would be meeting with the Shield of the King soon. He would be getting ready.

I shook my head. That was the last thing I wanted, to see him.

My eyes caught sight of my bag in the corner next to the saddles for the sahala. I couldn't stay here all day, but I didn't have to go back to the palace, either. No one wanted me there. The King knew I was the daughter of a traitor. That's why he looked at me like that yesterday. Being an elfess with a sword didn't help, but it made sense that the King wouldn't want the daughter of a goblain here, especially not when he was trying to protect against an assassination attempt. I wouldn't want me, either.

Zaran stared up at me. I met his yellow eyes.

I could go home. I should go back to my village.

Clicking my tongue at Zaran, he stood up and nudged me with his snout. I lifted the saddle and set it on his back. I grabbed the straps and cinched them underneath. I leaned on the sahala.

What would I do back in the village? Die of boredom. The local Keeper had expelled me from the school. Without Father's help, I wouldn't have a chance to get back in. Did I even want to get back in and be treated like a second-class citizen?

Not back home. There was nothing for me there. But where else could I go?

Anywhere. The options were endless. Live in Jennah? Take a trip north? I could go anywhere. For a moment, the idea gave me a sense of freedom, like a weight lifted from my shoulders.

Until I had another thought. *Maybe that is exactly what my father wants me to do.*

Feint. Strike. Use your opponent's aggression against them. This was a master elf with numerous weapons, and as I learned over the last day, a former Shield of the King well versed in the lies and deceptions of politics for gain.

Why did he tell me about my mother last night? The King never threatened to tell me anything. Was he afraid I would find out on my own somehow?

Or he told me on purpose last night so I would run away. He had tried to convince me to stay home and not come with him. For my safety. I had forced the issue. Felt like I won.

What better way to get me to go away, to keep me safe? Tell me about my mother, finally, but that he was responsible for her death. That would do it.

"Crit on the gods," I cursed through my teeth.

With a quick move of my hand, I leaned down and uncinched the strap, and the saddle slipped to the ground. I pulled the sword and belt off the ground and wore them once more.

Bursting through the stable door, I marched over the stones of the courtyard with tall buildings on either side, and I approached the palace. I took my scarf and covered my head.

Two guards stood at the entrance and moved to block my way. I put my hand on my sword and scowled at them. It didn't have any effect on them.

"I need to get back to my rooms," I said.

The guard exchanged glances and then regarded me. "Who are you?" one said.

"My name is Elowen, and my father and I came here last night."

Another exchanged glance, and the other guard said, "We have not been given instructions about any Elowen."

"I need to get in the palace," I said. "Back to our rooms and my father."

The first guard's brow creased. "If you had rooms in the palace, then why are you out here?"

"I just … I just decided to sleep out here, okay? Not important why. I need to get in there, please."

The first guard shook his head. "I don't think so."

My sneer had even less effect, and I didn't want to have to battle my way past a palace guard. Even if I won, the King would have plenty of reason to kick me out of the palace, no matter what my father said.

Beyond the guard, a figure passed in the hall. Was that the …?

"Hey!" I called out to the elf. A royal servant. The one from last night. He paused and turned to me, a look of recognition flashing on his face. He blinked and stumbled. "You. What's your name?"

The elf glanced at the guard while he kept moving down the hall toward us. "Refa." He gave a slight bow when he stopped behind the guard.

"Refa," I said. "You remember me from last night? You took me to my rooms, my father and me."

He nodded. "Yes."

"Can you tell these two that I have rooms up in the palace?"

The guard looked at him now, and Refa swallowed. "She and her father were given rooms last night. They are guests of the King."

The first guard narrowed his eyes at Refa. "Will you escort her to her rooms, then?"

"I will," Refa said.

The first guard looked at his partner, who shrugged. "Very well," the first guard said. "If you will escort her back to her father, she may enter."

I released a sigh when they parted and gave me space to enter. Refa waited and followed me while we walked into the main floor of the palace.

I slowed to talk to him. "Thank you." I kept my voice low. "I just need to see my father."

"I understand."

Refa was about my height, maybe a couple of centimeters taller, and seemed young, my age. We took the back stairway up to the third level, where the apartments were.

"I'm sorry if I was short last night," I said. "I was ..." What? Upset? I couldn't think of a word that could explain what I was. How do I explain my whole world falling apart in a matter of minutes? Well, I guess I could have said that, but he didn't need to know.

"Of course."

"How long have you been a royal servant?"

He frowned as he calculated. "Five years next month."

"That would have been after my father left. Did you ever know him?"

"General Natanel?" He scoffed. "Your father is a legend in the palace. His service with the Desert Corps and his reputation with the other servants in the palace from when he was Shield."

"Okay, okay," I stopped him. Was a mistake to ask that question. I didn't want to hear how much of a legend or hero my father was.

We reached the level of royal guest apartments, and he paused at the end of the hallway. I stopped a few paces from him and turned. "Are you busy with something else right now?"

His brow creased.

"You're busy," I said. "Probably with something important. It's okay."

"Why do you ask?"

I looked down the hall at the door to our apartment and then back. "I was just wondering if you would stick around. Just in case I need you to show me where to go or something."

"Ah," Refa said, like he understood. Even though I wasn't sure I did. "Whatever I was going to do doesn't matter. I am a royal servant. You are a guest of the King. You are my priority."

I cringed. "You sure you won't get in trouble? I don't know how all this works."

"Not at all. You want me to wait here?"

"Sure," I said. "Thanks."

Taking a deep breath, I made my way down the hall and opened the door.

Father stood in the common area, dressed in his Corps uniform, Qatal at his hip. He was in the middle of buttoning his uniform jacket when I burst into the room and slammed the door behind me.

He froze, his jaw slack.

"You're not getting rid of me like that," I said.

He recovered quickly. "Wen. What do you mean?" He went on to the next button.

I hovered by the door. My courage only allowed me to get so far. "You didn't need to tell me about my mother last night. Why did you?"

Finishing the top button, he took a step towards me. "You've been begging me to tell you about her for years, your whole life. I was finally free of my vows. I could give you what you wanted."

My vision blurred. "And then you could get what you wanted."

"What do you mean?"

Blinking, a tear ran down my cheek. I thought I had cried it out last night. Where did these tears come from? "You trained me. You don't think I know how this works? You're gonna make me say it?"

Father stood tall and straightened his jacket. "Say what?"

I bit my bottom lip before answering. "You never wanted me here. You told me so I would run away, run back home."

"I wanted you safe, that is true. And it is not safe here. That is also true. But that is not why I told you."

I huffed. "You knew that if you told me, I'd hate you, and by hating you, I'd leave. Is the story even true? Is what you said about her even real? Or did you make it up just to drive me away?"

My father flinched. Like I had punched him. "Elowen. I have never lied to you. Do I want you away from here? Safe? Yes. I told you before we left this is more dangerous than you realize. There are no heroes here. That was the truth then. It is still true. And what I told you about Talia ... I owed you the truth, no matter how you reacted."

Shaking my head, I said, "Well, it doesn't matter if you want me here or not. I'm staying. I'm going to the meeting with you this morning. And to the Trust after that."

"Why, Elowen? You don't need to do this."

"Yes, I do. What you told me last night made it clearer," I said. "The King and whoever else knew of my mother sees me as the daughter of a traitor with no place here. I don't know how yet, but I'm going to prove them all wrong."

Father took another step and looked into my eyes. "Listen to me. Please. You are not your mother. You are not me. You can be your own person, free of all this. You have nothing to prove."

"You're wrong. I do. And I will."

He sighed and lowered his head.

"Now, let's go to that meeting with the King," I said.

CHAPTER

S haul, the Shield of the King, stood taller than my father. Taller than the King.

Even this early in the morning, King Yacob dressed in finery, his black hair and light brown skin immaculate. My father's Desert Corps uniform, complete with a dozen medals on the left breast of the jacket, made him appear commanding in his own way, despite the signs of age.

However, Shaul wore only a simple tailored blue tunic, gray trousers, and leather sandals on his feet. A scimitar hung at his hip. His hair was shorn to a slight strip down the middle of his head. Despite the simple outfit, he looked the hero with handsome and ageless features and the way he stood like an immovable stone.

On his back was an ancient iron shield, his arms through straps that held it in place. It was the shield given to the Shield of the King. My father once wore it.

Did Shaul want my father here? His face betrayed no emotion.

We gathered in the same meeting room as the night before on the second level of the palace.

"Your informants," Father said to Shaul. "Have they given any indication of the timing of the attempt? The location?"

Shaul didn't answer at first. When he spoke, he barely moved. "No. Only that the goblain will make their move during the Festival."

"Is this one source?" Father said. "Or several? Have you been able to cross-check and confirm this information?"

"The information comes from one main source, an informant I trust," Shaul said. "None of my other sources have been able to fully confirm. Only that the rebellion will make a move. A major one."

Father rubbed his jaw. "You haven't received corroboration from other informants? How do you know it is real?"

Shaul lifted one eyebrow. "Because this source has always given me good information. Certainly, you had those when in your time."

"I did," Father said. "However, I still confirmed through other sources. Even good informants can be turned."

Lesson number one. *Trust no one.*

"I trust this source," Shaul said, like the subject was closed.

Father sighed. "Very well. Yacob, you said that there had been other attempts. I would like more detail."

Yacob nodded. "Last year, I had been visiting the Corps engaged in skirmishes with Faltiel in the north. On the return trip, one of the lieutenants assigned to my protection detail attacked me."

My eyebrows rose as Father grunted. "A lieutenant?" Father said. "In the Corps?"

"I dispatched him easily." Shaul gave a look of dismissal. "He didn't get close enough to do damage."

Father winced. "That is not the point. A goblain assassin infiltrated the Corps. To an officer's rank. Had he been turned? Had he been planning it for years?"

"He died within moments," Shaul said. "He didn't get a chance to tell us anything."

I watched my father stand straight. "It would have been better to wound and capture him." Father had killed that goblain in the desert because we didn't have time to torture him. It would have taken torture to get information from a zealot. Torture.

Yacob shifted his weight. "We vetted every officer in the Corps after that. Questioned their background and loyalty."

"I'm sure that went over well," Father grumbled, then spoke louder. "What about the other attempt?"

"Two months ago, I found an assassin here among the palace guard," Shaul said. "My source gave me that information, and it proved correct."

"Were you able to capture him? Question him?" Father looked from Shaul to the King.

"We did," Shaul said. "I questioned him thoroughly. We found one of the goblain cells in the northern quarter among the Ruchali."

"Did he give any information on any future assassination attempts?" Father asked.

"None on any future attempts," Shaul said. "But you know how these cells work. They are only given instructions on their mission and kept in the dark about other plans. Or they operate independently. Ruchali find it difficult to work together."

"That is true," Father said. "But now there is a leader, someone unifying them. This Hateph?"

"He is very active," Shaul said. "Though none of my sources have ever seen him."

"When we smell crit, there is usually a bosaur in the barn." Father's lip curled. "This is concerning. An assassin in the Corps, your palace guard, and one of your couriers. They are getting closer than ever before."

"And the Festival begins tomorrow." Yacob's eyes pleaded with Father. "This is why I asked for your help. No offense to Shaul. He has served me well. But the Kaila Festival is the pride of the city and the kingdom. Merchants, dignitaries, and people from all over the world will be here."

Shaul inclined his head. "And contestants for the Tournament. I concede that is an area of your expertise."

"The Festival, in general," the King said. "Natanel, you ran security for three of them. While participating in the Tournament. As you've said, the goblain have grown bold and close."

"They have," Father said. "They have also shown more long-term strategy. An officer, a guard, a courier. That was more than reactionary. That took planning and coordination on a level not seen in a couple of centuries."

Shaul sniffed. "Agreed."

Father rubbed his chin. "I still have some contacts in the city, independent from yours. I will see what we can find."

One of my brows rose. "What *we* will find."

Father paused, then nodded.

"I ran security for the last Festival," Shaul said. "But my main concern is the Tournament. These will be the greatest swordmasters from around the world. If the goblain have the resources to plan ahead to infiltrate the guard and the Corps, then they could do the same with one of the contestants."

Since my father had been the champion of the Kaila Tournament several times, I had heard stories of the competition. The contestants were sent by other kings, queens, and nations, and they stayed within the palace complex. If one was an assassin …

"You could simply change where they stay during the tournament," Father said. "Let them stay at one of the wealthy houses in the southern part of the city."

Yacob shook his head. "You know the purpose of the tournament. It is a statement of peace, a way to compete without going to war. Those contestants are personal guests of the King. Due to the recent skirmishes with Faltiel and tensions with Kryus, I don't think we can afford to offend other nations."

"That is even more reason to risk the offense," Father said. "Kryus and Faltiel have motivations to participate in destabilizing this kingdom."

King Yacob frowned. "That has been the concern."

"Which is why I agreed that the King call on you," Shaul said. "We have made room for you in the competition. You could return to the Tournament."

Father's brow creased, and I grew tense. "The courier said that Father wouldn't be back in the Tournament," I said. The other elves looked at me – the King with annoyance. Shaul kept his thoughts from his face.

"He was an assassin," Shaul said. "He didn't know. Even the real Baruch never knew the reason for your summons."

Father said, "True point. However, I am not the fighter I used to be. I haven't been training for the Tournament."

I squeaked, the image of a dozen goblain assassins in pieces littering the desert.

"It is a symbolic gesture," King Yacob said. "You are a hero to the city, well remembered. Your bouts would be more for entertainment and nostalgia."

Shaul waved a hand at Father. "You would be close with the other contestants, as an added benefit. A former Shield with the right eyes and ears, in case the goblain are also working with one of our enemies."

The King stared at Father. "I'm sorry to have called you out of retirement. But your kingdom needs you. I need you."

I glanced from my father to the King. "Excuse me, sir. What about me?"

The King cocked his head. "What do you mean?"

I took a deep breath, suddenly feeling the sweat underneath my arms. "I could enter the Tournament."

King Yacob and Father blinked.

After a tick of time, Shaul laughed. He threw his head back and guffawed. Once he was done, he smirked. "You can't be serious."

"Sure," I said. "You said you had a place for him in the competition already. But Father still has contacts in the city. He needs to be free to investigate, not be busy with the Tournament."

"An elfess of Jibryl in the Tournament?" Yacob shook his head. "That's never been done. I won't allow it."

I swallowed. "You have to, my King."

"Elowen," Father warned.

I reached into a pocket in my trousers and grabbed the Kaila Champion amulet. It hung on a ribbon and glistened golden in the light from the window. "This is my Father's. We all know the tradition. If the Champion gives the amulet to one in his lineage, they must be admitted to the competition."

"An elfson, sure," Shaul said. "Not a daughter."

Father stared at me for a moment. Then he grinned. "Actually, the tradition isn't clear. That is on purpose. Other nations, like Kryus and Faltiel, have different cultures that allow elfdaughters to fight in the tournament. The tradition doesn't say it must be a son. Otherwise, other nations would be offended."

"A technicality, surely," King Yacob said. "We would be a laughingstock."

"I assure you," Father said, "she is good with the sword. I trained her."

"My King." Shaul tone was firm and low. "We cannot allow this."

"Elowen makes a good point," Father said. "I brought her with me because I trust her, and she can help. She doesn't know my contacts. And even if I told her who they were, they wouldn't trust or speak with her without me there. It may take me days to make head-way in my investigation. I can't do that and be your sideshow.

"You wanted someone in the Tournament; she has the amulet, and she's been trained by a Champion. Even as an exhibition, if the people regard me as a hero, as you say, then my daughter will cer-tainly hold interest for them."

King Yacob bristled. Shaul looked disgusted, like he had to force down a burnt hornoth steak.

Father took a deep breath and met their glares with his own calm demeanor. "You asked me here for my expertise, and I agree this is a good solution. Ultimately, though, it doesn't matter. It is the tradi-tion and law of the Tournament for the sake of peace. You must allow it. You do not have the authority to stop it."

Shaul stood like a statue, his eyes blank.

The King glowered. The daughter of a traitor would represent his kingdom in a tournament in sight of the world.

"If you feel it is best," the King said.

"I do," Father said.

The King spoke through clenched teeth. "Very well. Shaul will make the arrangements."

Shaul's nostrils flared. "Yes, my King."

CHAPTER

12

Father and I left a few minutes later. After the door closed behind us and we made our way down the hall away from the guard, my breathing came short, and my hands shook. I placed my hands on the sword belt to keep them steady.

Holy crit of the gods, what did I just do?

I licked my lips, forcing deep breaths.

"You stole my amulet," Father said once we reached the stairs.

"Stealing is a strong word."

"You did not ask me."

"No, I didn't," I said. "It is my birthright. Do you deny it?"

Father led us up to the level of our apartments. "Birthright may also be a strong word. No, I don't deny it. Although you know full well that it has only been used by an elfson."

"A stupid idea, only for *elfsons*. What if a daughter is better? Wouldn't that give our kingdom a better chance to win the tournament? To prove our superiority to others?"

"Depends on your perspective," Father said. We reached the next level.

I rolled my eyes. "Just because it has never been done doesn't mean it shouldn't be done."

"That is true." He sucked in air through his nose. "You know I think highly of you and your skill. But be careful what you tear down. You may not like what is built in its place."

"An excuse to hold on to what is wrong. You know that."

Father stopped at the door to our apartment. "Here is what I know. Fighting in the tournament won't solve or change anything. Talia will still be your mother. I will still be your father. The Keepers will argue that you are the exception, not change the rule. The King will dismiss you."

He opened the door, and we entered the apartment.

I shrugged. "Maybe I'm not doing it for any of those reasons. Maybe I'm doing it to help you. And for me. To find my own destiny. My future won't be found by hiding and running."

The door closed behind us. Father hung his head. "Destinies are dangerous things. They hunt you. Then they find you, whether you run or no. Often they are not what we want or desire. I would be careful looking for your destiny."

"We'll see."

He nodded. "I will give you exercises to work on this afternoon."

My brow creased. "I thought we were meeting with the Trust later? And finding your old contacts?"

"We were. But now you have to train. You will be facing the best in the world tomorrow."

"I'll train tonight," I said. "I'm going with you."

Father stared into my eyes. I squinted back at him.

He sighed. "Very well. Are you hungry? They brought you break-fast." He gestured at a table with flatbread, dates, and other fruit.

"I could eat." The smell of food manipulated my stomach. "I'll need my strength if I'm going to win that tournament."

CHAPTER

The Trust met in the King's throne room.

Father and I entered the massive space with high, vaulted ceilings on the lower level of the palace. Regular pillars carved from pure white stone were spaced on either side of the broad aisle down the middle of the room. The wood that covered the floor swirled in chaotic patterns. White walls surrounded us.

King Yacob sat on the golden throne. The King lounged back, his elbow on the arm of the throne.

Father had given me the names of the members of the King's Trust, all elfmen, of course, and counseled me to keep my ears up as they spoke. One of them might be a traitor and part of the assassination plot or whatever the goblain planned. Or all of them. Father explained that it would make sense with so many enemies getting close to the King.

Shaul stood next to the King on the dais.

We lingered behind the three other members of the Trust, who stood on the floor before the five steps up to the throne. They wore robes, each a different color. The First Keeper, Fahim, was dressed in white. His long hair lay in one braid down his back, his white robe embroidered with golden pictures of planets and stars.

Paavo, the High Marshall of the Corps, wore a black robe embroidered with swords and spears in blue silk. Two swords hung on his belt, one long and one short, and his light hair was cropped on his head.

The Lord of Coin, Aiken, was hunched in his golden robe, his thick features clean and well-groomed.

Paavo glanced over his shoulder at us when we approached, his right hand on the hilt of the jeweled long sword. He nodded at my father. "General." His jaw tightened when his eyes fell on me.

Father inclined his head in return. "Marshall."

According to Father, Paavo had been High Marshall for nearly a century, holding his position longer than the Lord of the Coin or First Keeper. He was an elf of power and influence, the ruler of one of the most devastating armies in the world.

The King sat up. "Thank you for joining us, Natanel."

"Yes, my King," Father said.

Lord Aiken addressed Father. "What brings you to us, General?"

"He is here at my request," King Yacob said. "With all the conflict in recent months and the Kaila Festival preparations, I asked the Champion to assist us."

"The General is a hero, there is no doubt," the Lord of the Coin said. "But he is not a member of the Trust. He has no place here."

"It is the *King's* Trust," Yacob said. "You are all here at my leisure. And I find Natanel useful."

The Lord of the Coin's nostrils flared. He could have taken issue with that statement – the Trust was a tradition thousands of years old to advise the King and hold him accountable. The people of Jibryl loved their King, but they would revolt if the King dissolved the Trust. Citizens of the kingdom believed the Trust protected them if a king went mad.

As my father taught me growing up, that belief was misplaced. The Trust members were as capable of corruption as any elf. Sometimes more.

Father grinned. "Believe me. I will return to retirement as soon as my King allows."

The First Keeper glanced from me to the King. "I understand your desire for Natanel's presence, my King. But must we suffer his daughter as well? This is a place for elfmen. Not her."

"The King finds me useful," Father said. "And she is useful to me."

My back stiffened. "My name is Elowen. My lords."

First Keeper Fahim's brow creased. "How could she be useful? She's a child."

My father's stare hardened, and the Keeper didn't flinch. I almost did, and it wasn't even directed at me. "She is a skilled warrior and has been disciplined in her education."

Keeper Fahim's face flattened. "A Keeper allowed her to be taught? For what purpose?"

"Because she wished it," Father said. "That is purpose enough."

"You say she is a warrior?" the First Keeper said. "That is not the way of the Great Onamaker. Are we to allow the Cursed to live and serve in the Temple, as well?"

Father grinned again. This time it didn't touch his hard stare. "The parchments would disagree with you. She is taking my place in the Tournament."

The Keeper's jaw dropped. He gave an accusing look to the King. "My King, did you know of this?"

The King didn't answer right away. "Yes. She has the amulet." He waved a dismissal. "It is done, Fahim. We must finalize details for the beginning of the Festival."

Fahim stood stiff. "I must have my objection noted, my Lord. Officially."

Yacob sighed. "It is noted."

"I must also object," Marshall Paavo said. "We don't need this distraction. Not with the whole world watching and whispers of rebellion. We need the support of the people now more than ever. This …" His dark eyes measured me. He didn't seem impressed. "… will not garner that support."

"She has the champion's amulet," the King said. "And the distraction may be greater if we deny her and go against centuries of tradition. Your objection is noted." The King cocked his head at the Lord of Coin. "Aiken. Should I add your objection?"

"I have no objection," Lord Aiken said. "It will not affect the merchant's guild in any way. We have more to worry about."

"Very well," King Yacob said. "Now, let us move on to why we are all here."

Aiken began the discussion with how guests would be lodged and how many foreign merchants would be allowed. Those merchants had already turned in their applications and been approved months ago.

Many Keepers from around the kingdom traveled to Jennah for the Festival. First Keeper Fahim explained the need to ensure the city would shut down for the regular prayer and worship times each day and that the foreigners would be forced to comply.

The Marshall agreed to do what he could, but how could they control thousands from other nations? What would it look like to force others to follow their religious traditions? The City Corps would be out in force and had other more important concerns than someone refusing to pray in the morning.

Keeper Fahim seemed unsatisfied but accepted it.

Shield Shaul used the transition to discuss security concerns. He would have agents in strategic places working with platoons of Corps soldiers. Shaul asked to see the list of foreign merchants and their applications to personally vet them another time. Aiken was reluctant but agreed.

During the meeting, I caught each one glancing at me with not-so-veiled grimaces and looks of disgust. I did my best to keep my gaze on the King. I only failed twice and felt my face grow hot when my eyes locked with Fahim and then Marshal Paavo minutes later. I pulled the shawl on my head further over my eyes.

The King brought the meeting to a close. The Keeper said a prayer to Ona, his hands in the air. I wondered if every Keeper found a way to extend his religious supplication unnecessarily. Did they teach that at the Temple school?

Father and I stepped aside to let the High Marshal, the First Keeper, and the Lord of Coin exit the room.

Once they were far enough ahead of us, Father and I bowed to the King and made the long walk toward the guarded door to exit the throne room. The three members of the Trust were gone, and I waited until I felt we were out of earshot of the King and Shaul.

I brought my voice to a whisper. "I don't think they like me very much."

"You are the master of the obvious," Father mumbled.

"All but Lord Aiken," I said. "The Lord of Coin didn't seem to care."

"The others show their hate because they have agendas and morals, whether the right ones or not. They are loyal to those and easy to understand. Aiken has no loyalty to any idea of right or wrong. He will, however, sell your soul for a few silver serpents."

I sniffed. "Are you saying that I just angered the most powerful elves in the kingdom?"

"No. *We* did," Father said. "And remember, you were the one that wanted to be here."

CHAPTER

A wall separated the northern part of the city from the rest of Jennah. The Ruchali lived in the northern portion. A wide, open area covered with cobblestone and cement lay before the wall, further protecting against the northern region of the city's supposed dangers.

Father had changed out of his Desert Corps uniform and into a light tan tunic and trousers with simple sandals. He had me wear a longer robe over my own trousers and a more formal head covering.

We didn't bring our swords. Too conspicuous for the northern city, Father said, especially Qatal. We both had a dagger and several throwing knives in our pockets.

Four gates allowed access into the northern city. We approached gate three, and the guard eyed us. City Corps soldiers with armor, shields, spears, and scimitars. They stood in the middle of the gate, guarding both directions.

Two of the three guard stepped forward, and the third stayed behind next to an iron lever that controlled the metal gate.

"What is your business, sir?" one guard said.

"Good afternoon, soldier," Father said. "We are on the King's business." He reached into the inside pocket of his tunic and brought out a folded parchment.

The first guard unfolded and read it. His shoulders drew back. "The King's Seal."

"That is correct, soldier," Father said.

The guard handed the parchment back to Father, who folded and returned it to its pocket. The third guard moved the lever, and the gate creaked open.

"Do you need an escort, sir?" the second guard said.

Sure. We'll take an escort while looking for a spy for information.

"We will be fine," Father said. "Thank you."

The guard parted and allowed us through the gate.

I walked into the northern city for the first time in my life.

The streets were narrower, the buildings smaller. Still made of brown stone and wood, most required repair – holes in the roof, doors barely hanging on hinges. While I saw a few elfwomen, the children were everywhere with tattered clothes and covered in dirt and smudges.

We walked through the mud of the streets, my father leading the way. He wound through the buildings, taking a left at an alleyway where we squeezed past a number of young elves. I tried not to meet their eyes. But when I did, there was an emptiness within them that struck me like a smack in the back of the head.

Father rounded the next corner to the right.

I peered around us. "Where are we going?"

His stern glance told me that I was too loud. After passing into an area of the street bereft of people, he leaned close, whispering. "There are still a handful of my contacts that I never divulged to the King."

"You kept them secret from the King?"

His eyes narrowed. "This is a war of secrets."

"A war?"

"Yes, a war," he said. "Secrets have more power than swords or armies. Secrets control those weapons, where and how they are used. Everyone in the war of secrets is alone against everyone else."

"Trust no one," I said, more to myself than for him.

Father nodded. "Come. She is just around the next corner."

Taking a left, he led me to an even narrower street. We were far into the northern city by now, and I didn't know how to make my way back. Looking behind me, though, the spires of the palace were visible just over the roofs. I breathed easier and almost ran into my father as he slowed before a square building with open windows. I peered inside a dim room with tables with scrolls and leather-bound books. Was it a shop? A library?

Father paused at the wooden door made of mismatched slats. He sighed. Scanned the area. No one was visible on the street. Then he entered the building.

I caught the scent of pungent spice and smoke. I winced and coughed. A bone-thin elf sat behind a thick wooden desk at the far side of the room. She lounged in the high back chair with a long pipe in her hand. Her darker skin was marked with lighter patches. Scars? The long braids on her head tinkled when her head turned to regard us.

Her eyes were glassy, her eyelids half closed. When she saw my father, she froze. Her eyes opened to normal – her look of surprise? – and she finally sat up, turning to face us.

"Well, shog me," she said. "I'll be a crizzard's arse. I never thought I'd see you again."

"Bhelen," Father said. "How are you?"

She glanced around the room at the books and bared yellowed teeth. A smile. "Business is good. For the northern city."

A book shop, maybe, but the volumes were in disarray.

"I'm still alive," Bhelen added. "Isn't that enough?"

"For most of us, yes," Father said. "It is good to see you. Alive."

"Please don't be offended if I don't say the same." Bhelen took a drag off her pipe. "Or actually, please be shoggin' offended. I think I would like that." Smoke escaped her lips when she spoke.

Father nodded. "I understand."

Bhelen nodded at me. "Who is this? Your bedgirl?"

Father took a few steps further into the bookshop, and I followed on his heels. "This is my daughter."

After a pause, Bhelen's face became drawn and pained. "This is her?"

"Yes," Father said.

I cleared my throat from the annoyance of the smoke and stepped past my father. The desk was strewn with parchments, bottles of ink, and quills. Her glassy eyes were fixed on me. I extended my hand. "I'm Elowen."

She took my hand, her fingers covered with dried black ink. "Elowen. Talia's daughter." I tensed, hearing my mother's name. Bhelen gripped my hand. "Yes. I see it now. You look like her. It's been so long."

Bhelen released my hand, and I stood straight. "You … you knew my mother?"

She leaned over and addressed Father. "What have you told her?"

"He just told me about my mother and what happened," I said. "Last night."

Chuckling, she said. "Ah, yes. Natanel, the Champion of Kaila. Great with a sword. Even better with secrets, no? A true master." She took another drag off the pipe, her head surrounded in smoke. "Yes, child, I knew her. We were good friends. A part of Natanel's network of spies and informants, we were."

I shifted my weight. "What can you tell me about her?"

Bhelen leaned back and gestured at the room. "More than all of these scrolls and books combined. We grew up together." She squinted. "I'm surprised you brought her here to me, Nat. What are you up to?"

Father spoke with a firm voice. "I need to ask you some questions."

"Ah," she said. "Of course you do. You know, I was surprised all those years ago that agents didn't bust down that door for me after they burned down that village, killing everyone."

Father grunted. "You weren't a part of it. I never told them about you."

"I figured," she said. "You've kept me in your pocket for such a time as this?"

"No," Father said. "I was trying to protect you, protect all my sources. One was compromised. If they had learned about the others close to Talia, they would have killed them. Killed you."

"But you're here now," Bhelen said. "Why?"

"Wait," I said. "I want to hear more about Talia. About my mother."

"Not now," Father said.

"No," I growled. "Now."

Bhelen grinned. "Be patient, child. We will talk in a moment. And I will tell you what you want to hear. Whether he wants to endure it or not." Her grin disappeared when she turned to Father. "Ask your questions."

Father stepped toward her, his hands down but close to hidden weapons. "There have been assassination attempts on the King over the last few months. What do you know about them?"

"I've heard rumors that they happened," Bhelen said. "But I know nothing about who was behind them."

Father cocked his head. "Nothing? That is hard to believe."

"Shog what you believe," she said. "I'm not as connected as I once was. After Talia, I didn't have the stomach to keep working those contacts. And you disappeared. No one tells me anything. And I don't ask."

Father's lips became a line. "What of this Hateph? You know any-thing of him?"

Bhelen took a long draw on her pipe. Her eyes blinked slowly. "You're chasing ghosts, Natanel. You know better. The goblain don't unify."

"But you have heard of him," Father said.

"They speak of him in the northern city." Bhelen shifted her weight in the chair. "In hushed tones. Like he's been blessed by Ona himself."

"You've seen him, met him?" Father said.

"I told you," Bhelen said. "He's a ghost. You know as well as I do that whatever machinations exist probably have their source in the Trust."

Father raised an eyebrow. "You have information on this? Of treachery in the Trust?"

Bhelen laughed. "No. I only know how your people operate. And I know the King. He's done plenty to make enemies within and without."

Father didn't speak for a moment. His silence said enough.

"What about other moves against the King, against the Empire?" Father said. "Any rumors? Anything?"

Bhelen shook her head. "I have nothing to give you. Nothing that will help you."

She and Father stared at each other for a few drawn-out ticks. "Very well," Father said. "Come, Elowen. The hour is late. We need to get back before nightfall."

She snorted. "Yes, before the roaches come out. Or are you more afraid of the ghosts?"

"Come." Father turned to leave.

"Wait," I said. "I want to hear about my mother."

"I did promise her, Nat," Bhelen said. "We won't take too long."

He stopped moving for a moment. "Very well. I'll wait outside."
Then he left.

CHAPTER

15

The room fell quiet, and I didn't know what to say.

Thank the Ona, Bhelen spoke first. "The Champion of Kaila. Such a warrior. Did he tell you how he got his sword? Qatal?"

I frowned. "No. How?"

"Not my story to tell. We are here to speak of your mother. Would you like to sit?"

I glanced around the room. Every surface was covered with a scroll or pile of books. "No, thank you."

"Suit yourself. What would you like to know, child?"

"Anything," I said. "Father never told me about her."

Bhelen rolled her eyes. "There's much I could say. Where do you begin when describing a person? I could tell you she was intelligent, well-read, and fiercer than a flying trodall hyped on hatespice. But that doesn't begin to tell you anything."

"Maybe where she came from?"

"Ah. The chronological option," Bhelen said. "Fine. We grew up in a village far to the north, near the border of Faltiel. She hadn't been made for small town life. I was her only friend. She taught me how to read, so we were both oddities in our village. Talia believed that if we moved to Jennah, we could find more opportunities and make a way for ourselves. But we were Ruchali. When we arrived, well …" Bhelen waved around her. "We had to live here in the northern city.

"But still, she trained herself and learned and fought. Talia was a fine warrior on her own."

"So am I. My father trained me."

"He did?" Bhelen said. "Surprising, that is. Good for him, I guess."

"I have entered the Kaila Tournament."

Bhelen's eyes narrowed. "Impossible."

"I used my father's amulet. I begin tomorrow."

She laughed loudly, wiping a tear from her eye. "Well, you are your mother's daughter, after all."

I shook my head. The daughter of a traitor.

She clicked her tongue. "Talia and I started this bookshop together. I ran it. Especially when she began working with the Knights of Truth."

"The goblain?"

"The *Knights of Truth*," Bhelen said. "The Ruchali that fight for our freedom and rights against the Killer King."

"She was always a traitor? She was always working with the … Knights of Truth?"

"There you go with those words, child," Bhelen said. "Traitor to who? When a kingdom steals your children or kills them because they are deemed defective in some way, cursed, is it a betrayal to fight that King or kingdom? She never thought of herself that way. You say you are a warrior. Wouldn't you fight a crit kingdom that murdered the ones you love?"

"I … don't know."

"Of course you do." Bhelen sighed. "You just don't want to say it. I probably wouldn't, either. But Talia did fight."

I lowered my eyes.

"For a time, she did love your father." Bhelen's voice was low, softer. "She thought maybe he would see and understand. But she was wrong. His duty overcame him and ruled him. When that became clear, she was going to stop working with him and go into hiding. And then she found she was pregnant."

"With me."

She nodded. "With you. No one planned for you. And yet here you are." Bhelen sucked on the pipe, leaned her head back, and blew out a long stream of smoke. "You favor her, surely. I miss her."

"I wish I knew her enough to miss her."

"Me too." Bhelen lowered her gaze for a moment. I could feel the sorrow in her from where I stood. Then she lifted her eyes. "Your father was correct. The hour grows late. You should leave before dark."

I turned and walked to the door. I paused with my hand on the leather strap handle. "Did you tell the truth? You know nothing of the assassination attempts on the King? You know nothing of Hateph?"

"I spoke the truth," Bhelen said. "Hateph is no one. A ghost. I also spoke true when I suggested you seek your enemies in the Trust. They are no friends of the King. Never have been. Your father knows this more than anyone."

Trust no one.

"I understand," I said. "Thank you."

"You come back anytime. You're always welcome. We are family, you and me." She hissed. "Just don't bring your father back with you."

"Okay." I opened the door and left.

CHAPTER

My father was silent as we made our way back through the northern city to the same gate. The sun began to lower in the sky, hiding behind the city walls by the time we arrived. The guard allowed us through.

Once in the central part of Jennah, I spoke to him in a low voice. "Is it true what she said?"

Father's limp seemed more pronounced as we neared the southern market, different shops and housing hovering over us on either side. "What did she say?"

"That the kingdom of Jibryl stole their children, killed others."

"We have been at war, one way or another, with the Ruchali for thousands of years," Father said. "There has been violence on both sides. Did she tell you of the countless times the goblain have killed innocents in the streets of this city? Of the villages of Jibrylans in the north that their so-called warriors have decimated?"

"No."

"She wouldn't," he said. "That wall exists for a reason."

I remained silent for a few minutes. We turned onto a wide street that led to the southern market square.

"What will we do now?" I asked.

"I have other contacts," he said. "I will contact them tomorrow."

"You mean *we* will."

"No. You will be fighting in the tournament."

"Not all day," I said. "My first bout is in the morning. I don't fight until the next day, and that's if I win."

"We shall see."

"Bhelen also mentioned betrayal in the Trust," I said. "Do you have any idea who that could be?"

"We won't place much stock in what Bhelen said until I can check with other sources," he said.

"Okay." The southern market square shone golden with the orange sunset spreading across the western sky. "Father?"

"Yes?"

"Why did you take me to her? Was it to learn more about my mother?"

We turned right along an open pathway through the merchants. The palace of the King rose before us.

"No," Father said. "And yes."

"Thank you."

He said no more after that.

CHAPTER

17

The contestants for the Tournament arrived that evening. I gathered my bags and moved into another building situated next to the stables, with more guest apartments set up for foreign dignitaries and other visitors connected to the swordmasters.

Sixteen contestants and their entourages began to enter the housing area, directed by the palace guard and servants. One after another, a contestant arrived in the lobby; the elves wore fine robes and finer swords. Humans came dressed in tunics, trousers, and boots of high quality and clean leather. Heavy furs and leathers covered the dwarves.

Each contestant had at least one weapons-master or assistant of some kind. A few had several, carrying luggage and other effects.

A human woman passed me, slightly taller than me. A boy child followed her with an older woman behind. A nurse of some kind?

The contestants didn't need the fine clothes or attendants for impact. Their very presence intimidated everyone except for each other. These were masters of their craft, the greatest blademasters in the world.

I stood in the lobby near the door in my worn robe and a simple sword at my hip, my canvas bag slung over my shoulder.

"Can I help you, ma'am?"

I blinked and started, turning to the voice. Then released a breath. "Refa."

The palace servant gave a slight bow and smiled at me. "At your service."

I nodded at the contestants and servants moving through the lobby. "They are from all over the world. I've never seen a human before. At all. And there was a woman with her kid earlier."

"That was Mia from Lior, her son, Lucas, and her aunt Shallam," Refa said.

"You've met them?"

He chuckled. "No. But the servants must know everyone who enters the palace; their names and purpose."

"Wait. You know everyone's name here? All the contestants and their people?"

"Part of my job," he said.

"Impressive." I grinned at him. "Good to see a friendly face."

"I am glad to be of any help." He gave a flourish.

"Are you assigned to one of the contestants, or are you just visiting?" I asked.

"I am here to escort you to your room, madam. Was that not clear?"

"Um, no. Not clear. They assigned you to me?"

"Actually," he said, "I requested to be assigned to you."

My brows rose. "With all these warriors from around the world, you requested me?"

"I did," Refa said. "I thought you might want, what you called it, a friendly face."

"You don't have to be so kind. It may be a short assignment. I may not survive past tomorrow."

"Perhaps," he said. "Stranger things have happened."

I leaned in closer. "Probably why you requested me, right? Short assignment, quick time to vacation."

"I work in the palace, and it is the Kaila Festival. There is no such thing as a vacation."

"That makes sense," I said.

"Shall I carry your bag to your room?"

I glanced over my shoulder at the bag. "I think I can handle it."

"Not a problem," he said. "Glad to do it."

I slung the bag down and handed it to him. "It's all yours."

"Thank you. Follow me, please."

Once Refa, a palace servant, took my bag and led me through the lobby, contestants began to take notice of me. The brow creased on an elf from Kasem. A Faltielan elf followed me with mouth agape. A Kryan contestant dismissed me with a look of disgust. I tried to keep my eyes forward.

We reached the wide staircase that wound up through the middle of the building. Ascending, I said, "They didn't know I was a contestant."

"They do now," Refa said.

He led me to the fourth floor and then to the last door on the left. Opening the door revealed a spacious but simple room lit by two oil lamps.

Refa left the door open while he placed my bag on the bed near the far window. The night sky and three moons shone through. A plate of cheeses and flat breads sat next to a carafe of red wine on the table next to a short couch. I didn't realize I was so hungry until I saw the food. My stomach gave a gurgle.

Refa stood in the middle of the room. "I will not be staying in the room with you, as some servants will for other contestants. For obvious reasons."

"Of course."

"Do you require anything else before I go?" Refa asked.

"I don't think so," I said. "But I do have a question."

He stood and waited.

"If you're … assigned to me," I said, "how do I get ahold of you if I do need something?"

"Good question. I will be staying in a room just down the hall, a small servant's quarters. That button …" He pointed to a golden button near the door. "… buzzes into my room. I am only a few steps away."

"Okay," I said.

He nodded and began to leave.

"Wait," I said. "One more thing."

Refa stopped. "Yes?"

"I know how the King and others feel about me being here, being in the Tournament. To be honest, none of the other servants would help me, right? They made you do this."

"I did make the request." He didn't offer more.

I raised a brow. "But it is true that others didn't want to."

Refa paused before answering. "As I said before, I felt you needed a friendly face."

"I'll take that as a yes." I snorted. "They don't believe I should be here at all. And looking at those other warriors tonight, I'm starting to think they're right."

Refa continued to stare at me.

"I mean, I forced myself into this competition because I wanted to prove something, to crit on my father and the King and everyone else," I said. "Didn't think it all the way through."

I didn't mention the possibility of assassins among the contestants. He didn't need to know that.

"Here is what I know," Refa said. "If I may …"

"Please."

"First, if you got into the competition to, as you put it, crit on your father and the King, then it seems you've accomplished your goal already." Refa smirked. "From my perspective."

"Funny. Is there a second?"

"Yes," he said. "Second, I witnessed an amazing feat last night."

My brow creased. "What was that?"

"An elfdaughter left a palace and slept in a stable with two sahala like they were old friends."

I shrugged. "We are."

"That is not normal. I have never even heard of such a thing. I don't know many elfmen that would brave such a thing."

"My father would. And has."

"You are probably correct," he said. "But if a fierce war lizard counts you as kindred, then it may be your opponent that should be concerned." He bowed. "That is only the view of a lowly servant."

"Right. A lowly servant." I nodded. "Thank you for that."

"It is my duty to serve," he said.

"Thank you. Oh, and you know *my* name, correct?"

"I do," he said.

"Then call me Elowen, please," I said. "I would like that."

He bowed once more. "Yes, Elowen. Good night."

Refa turned and left, closing the door behind him.

CHAPTER

"What do you mean I'm fighting first?" I squealed at my father.

We walked through the central city courtyard and turned north, shouldering our way through the throng of people.

Jennah had grown two or three sizes overnight. People from all over the world had come to the city for trade, entertainment, celebration, or religion. Most visitors were elves from the other three elven kingdoms, but dwarves and humans bustled among the crowd, as well.

"You took my place in the tournament." Father had to raise his voice over the din of people around us. "I was to be an exhibition, not a serious contestant. Now it's you."

Leaving the courtyard, Father took me along the main street that led to the massive building a kilomitre or so away. The arena. The crowd thinned slightly on the street.

"They could have rescheduled the bouts," I said.

"That would have thrown off the whole tournament and upset other contestants and nations. There are five rounds, and the seedings are very political. Even the one you're fighting in an hour was carefully chosen."

"You know who it is?" I said.

Father frowned at me, the *silly question* look. "You will face Xong, one of the two contestants from Kasem."

Eleven nations sent contestants to the Tournament – four elven, two dwarven, and five human. To get to the sixteen open seats, all four elven nations sent two contestants, and one of the human kingdoms, Erelon, sent two. All others sent one.

I was the second for Jibryl, the position meant for Natanel, the Champion of the Kaila.

"You know anything about Xong?" I said.

"I have heard of him."

After a moment, I said, "And?"

"For those that send two contestants, like Kasem, they usually send one of their top masters and one making his way." He huffed. "Or her."

I groaned. "Let me guess, Xong is the master."

Father nodded. "He is over a millennium in age and a famous student of Akeno."

I stumbled and almost fell. "Akeno?" Elves all over the continent read heroic stories of that ancient swordmaster.

"Yes."

The arena loomed over us while we drew closer. What had I been thinking? A thousand-year-old elf trained by Akeno?

I stopped in the middle of the street, gazing up at the flags flying from the top of the gigantic stone arena.

Father turned around and stood before me. "Elowen."

Blinking, I met his eyes.

"You chose this, remember," he said.

"If I didn't remember, you'd keep reminding me."

"These are some of the greatest warriors in the world, highly trained, many of them battle-tested. I didn't enter the tournament until I was 326 years old. I didn't win until twenty years later."

My eyes narrowed. "This is really encouraging. Thanks."

"I'm not trying to encourage you," Father said. "What would a lie mean to you now? You've heard me talk about this tournament. It is dangerous."

"How dangerous?"

"It is rare, but people have died." Father took another step closer. "Listen to me. You've been well trained. You may not win the first bout, but acquit yourself well, last a few minutes, and you can still gather with the other contestants, which was the point all along. To give you access to possible threats to the king."

My mouth became a line. "You think I'm well trained."

"That's a compliment to *me*, by the way," Father said.

"I caught that. You think I'm good enough to win?"

"I think you're good enough to survive," he corrected. "And that is the goal. Remember, this is a bout with the sword, but there are other weapons in that arena."

"Like what?" I said. "Knives? I thought other weapons weren't allowed on the platform."

"Just be careful and keep your eyes open. You'll be fine."

He turned and led me back through a separated door away from the main crowds and into the underbelly of the building. The tunnel opened to a larger room where the contestants gathered, a few with their weapons-master or a servant. Most were alone.

I only recognized a few of them. Claudim was the other contestant from Jibryl. He glared at me the moment we entered the room. Mia from Veradis, which Refa pointed out the night before, was the only other female in the room. She nodded at me.

And there was Julius.

Julius was an elf from Kryus and the current champion, winning the last two tournaments. He had pearl-white skin and long dark hair flowing past his shoulders. Julius lounged in the corner, dressed in a simple robe. He was the only contestant not to give some reaction when I entered. Most were dismissive toward me. Two of the elves were hateful, one from Kasem I assumed to be Xong.

Father and I hovered at the entrance to the room. He pointed to a space to the left, one not taken by a contestant. It had a chair and pegs on the wall with items gathered there. "There is your tournament sword and armor. I requested a sword the same length and weight as your own. The armor should fit you. I must leave you now and sit with the King and his family. You have any questions?"

After a hesitation, I shook my head.

"Very well," he said. "Ona be with you."

"And with you."

Father left, and as piffed and disappointed as I was with him, I never felt more alone.

I forced my feet to walk over to the corner. A stool was set before the open closet area that held what I would need for the bout. I took off the belt that held my own sword. Lifting the tournament sword, father had done well. Its balance and weight were a perfect copy of my own, but the blade was blunted.

While blunted, the blade could still injure if struck against the body with enough force, hence the armor. Many contestants suffered broken bones and lacerations.

Setting the sword back down, I dressed in the padded breastplate made for an elfman, and I cinched it more at the waist while tight around my chest. It worked well enough. Should I take my present head covering off before wearing the helmet? Shrugging, I tried it over the thin cloth, and with some adjustment, it fit fine, so I left it.

My eyes wandered to Claudim, already dressed, and I caught him staring. I stared at his breastplate. A Desert Corps hornoth was painted across the chest, the same legion as my father. Scanning the room, most of the contestants had some sort of emblem emblazoned upon their breastplate – an eagle, a lion, and others.

The armor I wore was bare. Was that done on purpose? Did Jibryl not want me to represent them?

I straightened my tunic and trousers for comfort and movement. Then I sat on the stool, doing my best to breathe and remain calm and centered.

One by one, the contestants filed out of the room, a different door than where Father and I entered. This exit led to the arena.

All of the swordmasters left until I was alone with one of the humans, Mia. She finished tightening the straps on her own armor.

Mia met my eyes. "Did you volunteer for this, or did someone force you to fight?"

I blinked and frowned. "I volunteered. No one forces me to fight. I'm not a slave."

Then I snapped my mouth shut and cringed. Many humans were slaves throughout the elven empires, especially Kasem and Kryus.

Mia appeared unfazed. "Good. I would hate to think someone forced you into this."

I frowned. "Did someone force you?"

She chuckled. "Me? No. Back in Veradis, we had a separate competition to have the honor of coming to this tournament. I had to fight some of my country's best to get here."

"What are you saying?" I bared my teeth. "That I don't belong? Because I had to use the amulet to get in?"

"Not at all," Mia said. "I did not mean to offend you."

I nodded and adjusted my belt again.

"I met your father once, years ago," Mia said.

"You did?"

"I was young, maybe two or three, and it was two Kaila ago," Mia said. "My father was a contestant, his last year. I got to meet the great

Natanel. It was an honor. He was kind to me, a human child and a girl. I'll never forget meeting him."

I paused before speaking. "Your father trained you?"

She nodded. "As yours did, I suspect."

"Yes. Is your father here?"

Mia's eyes fell. "No. He died five years ago."

"Oh, I'm sorry."

"Me too," Mia said. "But he died doing what he loved."

He got to do what he loved? What would that be like? "What was that?"

"Fighting for what he believed in," Mia said. "Choosing to use his sword for what is good and right. I miss him."

"He was … free to fight for what he chose?"

Mia nodded. "It is rare in this world, I know. But he did."

"And you? Do you also?"

Mia reached over and touched her sword that leaned against the wall, the tournament blade in her other hand "I do."

My brows creased.

Mia stood and walked to the exit to the tunnel that led under the bleachers to the fight field. She paused there. "As to whether or not you belong here, that is not for me to say. It's not for anyone to say. Not even you."

I frowned up at her.

"There's only one way anyone will know, including yourself." She leaned closer to me. "You will prove it. Out there. In front of the world." She stood straight. "Maybe that's not comforting. It is true, however. With the great Natanel's training, you may be more ready than you think. Come on. It's about to start. You're first, I think."

Mia smiled and disappeared into the tunnel.

CHAPTER

19

The tunnel was dim with torches giving low light. I passed through the tunnel. While I walked, the crowd announced itself with a whispering roar that increased in volume until the noise was a physical force. The end of the tunnel shone like the sun. I walked into the light and onto the field, using my left hand to shield my eyes.

My right held the tourney sword.

Thousands of people yelled and screamed in the stands of the arena, and I walked past a short bleacher section where the contestants all sat. I hovered near the front. A platform sat in front of me on the center floor of the arena, and just beyond the platform was another sitting area where the royal family congregated. My father and Shaul sat among them with guard all around.

Xong stood on the raised platform. He wore a light tunic and simple trousers, a brown leather belt around his waist. His head was bald, his tan skin glistening in the bright sun.

An elf in a blue and red robe approached me, his hair close-cropped on his head, his darker Jibrylan face scowling down at me. "It is time to start. Get on the platform." The referee.

He moved to the side to allow me to pass.

I licked my lips, looking at the referee and then over my shoulder at the contestants. Last, I turned to see the King sharing the referee's scowl. The crowd shook their fists at me. My father's face was blank.

There's only one way anyone will know. You will prove it.

I rolled my shoulders, took a breath, and ascended the stairs up to the platform.

The stone platform was a large circle, and Xong stood at the other end, his sword held at his side. I waited on the opposite side.

The referee stepped onto the stone next to me. "You know the rules? You've been to the tournament before?"

I nodded. "Fatal strikes are to the torso and head. It is up to the competitors to yield if they can't continue."

"What happens if you leave the field?" he asked.

"Forfeit." I met his gaze. "But I will not run."

"We'll see." He glanced pointedly at Xong. He turned back to me. "I will call fatal strikes. No one else. Keep fighting until that happens, or there is yielding or forfeit."

"I understand."

He nodded, the scowl never leaving his face, but he left me there to take a position in the center of the platform. The referee waited for the King.

King Yacob stood, and at that movement, the crowd fell silent. The King raised his arms and said, "Welcome one and welcome all to the Festival of Peace and Beauty, the Kaila. We gather for the good and benefit of all to entertain, educate, and host our friends from around the world. We begin the Festival with the great tournament. The first bout."

Yacob's smile seemed painted on.

"From the great land of Kasem," the King said, "we have Xong, a legendary warrior of many battles."

The crowd cheered.

"Many of you remember the great champion, Natanel, the Son of Wahid," the King continued. "One of our greatest generals."

The crowd's cheers grew louder.

"Fighting for Jibryl today is Natanel's daughter," the King said. "Let the Kaila commence!"

And he sat down.

He didn't even say my name.

I knew I wasn't a legendary warrior. The only battle I ever fought was in the middle of the night, and a sahala had to save me.

But he could have said my name.

My fingers tightened on the hilt of the sword in my hand.

The referee bowed to the King. Then he turned to Xong. "Contestant, are you ready?"

Xong gave a nod of his head.

The referee turned to me. "Contestant, are you ready?"

I widened my stance, set my sword out in a diagonal guard, and peered at the referee. "I am."

"Very well." The referee backed to the platform's edge, raised his right arm that held a long white cloth, and swiped it down through the air. "Begin."

The crowd made noise, but I pushed them from my mind. I crouched lower, getting a better center of gravity and balance, and stepped forward a pace to ensure I didn't get pushed off the platform when Xong attacked.

Except he didn't.

He stood there, holding his sword in both hands, the blade down, his eyes pointed at the ground.

Frowning, I continued to wait. Was that his stance? His style? To stand until the other attacked?

Another few ticks of time passed, and the crowd began to stir, first with silence then with murmurs. Then they started to boo. One or two began, then it swelled.

The crowd wanted action. They bought their tickets to see a battle.

I squinted over at Xong. "You just going to stand there?"

His gaze lifted to my own. "I was meant to fight a champion. Not a child."

Ah. My father was supposed to be his opponent. The legendary Natanel. It insulted him to have to fight me, an elfdaughter, no one.

"Sorry you're stuck with me," I said. "You're just going to stand there?"

"I am."

I gritted my teeth. "What do you expect me to do? Attack you?"

"You can," Xong said. "Or you could step down from the platform."

"But then I'd be eliminated," I said. "A forfeit."

"Yes."

The referee spoke to me. "Daughter of Natanel, you are free to step down from the platform and forfeit this match."

Even above the rising boos, the crowd heard that. They shook their fists and cried out, "Get off the platform!" "Forfeit!"

Those were my choices? Forfeit the match or attack a swordmaster? Xong would be better trained on how to turn my aggression against me. My whole plan was to try to stay on defense, measure Xong's skill, and look for weaknesses. That plan was lost in the dunes now.

I relaxed a bit, keeping my sword up just in case, and looked over at my father. He maintained his lack of expression. The King's glower had deepened, if possible.

My father. *Even a novice can beat a master on the right day.* I had fought a swordmaster and champion every day of my life.

I came up with a different plan. And not a very good one.

"Crit it all." I moved forward, twirling the blade in my hand, walking to approach from his left.

Xong raised an eyebrow at me but otherwise didn't move.

I kept my movements deliberate and smooth until I got within three paces of him. Then I lunged at him with a wide swing of my blade aimed at his head. His own raised in a flash – so fast – and met my blade with a clang. I let the sword bounce off his and turned it for another slash he blocked before my feet fully hit the platform.

The crowd cheered.

Crouching, I pressed him with two more strikes, one high and the other low. I slid to one side and then the other, alternating my angle while giving him a light touch and a straight stab, all of which he deflected without much effort.

Then his brow creased, he turned my next strike, and he began his own attack.

There it is.

Xong's forms were efficient, honed by years of training. No energy was wasted. He breathed easy. It took all of my speed and calm to divert his attacks – trying to upend me with a low swipe, a slash at my opposite knee, and a fierce chop at my head, which would have taken my head off if it connected, dull blade or not. But I stood my ground.

He adjusted his angle, taking a step away from the edge of the platform, coming at me from the side, his blade a blur. He shifted his hold on the hilt, rocked to the ball of the back foot, and moved his sword along the horizontal. A strong move.

Now.

I met his blade with mine, the blunted steel blades ringing.

Then I released my sword. The sword went end over end and landed on the stone platform a mitre beyond me.

The crowd gasped.

A hint of a grin showed on Xong's face. He stepped forward and stabbed at my padded breastplate, looking to end the bout then and there. His blade met only air when I slid to the side. The lack of resistance to his blade caught him off balance, his momentum carrying him forward.

With speed born of desperation, I grabbed his wrist with my left hand and spun my whole body, pulling him to continue in that direction. Along my spin, I tried to elbow him in the back of the head, a little extra push.

He was a master. It wouldn't be that easy. Beginning to recover, his feet shuffled, and he turned in midair, blocking my elbow with his left. Xong twisted to strike at me with his sword. I swatted the flat of the dull blade across my body with both hands. At the same time, he was still leaning backward when I jumped forward and kicked him full force with both feet in his chest.

Xong's arms flailed, his sword reflecting in the morning sun, his eyes going wide while his feet left the platform, and he lost complete control.

I landed on my arse and hopped up in a crouch in time to see him bounce off the side of the platform, his arms and legs scrambling. He fell the mitre distance to the field below.

The crowd was silent. The whole arena was silent.

"I can't believe that worked," I said under my breath. *There are other weapons in that arena.*

I stood and took the few steps to the edge of the platform. Xong looked up at me from the ground, baring his teeth, and holding his chest. His padded armor probably saved a few of his ribs from being broken. His glare would have killed me if it could.

I bowed down to him. "Well fought Xong from Kasem. You honored me with the bout. Ona be with you."

I picked up my dull sword from the floor, strode to the center of the platform where the referee waited for me, and stood next to him.

The referee grabbed my wrist. "My name is Elowen," I mumbled so only he could hear.

He grunted, and lifted my arm. "Victor of the bout. Elowen, the daughter of Natanel."

In the ancient stories of Selina the Brave and other heroes, there would have been a rousing roar of joy for me, changed hearts, and glory for the winner.

The crowd that day sat stunned and gave me a half-hearted smattering of applause. The King's jaw had dropped. He closed it and gave me two claps. My father still didn't show any emotion on his face, but he did clap for me.

The referee lowered my arm. I sniffed, turned on a heel, and left the platform to join the other contestants on the bleachers nearby. Enduring a few glares and frowns of confusion, I moved to sit on the second of four rows in one of the empty spots. Mia winked when I caught her grin. One of the dwarves nodded at me in respect and said, "Well done, young one."

Xong dusted himself off and sat on the opposite side on the third row with one more parting glance.

Julius, last year's champion, sat in the top row. He chuckled behind me. It was not a kind sound.

CHAPTER

"But you told me that there were other weapons in the arena," I said. "Isn't that what you meant? Hands, feet, clothing?"

We made our way north from the square again in the afternoon, a cool breeze across our faces. The wall between us and the northern city faced us after we took a right on one of the streets.

"Yes," Father said. "But I meant to watch for others to use them. Not you."

"There aren't any rules against punches, kicks, those types of things, are there?"

"No," Father said. "No official rules."

"Then why are you acting like I did something wrong?"

The third gate loomed before us at the end of the street. We used a different entrance to reach Father's contacts in the northern city today.

My bout had been the first of eight, all sixteen contestants fighting in the first round. The round ended in the early afternoon with eight victors and the other half eliminated from the competition.

Ogden, the dwarf that nodded and spoke to me, won the second bout against one of the humans from Eleron. Mia won her bout. As did Claudim. Julius won his battle within a few moments. The crowd roared when he was proclaimed the victor, almost as loudly as they had for Claudim, the other contestant from Jibryl.

Father and I went back to the palace complex to change, gather our daggers and throwing knives instead of swords, and return to the northern city.

"I told you to simply survive," Father said. "You weren't supposed to win. You were just supposed to get in the tournament, make connections, and watch for anything suspicious."

My heart sank to the emptiness in the pit of my abdomen. "But I won."

"You embarrassed a swordmaster and tricked him," Father said.

"I looked for a weakness like you taught me. And exploited it. His pride. He underestimated me."

Father stopped in the street. "You believe you could have beat him otherwise?"

"It was a feint," I said. "I drew him forward, exposed him, yes, but that's good strategy, right?"

"Do you believe you could have beat him without it?"

I sighed. "I don't know. That's like asking me if I could win without good strategy, fighting to win."

"You are fighting to win the wrong battle," Father said. "Your goal isn't to win the bout, beat your opponent, or even win the tournament. Your goal is to protect the King. And that means looking for a very real assassin that might be among the contestants."

My mouth became a line. "I can do both."

"No, you can't. Two different goals divide your attention. You're focused on proving everyone wrong, that you can be a warrior and an elfdaughter. What happens when you allow something to distract your focus?"

The answer from years of lessons came to my lips without effort. "Divided focus loses the battle."

"That is why we attempt to distract and divide our opponents," Father said. "Do not fall into the same trap, or we will lose this battle. This is not a tournament. The consequences are much greater."

I nodded. "I understand."

"Good," Father said. "Now, let's try to reach my contact before it gets late."

The guard noticed our approach, and we moved through the gate easily as we did the day before with the missive and the King's Seal. Once on the other side of the wall, Father led us along a different path through the run-down homes and buildings.

"We are close," Father said.

After a few minutes, we turned another right. Father skidded to a halt and reached out with a hand to stop me. I followed his stare to a building fifty mitres on the left. It had been burnt recently, now only a skeleton of blackened beams and browned piles of stone.

A black figure lay on the dirt in front of the burning building. It took my brain a tick to recognize that it was a body.

Father scanned up and down the street, his other hand hovering near his hip where a dagger waited. He crept up the street, and I followed. Now within twenty mitres or so, he stopped and stood against the wall of a shop across from our burned target.

The street appeared devoid of life.

"This happened yesterday, probably last night," Father said.

"Who is that?" I breathed. My heart pounded in my chest. I reached into my tunic and grabbed one of my two long daggers.

"I will assume that is my contact. His name was D'Nuan. A jewelry merchant. Not wealthy. Dealt mostly in cheap baubles."

D'Nuan wouldn't be doing that now. I whispered a prayer to Ona. "Was this the goblain?"

Father nodded.

"Did they know we were coming?" I said.

Father snorted. "The city knows I've returned for the tournament. It is possible some of my old contacts were compromised over the last twenty years."

"Bhelen?" I said.

Father shook his head. "I never told her about D'Nuan. It's imperative to keep them independent so that if one is compromised, you don't lose all of them."

I stared at the motionless charred body. "Did this one know mother?"

"No. Talia didn't know him, but it could be connected to us. Or a coincidence."

"Probably not a coincidence," I said.

"No. Probably not."

I blinked to keep my thoughts focused on the moment and off my mother. "If this does have something to do with us, we should go. The goblain could still be here."

"They've been here the whole time," Father said.

"What?"

"If you can fight your way free, then make your way back to the palace. I'll be right behind you."

My head swiveled. "What are you talking about? I'm not ..."

Noise came from above me, and I looked up.

A figure in black dove from the roof. I cried out and spun to my left, pulling the dagger from my tunic. The goblain landed next to me but gurgled and straightened. He fell over with a throwing knife in his back.

Father held a knife in each hand now, and he threw one when another came from the roof above us, hitting the goblain in the eye, the elf wiggling in death the rest of the way down.

A goblain emerged from the alley to my left. I tossed the dagger to my left hand and reached into my tunic for a knife, removing and throwing with my right in one motion, hitting the goblain in the middle of the chest. He coughed, dropping his sword. I stepped forward and ran the dagger into his chest next to the knife.

Figures appeared from alleys and dropped down from the rooftops across the street, and emerged from doorways. So many. Way more than the throwing knives we brought. Father had commented in the desert *they should have sent more.* They didn't make that mistake this time. I guessed at least thirty, half with short swords and others with clubs. A few had short bows and arrows.

Father picked up the goblain sword next to him with his left hand and held a throwing knife in his right. I reached down and lifted the blade from the one I had just killed. My father stayed against the wall, keeping at least one direction protected.

"I'm going to fight a way through," Father said. "I want you to run back to the wall and the southern city."

"I'm not leaving you," I spoke through my teeth. "We'll get out together."

Father glared at me. The goblain encircled us. No time. "Follow me."

He pushed off from the wall, a short sword from one of the goblain now in his left hand and a throwing knife in his right, and sprinted at an angle toward one of the goblain with a bow. The elf lifted the bow to fire, but Father's throwing knife spun in the air and stuck in his neck before he could get a shot off.

The other goblain rushed in. An arrow from behind me skipped off the dirt street. I threw two knives in the twenty mitres it took us to get to the dead bow-elf – hitting the other bow-elf in the shoulder and killing a second that closed in on us.

Father knelt enough to grab the bow and the quiver off of the dead, and while he still held the short sword, he turned and began firing at the others, starting with those closest to us. I took position behind him, protecting his back. Goblain screamed as they died with arrows in their chests, and three died while the others rushed us.

A goblain appeared, swiping a club at Father. With the sword in my left hand, I severed his arm at the elbow and jabbed him in the chest with the dagger now in my right. Father killed two more with the bow.

I ducked an arrow that sailed overhead. I spun to see another bow-elf further up the street. I darted past my father to attack the last elf with a bow.

"Elowen!" my father called. I ignored it.

Goblain waited between me and the bow-elf, and I angled my approach to keep them between us so the arrows wouldn't have a direct shot. One goblain tried to grab me, holding his sword high. I stabbed his forearm with the dagger and slashed with the short sword across his face. He cried out and fell away to reveal one behind him with a club.

The club swept down at my legs. I hurdled it, and with my forward momentum, I slammed both knees into his chest. We fell down together, me landing upon him and crushing his ribs when we hit the street. I rolled forward, and when I came up to a crouch, an arrow from Father sailed over my shoulder to hit a third goblain in the chest. When he fell, the bow-elf stood just beyond, staring straight at me, an arrow knocked. He began to lift the arrow and hesitated.

Why had he hesitated? He had a clean shot.

In his hesitation, I threw the dagger underhand, and the blade sunk into his shoulder. Jumping to my feet and running, I reached him in another two steps and sliced the sword across his neck. I grabbed the dagger from his shoulder, placed it in my leather belt, and snatched the bow and quiver.

Pulling an arrow, I turned to the nearest goblain and fired. The bow was old, and the arrow wasn't perfectly straight, wobbling in the air but still finding a thigh. Nocking another, I shot at the next one, aiming better and hitting him in the stomach.

Father spoke from behind me, close. "The alley. Get us moving."

I turned to the left and ran toward the open alley past the burned shop and the blackened body of Father's contact, Father following. A goblain tried to cut us off, but I shot an arrow into his chest.

We made the alley. I waited for Father. "You lead the way back," I told him.

He no longer held the bow – the arrows spent. He made it into the alley, his limp more pronounced, now holding a short sword in both hands.

I fired at three more goblain, hitting two. A quick count told me nine goblain chased us into the alley, running through the bodies that littered the streets.

Turning on a heel, I ran and caught up with Father. He took a left at the other end of the alley, down a street toward the south. The street wound to the east, so he took another right. At the corner, I paused to look behind us – a handful of goblain closed in. I shot three of them.

With only two more arrows left, I spun and ran after my father. He had slowed while I paused to shoot back, and there was now a gap between us. I pushed my legs forward.

And three goblain dropped down between us, only a pace from me. One ran toward Father with a short sword held high. The other two sprang at me. I swiped across with the short bow, knocking the club aside on the right; in doing so, I allowed an opening on my left for a goblain with a short sword.

The goblain didn't stab me, as he easily could have. He grabbed me with his free hand and pulled me toward him, lifting the hilt of the sword to slam it into my face. I ducked it, moving to lean my shoulder into his chest, but the other elf clutched at my shoulders from behind and kept me from any momentum.

That close, he could have brained me with the club. But didn't.

Footfalls sounded behind me. How many more were there? I twisted and slashed with my sword across the abdomen of one that held me. With the bow, I hooked it over the head of the other. The bow and string caught on his neck, and I yanked him down with my body weight.

Two others drew close from behind. I let go of the bow while that goblain hit the ground, and the other fell back with his hands holding his bloody midsection. Still in the middle of my spin, I now faced the other two and launched the short sword at one of them. He attempted to dodge, but the blade caught his shoulder and knocked him against the alley wall.

The other swung at me with a long wooden plank. I jumped further into him and struck at the inside of his forearm with both of my hands. The bones of his arm snapped, he cried out, and I elbowed him under the chin. His head snapped back, teeth clacking, and he fell.

I turned to face any other attackers, and my father stood there over a bleeding goblain.

Scanning the alley, no goblain stood. Only dead and bleeding bodies. My father had killed the others.

Except for the one I had just elbowed. He groaned and stirred.

I was panting all of a sudden. Or maybe I had been the whole time. I leaned against the wall of the alley, my head down.

Father glanced at me. "Are you hurt?"

I shook my head.

"Good," Father said.

My father was covered in blood. "Are you?" I asked.

Father shook his head. Not his blood.

He took a few limping steps over to the only living goblain in the alley and took a dagger from his belt. "Find your way to the south, Elowen. It will be dark soon. There may be more."

More? "What about you?"

"I will be right behind you." He stared down at the one living goblain.

"If there could be more, then we should both go."

He crouched over the goblain. Father groaned as he settled. He pulled the hood off of the elf and grabbed the front of his tunic, lifting him off the ground and placing the dagger at the neck. The goblain's eyes bulged, and he bared his teeth.

"I will be right behind you," he said again. "First, we must have a conversation."

Conversation. Back in the desert, only a few days ago, he killed the assassin quickly because there hadn't been time to get information out of him before the others had attacked us. Zealots were resistant to questioning.

Questioning.

"You're going to torture him," I breathed.

"Wen," Father said. "Please. Go. I don't want you to see this."

I pushed off the wall and stood straight. "If you don't want me to see it, then maybe you shouldn't do it."

He sighed but didn't look at me. "You know I have to do this."

In the back of my mind, especially since the desert, I knew my father had done things he wasn't proud of. Even torture. But now it was real. It was in front of me.

I stared at the goblain on the ground, his fear and anger directed at my father, at me. This was my enemy. He wanted to kill us, to hurt us. They had killed Father's contact. They tried to kill us in the desert. They wanted to murder the King.

This was my enemy. I should hate him. But in that moment, I saw an elf. An elf about to be hurt. Tortured.

How many had I just killed? I didn't even know. My father even more. But we had been attacked. We had killed in self-defense, to live, to survive.

This was different. Causing pain to the defenseless, to the unarmed, felt foreign to me. And I was about to watch my father do it.

"No, I don't," I said. "You don't have to do this."

He shook the goblain beneath him, angling the dagger better to the throat. "I do. Please. Go."

"Come with me. I'm begging you."

Father turned his head and glared at me. "Leave."

When he turned his head, however, the goblain gripped the hilt of the dagger with his hand. "For the Hateph!" the elf said. And pulled the blade of the dagger toward him.

The sharpened steel slipped into the goblain's throat.

Father cursed, ripping the blade back. Blood sprouted from the hole in the goblain's throat. His eyes went blank while he gurgled, choking on his own blood. Father released the tunic and let the elf fall to the ground.

The goblain lay still.

Father's shoulders slumped. He wiped the blood from the dagger on the goblain's tunic and stood.

He limped past me down the alley without a word or a look.

I followed.

CHAPTER

F ather and I hadn't talked on the way back. We had stopped at
a dirty public water trough – for animals or people, I didn't
know – and cleaned most of the blood from our hands.
Father's tunic was covered with blood, so he stripped to his under-
shirt and threw the tunic aside. I carried what few weapons we had
left.

The guard watched Father with skeptical eyes, but the King's seal
and Father's glare convinced them.

We entered the southern city. I released a breath. We made it to
the palace courtyard near the stables after the sun fell behind the city
walls.

Father stopped. "I will continue the investigation alone."

I frowned at him. "What does that mean?"

"It was a mistake to bring you today."

"A mistake?" I scoffed. "You might not have survived without
me. They're obviously looking for you. Did you see how many they
sent? You can't go back in alone."

He shook his head. "There are things I have to do to get the
information I need. Things you don't have the strength to do."

My nostrils flared. "Don't have the strength? I have to be strong to torture people?"

My voice had raised, and Father made it a point to scan the courtyard. No one in sight. He kept his voice low. "I told you not to come. I told you that there were no heroes in the battle I have to fight."

"Battles that require torture?"

"Sometimes, yes," Father said. "This is a war of information. We must protect the King."

"At what cost?"

"At any cost," he said. "The goblain are willing to sacrifice it all for their goals. To protect the kingdom, so must we."

"Then what makes us any different from them?"

Father's jaw tightened. "We are protecting our people, our way of life. We build. They only seek to destroy."

I shook my head. "Lying. Burning down a village. Keeping the truth about my mother from me. Torturing people. Those kids in the northern city were starving. That's how we build?"

He stayed silent for a few heartbeats. "One day, you will understand. I've stared into the face of evil, of deep darkness. I will do whatever it takes to keep those monsters at bay."

"Even if that means becoming one of them?"

He nodded. "That is the way of this world. That is how it has always been."

I hung my head. What could I say?

"This is why I didn't want you to come," he said. "You don't have to face that darkness, that evil. I have faced it so you wouldn't have to."

My sight blurred with the beginning of tears. "So I won't have to face those monsters?"

"Yes," he said.

"What if I lived with one?"

Father recoiled like I had slapped him. His eyelids fluttered before he stood stark and rigid before me.

"I will go into the northern city alone tomorrow," he said. "Keep your eyes and ears up in the Tournament. You can do the most good there. Tomorrow night, we will meet, and you will report to me."

My father walked away and into the side entrance to the palace.

I stood alone in the dark courtyard for a few moments. When I blinked, a tear fell down my cheek.

I willed my feet to turn and walk toward the guest building at the far end of the courtyard. I kept to the shadows, my head down.

Voices reached me from far to the right. I paused and lifted my head. They came from the stables. My frown deepened, and I decided to go check on the sahala. My feet made no noise, another thing my father trained me to do – tread lightly without any sound.

I came at the main stable door from an angle, so I couldn't be seen by anyone that was inside. The voices grew louder while I drew closer. I couldn't distinguish words. Upon arriving at the stables, I peeked around the edge of the door.

At the other end of the stables, two people stood. My vision adjusted to the dark to recognize them – Aiken, the Lord of Coin, and Julius, last year's champion of the Tournament.

They spoke in low voices, Aiken more animated than the calm Julius.

I couldn't get any closer without giving myself away. Father said to report to him tomorrow.

Still silent, I turned and made my way to the guest building, sure I wasn't seen by anyone else. Once I entered, I trudged past a handful of contestants in the lobby, Mia one of them. She smiled at me. Odger, the dwarf, raised a mug of ale in my direction. I didn't respond to either one.

Pulling on the banister, I climbed the stairs up to my level and made it to my room.

Darkness. Evil.

I had a thought there might be an assassin waiting for me in my room, my heart hitching at the fear. But what did it matter? I opened the door to the room and strode in.

A figure huddled over the table next to the short couch, and he started when I entered. I tensed, but when he stood and turned, it was Refa.

Relaxing, I took a step toward him.

"I-I apologize, Miss Elowen," Refa said. "I noticed you weren't back yet and thought you might be hungry."

Sure enough, another plate of food was on the table next to the couch, flatbreads, and strips of jerky. "That is very kind. But I'm not hungry." I should have been, but I wasn't.

After taking another step toward him, some clothes had been laid over the back of the couch. I gestured at them. "What are those?"

"Ah. Some fresh clothes. I saw that you only had one change of clothes, so I brought you more. I hope they are in your size, Miss."

"I told you." I walked up to the items. "Stop calling me Miss. Just Elowen." I touched the clean, new, sturdy tan and light brown trousers and tunics. "Again, you're kind."

Refa bowed. "Doing my job, my duty."

"Well, I appreciate it." I faced him. "I'm pretty tired, though. I think I'll turn in."

Refa nodded. "Of course. I apologize. I will see you in the morning."

"Thank you," I said.

Refa left the room and closed the door behind him.

I walked to the bed and fell facedown upon the soft cotton sheets. My body ached, every muscle and joint. I closed my eyes.

I had to fight another swordmaster at the Tournament tomorrow.

CHAPTER

The sky was grey with a hint of the sunrise to come when I walked to the arena. Entering through the tunnel, I went to the room where the contestants would dress for the bouts, although I was the first.

I had slept hard for hours and woke famished sometime in the middle of the night. I roused my stiff limbs to get to the other room and eat some cheese and a daffapple. Once up, however, I couldn't go back to sleep. I stared out the window, trying to rest, but it wasn't going to work. Dead and bloody faces of the elves we killed yesterday watched me when I closed my eyes.

Elves *I* killed.

Cleaning and dressing for the day in fresh clothes, I made my way to the arena.

One by one, the other contestants entered the dressing room. I had already prepared and waited. Only eight would fight, the winners of the first round, but all sixteen would enter through the same room, even if just to wait for the bouts to begin.

Two rounds would happen today. Four bouts in the morning. After a break for lunch, the semifinal round would take place.

The final match would be tomorrow.

I didn't expect to be in the finals. I didn't expect to make it out of the first bout this morning, which was against Imam, a large man from the human nation of Lior. My victory against Xong had been lucky. A trick, as my father said. Not exactly cheating but taking advantage of his pride. Embarrassing Xong might not have garnered me many friends.

Yes, he should have taken me more seriously. If I wanted the others to take notice of me, then I had achieved that. The others would not make the same mistake.

Looking at Imam when he entered, a mountain of a man, I'm not sure that had been the best idea. No, I didn't expect to win.

But that wasn't why I was here. *You can do the most good there*, my father had said last night. With pain in his eyes. Pain as real as if I had stuck him with a dagger myself. I called him a monster. The evil in our home.

What's worse, I had meant it.

Maybe I should do my job here.

I examined them as they arrived. I was supposed to be searching for a possible assassin here among the contestants. And report back to my father tonight.

Jibryl had fought with each of the elven nations over the last century. Any of the contestants from the kingdoms of Kryus, Faltiel, or Kasem could be turned or have a reason for revenge – a family member killed in a battle or a raid.

Julius arrived, gliding like a ghost. He had met with one of the Trust last night, Lord Aiken. He wouldn't give up his reputation and shame himself for such an act, would he? Or maybe that was the perfect plan. Someone we would least expect.

Odger the dwarf entered. The dwarven kingdoms were so isolated I couldn't even remember the last time there had been a significant conflict with one of them. Maybe the Great Desolation thousands of years ago? He winked at me again before heading to his stool to get ready for the day.

Jibryl hadn't much contact with any of the human kingdoms except for Eleron, but humans were notoriously corrupt and violent. Would enough coin sway one of them? Coin from Aiken and Julius, maybe?

Mia entered, and I made a point to nod at her and smile. She had won yesterday and now applied her armor. She picked up the blunt tournament sword but didn't put her own aside as others had done. My brow creased. I had been so busy trying to make it through the day before that I hadn't really noticed her blade.

She caught me staring at her sword, and while I averted my eyes, she chuckled and crossed the room. "You can ask me, you know."

My face got hot. "It was just odd to see that you took your sword out to the field when everyone else left theirs here." She had stuck it blade down in the field before stepping onto the platform yesterday.

"My sword is a part of me," Mia said. "I can't use it during the bout, of course. But I keep it close."

Looking at it now, it was a simple sword. No jewels or unique inscriptions. "Is it old? Part of your family?"

Mia cocked her head. "Yes and no. It isn't old, not in the way you think. It has only belonged to me."

"What makes it a part of you, then?"

"Ah, a good question," she said. "I had to fight the greatest battle of my life, the most important one, to get this blade."

"What battle?"

Mia grinned. "The one with the darkness in my own heart."

My brow creased. "And you won?"

"You could say that." She took her sword and held it with two hands. "Would you like to hold it?"

I stood, reached out and took the hilt of the sword, and rested the blade in my other hand.

My breath caught. It felt heavy. Too heavy to be a real sword. Heavier than any weapon I had ever held before. I strained to keep it upright. How did Mia fight with this?

Mia watched me for a moment and then took the sword back. I gave it to her gladly. She held it like it weighed nothing.

"Where did you get it?" I said.

"That is a long story," Mia said. "One we don't have time for right now. Ask me again another time. I should go. I have the first bout. You coming?"

"I will be there in a few ticks." I forced a smile.

"Very well," she said and left.

Taking a deep breath, I checked the straps that held the padded armor in place and made sure the helmet was firm and comfortable.

Then I went out to the field.

I emerged from the tunnel and heard a mix of cheers and boos. Mostly the boos. It took me a moment to realize that the crowd reacted to me. I hesitated, gritted my teeth, and walked forward, forcing my chin up.

Reaching the area where the contestants sat, I paused at the bottom, scanning the options. I could only see one empty space, which appeared like two, until I saw a hairy head pop up over the shoulders of the people in front of him.

Odger grinned, his yellowed teeth showing under his mustache. He raised a hand and waved me up, pointing at the seat next to him.

My mouth became a line, and I took the stairs to the third row and sat next to him.

Odger dropped back to his seat. "Saved it for you, I did."

I took a deep breath, the beginning of a sigh, but that was a mistake. His stench was a combination of sweat and fermented cheese. I stifled a cough and stammered out, "T-thank you."

"My royal pleasure." He gestured to the crowd. "Don't worry 'bout them, no. They don't favor me none, either. You did what you had to do to win. No shame in that."

Odger looked around and then leaned in closer. I grunted at the smell and leaned away.

"Serves that Kasem elf right," he said with a lower voice. "He is a prideful one, that is. Thinks just because he was trained by that Akeebo or whatever, he's so great."

"Akeno," I said. "The master's name is Akeno."

"That's what I said." Odger sat straight. "All these elves need to be taken down a notch anyway. That's why I'm here."

I frowned.

"Oh, but I didn't mean you, no," Odger said. "Ya may be an elf, sure, but I'm rootin' for you. You're showing them they ain't all they think they are. You stick with me, and we'll both show them."

He laughed, and I forced a smile. I didn't see the humor.

When I looked at the crowd, Father sat right behind the King. Yacob and his family – his wife with an ornate head covering and high crown beside his daughter. I averted my eyes from my father and found another familiar face. Back in the corner, among the servants, Refa stood in royal palace attire. He had been watching me and smiled when our stares met.

I breathed easier and smiled back.

Shaul, the Shield, sat next to the King, and the Trust were in the row behind Yacob, along with Father. The Trust all eyed the platform at two foreigners about to battle. Fahim, the First Keeper, glowered at Mia like a snake about to strike. General Paavo was unreadable, as usual, and Lord Aiken seemed disinterested, gazing down at his own attire.

My eyes narrowed at Lord Aiken. Father said he was least likely to support a coup of any type, but he had been meeting with Julius from Kryus the other night. Could his close connection to the King's family make him a prime target to turn traitor? People would suspect him less, but money could be a powerful motivator.

The King stood and nodded at the platform.

The referee bowed, walked forward, and stood on the stone platform, and the crowd quieted. "The first bout is Mia D'Alor of the nation of Veradis and Ruvaen, son of Lezan, from the land of Faltiel."

Mia stood from her seat and made her way down to the field, as did Ruvaen. While they were two different races and genders, they looked similar in their tan skin tone, dark hair, slight build, and height. Except for Ruvaen's pointed ears, they could have been brother and sister.

Ruvaen wore forest colors of green and brown, his hair thick and shoulder length and held with a leather headband. He stepped up to the stone platform first.

Mia came to the edge of the platform and stopped. She took her personal sword, the one I could barely hold, and stuck it in the ground blade first. With the blunt sword in hand, she sprung to the platform.

The referee checked with both Mia and Ruvaen to see if they were ready. They both assented, and the bout began.

Yesterday, with my nerves and processing my own bout and how I had actually won, I hadn't been as intentional in examining the styles of the other contestants. Stupid of me, especially considering I would have to fight one of them today.

While I didn't expect to win against another swordmaster, I never knew what would happen. And I could learn something from others who had years of experience more than me, centuries more in some cases.

Mia and Ruvaen engaged, hesitantly at first, as many do, and I had expected Xong to behave yesterday. Soon the hesitation disappeared, and both fought with vigor. Mia was both smooth and sharp, constantly changing angles and looking for holes in Ruvaen's defense.

Ruvaen stayed in the center of the platform for much of the bout, moving only to keep her in front of him, although he used more flourishes.

Odger sniffed. "What do you think?"

I leaned down. "What do you mean?"

"The bout," he said. "Who do you think will win?"

They seemed evenly matched, but Ruvaen seemed faster, more confident, and more focused. Mia moved more and appeared to be tiring. "If I had to guess, Ruvaen." I hated to admit it, though.

"Care to bet?" He grinned.

"No," I said. "What are your thoughts?"

His eyes narrowed. "It is close, but I give the slight advantage to Mia."

My brow furrowed, and I sat up straight.

Within a few more moves, Mia suddenly found more energy and speed. She was able to turn inside one of Ruvaen's strikes and stab him in the chest with her blunt sword.

The referee called the bout and declared Mia the winner. She moved to the semifinal that afternoon. The crowd cheered.

I clapped. "How did you know?"

Odger shrugged. "Could have gone either way, but that Mia is dangerous, she is. There's more to her than we've seen." His grin widened. "And I wanted her to win."

Mia lifted her personal sword from the field and came to sit with the contestants, wiping sweat from her brow and hands.

"Well, I'm up," Odger said. "Wish me bright eyes?" He stood to his feet.

"Of course," I said. "Bright eyes to you."

With his grin still in place, he shuffled past me and down to the field. The referee announced Odger of Jurgen and Conor M'Cear of Eleron, a tall red-haired human with light skin.

Odger's blunt sword was wide and flat at the end. He seemed eager to get to the bout, and after the referee started the match, Odger rushed forward with his head down and the sword whipping back and forth. Conor seemed ready for it – perhaps he didn't waste time as I did yesterday. The human slid and hacked from the side, which Odger somehow deflected.

Dwarves were the shorter of the three races but the strongest. Some humans could be as strong, but the heftiest of dwarves were the stronger. Conor was muscular but lanky, not able to directly block Odger's forceful style.

Conor spent much of the match dodging and moving out of the way to strike from another angle. Odger was able to move quickly and yet stay in control. More than once, it appeared Odger would run right off the platform, but he could stop and turn on a silver coin. That control allowed the dwarf to counter Conor's attacks.

The dwarf's strikes were calculated and measured, even during his mad rushes. The insane appearance of his method was only to intimidate and distract. The more I watched him, the more his forms belied his mastery and skill.

Conor possessed the longer reach but could not connect a strike. The human didn't get far enough out of the way at one point, and I could see the inevitable unfold. Odger changed direction with such ferocity that his sword connected to the human's abdomen and knocked Conor two meters to his back.

The crowd cheered and rose to their feet. They chanted, "Giantbreaker! Giantbreaker!"

The referee declared Odger the winner, and on to the semifinals. He would fight the victor of the previous match – Mia. Both contestants came back to the designated bleachers. When Odger slid by me, I leaned away, not to let him by but because the stench had grown and hit me like a fist in the face.

He sat down, beaming like he had won a billion gold coin.

I tried not to breathe through my nose. "Giantbreaker?"

"Ah, some call me that, they do."

"How did you get that name?"

He laughed. "How do you think?"

Julius of Kryus was called for the next bout along with his opponent – Claudim of Jibryl.

The crowd, mostly elves from Jibryl, roared when Claudim was announced. I cringed at the noise, and I understood it. This was Jibryl's chance to bring the championship back to their kingdom. Claudim was the best swordmaster we had to offer. Beating last year's champion would be a boon, indeed.

The match started, and even as they walked toward one another, I knew the winner. The crowd cried Claudim's name, but I had watched a swordmaster and champion train and spar my whole life. I had never seen anyone move with such efficiency and calm as my father until now. Until Julius. Every contestant exuded confidence and danger, but Julius moved like a hunter, like a ghost and a snake in one. Waiting. Watching. Venomous.

Claudim showed no fear. He darted forward for a few strikes that never connected. Julius didn't meet blade to blade. He didn't have to. He just moved and appeared in a different spot all of a sudden.

It didn't take long. Julius attacked, and within three strikes Claudim's sword was on the floor of the platform and Julius had smacked the chest of his opponent with the flat of his blade. Claudim stood frozen with bulging eyes.

Julius turned and walked to the middle of the platform.

The crowd went silent in a heartbeat or less. Mouths dropped. It wasn't until the referee declared Julius the winner that the crowd clapped or made noise.

Claudim and Julius made their way to the bleachers. Neither had broken a sweat.

Julius might be better than my father. Scary thought.

Then the referee called my name for the next match.

CHAPTER

Imam of Lior stood in the bleachers, and it took a moment for him to finish rising, his broad shoulders blocking most of the crowd from my view.

He had beaten the other elf from Kasem, Kaden, yesterday in his bout, which meant Imam and I were pitted against one another today.

"You best be going," Odger mumbled.

I blinked and stood, descending from the bleachers down to the field. Imam and I faced each other from opposite ends of the platform.

Imam had to be at least two mitres tall, with thick muscles and dark skin, another shade darker than any Ruchali. He wore no shirt underneath the padded armor. The top of his head was bare of hair, only some dark fuzz above his ears that wrapped around back, which I guessed happened to humans. Strange that human men would go bald. Never happened to an elf that I knew. A thick mustache and beard framed his narrow mouth.

The referee turned to Imam. "Contestant, are you ready?"

Imam rolled his massive shoulders and nodded.

The referee turned to me. "Contestant, are you ready?"

I couldn't turn my head and look at Father; that might dissolve my remaining courage. What was I thinking? I should have lost yesterday on purpose. This human could kill me with a blunt sword. Or a fist or elbow.

"Contestant?" the referee repeated.

"Yes, yes," I said. "I'm ready."

My mouth was dry, and sweat dripped from my armpits.

"Begin," the referee said and moved out of the way.

Imam moved forward, and I shifted into my stance, trying to stay relaxed while he approached.

When he attacked, I was ready and met his blade with my own. His muscles didn't seem to strain, but the blow reverberated through my forearms anyway. I gritted my teeth and lowered my stance to give more leverage.

He struck a few more times, testing my defenses and reflexes. I countered the last strike with a three-slash combo of my own. He deflected them all easily. Great. Big *and* fast.

At that point, Imam was tired of the testing – apparently, he felt that he had enough response to truly begin – and he came at me. I stepped back, lifting a leg over a low swipe, and blocked another on each side. He swung overhead and down while I recovered, and I had to use my blade to take the full force of the blow. If it had hit my head or shoulders, my day would have been over, maybe my life.

My arms ached from taking the power of his attacks, but I growled and sent a flurry of strikes at him, feinting and stabbing, high and low, soft and hard. He didn't even take a step back. He met each one, and my sword bounced off his blade like he played with a child.

Overwhelmed, I felt helpless, useless, and beaten. He was stronger and had a longer reach. My body was also exhausted from the bloody battle in the northern city yesterday. It was only a matter of time before I lost.

I wasn't there to win, anyway, as my father liked to remind me. The goal was to survive. There was no shame in losing to Imam in the second round of the greatest sword tournament in the world.

He was a master, after all. Human or not, he had beaten a master to get here.

Then again, so had I.

Breathing hard, I retreated to get some distance and regroup. The tunic under my padded armor was soaked with sweat. I wiped my brow with the back of my arm to keep the perspiration from my eyes.

I stayed a few paces away from him, outside of his long reach, and stalked around the edge of the platform. He turned to face me, sweat glistening on the sides of his face, his visage patient but confident. Did he know I was like a child to him? Of course, he did. A master would.

Like a child.

I had been a toddler when a swordmaster began to teach me, barely able to hold a wooden stick but trained to defend and strike. I was ten years old when father let me use a blunt sword like this one. He didn't hold back when we sparred, not even then.

He had been far stronger. His reach far longer. Taller. More skilled. He taught me how to beat him. Or at least make it a good match, so he wasn't bored.

Be like water, Wen. Have you ever thrown a stone in a river? The stone might make a big splash and cause massive ripples, but within moments, the river is back to flowing forward. The water doesn't resist the stone. Over time, however, whatever rough edges that exist on that stone will be smoothed. The jagged parts will no longer exist. Given enough time, moving water will wear the stone down to a pebble or sand.

Being a child, I had asked him, *What if it is a large stone, big enough to dam the river?*

Then the whole river finds another direction, he had said, *burrows through soil and dirt and trees to dig another trench for itself. Perhaps the stone becomes an island. Either way, the river will not be stopped. Water will win in the end.*

With a stronger opponent, you cannot win with resistance, he continued. *Find another way, or make one. It may take time, but that is how you can win. Be like water, Wen.*

Be like water.

I had never beaten him, but I did train like that for years. I knew how to do that.

Pretend Imam is my father. Maybe beat him this time.

I accepted the challenge. I would not meet Imam's strength with my own. I would be water.

I stepped into the platform's middle, ensuring I had room to move without getting caught at the edge and pushed off. I stayed light on my feet, with my sword at my side. I kept moving. And waited - like water.

For the first time, he frowned, noticing the obvious change in my method. Then he attacked. I turned to the side and stepped back, his sword meeting air. He slashed horizontally, and I leaned back, the blade coming within a millimitre of my nose.

The crowd did not exist in my mind. The other contestants, my father, the King, assassins, none but my opponent and me. I emptied my brain of all other distractions, and thoughts. Water doesn't think. It reacts. It keeps moving forward, somehow.

Whether forward or back, I didn't stop moving.

Most of Imam's strikes or attacks found only the wind. His blade whistled, and I contorted or bounced out of the way, being the splash of water but returning to my movement. Those strikes that did meet my blade only redirected his strength in slight angles that ensured his weapon would continue on that path.

Time seemed to slow. I don't know how, but in that space and acceptance, that focus, there was an awareness I hadn't had before.

I noticed a slight muscle tense and knew what Imam's next move would be.

It could have been a few minutes or an hour; I don't know how much time passed. Water waits. Takes its time. I don't even know if he got tired or frustrated. I only moved and reacted.

But then, there it was. The opening. I spun, his blade going wide when it glanced off of mine; and I let it go. His right arm was too high on the other end of the turn. He leaned forward too far. If I had been matching him strength for strength, I would have missed it. I wouldn't have been able to reverse my sword in time.

Because I was water, I was able. The split tick of time froze, the opportunity like a wink at me.

With a flick of my wrist and a twist of my arm, my blade stabbed Imam in the middle of the chest on his padded armor. My left hand followed with a flat-handed strike.

Water can be soft, but at great speeds, it can be hard, as well. Harder than stone.

Imam snorted and gave a loud grunt when the air left his lungs. His arms went straight. His midsection shot back.

Amazingly, Imam's feet shuffled, and he stayed upright. Bending over, he caught his breath and then looked up at me with narrowed eyes.

I stood straight, my lungs heaving with effort, and for the first time, I turned to the King and the crowd, all silent as death.

In the next heartbeat, the people in the stands stood to their feet and erupted in applause.

I gasped at the sound. My eyes found my father's, and he grinned at me. He nodded in respect.

The people of Jibryl cheered for an elfess.

I glanced over my shoulder at the referee. Scowling, he walked forward and met me in the middle of the platform. He waited until the crowd noise lowered.

"Elowen, the daughter of Natanel, is the victor," he said.

The crowd cheered again.

A contestant from Jibryl was still in the Tournament. Our people could have another champion of the Kaila Tournament.

Me.

To do that, I would have to beat Julius in the next round.

CHAPTER

24

When they served us lunch, I wanted to eat every piled platter.

After fighting with dozens of goblain yesterday, barely eating this morning, and the match with Imam, I could have curled up in the corner and slept the rest of the day. Raging hunger kept me upright, though. I changed into fresh clothes before arriving at the dining area.

The royal servants laid out platters of meats, cheeses, fruits, and flatbreads on a long table in another meeting room under the bleachers of the arena. The King and his family sat at a table on the far end of the room with Shaul the Shield and twelve guards around them. The servants brought him food.

Father stood nearby the King, Qatal hanging from his belt.

The King's Trust gathered around another table perpendicular to the royal one, a handful of guard around them. I glanced at Aiken, the Lord of Coin, who gave me a slight bow when he noticed me.

"Do you need me to get a plate for you?" the voice came from behind me.

I turned. "Refa. No, I can manage." I glanced down at the tunic and trousers. "I do need to thank you for the fresh clothes. They fit perfectly."

Refa gave a bow. "Gladly doing my duty."

I chuckled. "I'm not sure about that, but again, thank you."

"Of course," the servant said. "Please let me know if there's anything else."

"I will."

He leaned closer, lowering his voice. "You made your kingdom proud today."

I might have stood a little taller. "Thank you."

"No. On behalf of Jibryl, thank you." Refa moved on past me while I headed to the food.

I piled food on my plate – some hornoth steak cubes, roseberries, and three flatbreads. With a mug of clear water, I wove through tables to an empty one. I passed Mia and her son at one table, Odger and Conor at another. Forced smiles lasted until I reached the table, sat alone, and hunched over my food, shoving it into my mouth.

A figure appeared across from me like a shadow. "That was impressive," the voice said.

I looked up, my jaws filled with half-chewed food. Julius leaned back in the chair. I raised a brow at him.

"Many thought your inclusion at the Tournament a joke," he continued as if I didn't look like a garden serpent that was trying to swallow a war lizard. "Your stunt with Xong, while clever and effective, didn't improve those thoughts among many. Today, however, you showed skill. You showed that you belong among masters."

Drool started to escape my lips, and I sucked in air through my nose as I started chewing. I gulped a large portion of it down. It got stuck in my throat for a moment, and I almost choked, but I swallowed so I could sit straight and say, "Thanks."

"You are welcome." Julius brushed his robe during a pause. "Were you able to hear much of our conversation last night from the stable door?"

I choked, then turned my head so I wouldn't spew bits of food on him. I managed to keep most of it in, swallowing the remnants in my mouth, and I took a swig of water from the mug.

With a deep breath, I said, "I'm sorry. What?"

"Last night. Come now. You were at the stable door last night while I spoke with the great Lord of Coin." He smirked. "What did you hear?"

Should I lie? I strained for a moment to manufacture some excuse or explanation or maybe just deny it. But what was the point? He obviously knew.

"I-I didn't hear anything," I said. "It seemed like a private conversation, so I left you alone."

Julius nodded. "I see. Do you know my role in my kingdom?"

I hesitated. "No."

"I work beside one of the greatest generals the world has ever seen. My role is one of military intelligence, primarily, although it has expanded in recent years."

My brow creased. "Okay."

"It is not a secret," he said. "I mention this only because I don't want you to think I am an idiot."

"I don't think you're an idiot."

"Ah, good," Julius said. "Your inclusion in the Tournament looks like a publicity stunt, but I have heard the rumors of rebellion in your kingdom. The Ruchali people are restless, from what I understand."

He waited like I was going to respond, but I didn't.

"That is also not much of a secret," he said. "Neither is the fact your father was once the Shield of the King, and he is here after being retired for many years. You can play innocent if you wish, but your

presence is strategic. Standing at the stable door last night was intentional, as well. You sure you heard nothing of note?"

I shook my head.

"Very well," Julius said. "You know, politics is a funny game. Not
many play it well. It frustrates me. Many in my own nation have
their machinations, and we must learn the rules to protect ourselves
and operate in this world. Fighting face to face with a sword is much
simpler, more elegant, more preferred than sneaking in the dark,
wouldn't you say?"

I took a moment before answering. "Yes."

"Good." Julius stood. "You beat a master today, Elowen, daughter of Natanel. Not with a clever trick but with superior skill. Do you
know what that makes you?"

I sniffed. "No."

"A master. I look forward to our match this afternoon, Master
Elowen."

He turned and left.

I was nibbling at my food when my father sat down across from
me.

I sighed. "Really?"

Father cocked his head at me. "What?"

"I sat down at a table all by myself to eat, and no one can leave
me alone?"

"You want me to leave?" he said.

I stared at him. "No, you can stay."

"I was going to stay anyway, but thank you."

I rolled my eyes and put a hornoth steak cube in my mouth.

Father gestured behind him at Julius, who now stood across the
room. "What was he talking to you about?"

I whispered when I told him what had happened the night before.
"And he let me know he knows."

He rubbed his chin. "You didn't hear what they were saying?"

I shook my head.

"Lord Aiken," he said. "He has the closest relationship to the King and the most power among the Trust because of it. I will have to look more into him, see if there is any reason he might have to support a coup."

"Besides money?"

Father shook his head. "He has all the money he can get his hands on. It would have to be something else. Power? Revenge? Acting on another's behalf to change the royal line? I will look into it."

"He is sitting right behind the King in the crowd," I said. "I would watch him."

"I will," Father said. "But he won't lift a finger. Even General Paavo wouldn't take violent action himself. None of the Trust would if they were involved. They might get an assassin as a servant and get them close."

I spoke while chewing, my brow raising. "A servant?"

"Yes. The royal family chooses the servants near the King and the Trust, but if one of the Trust could get an assassin within the palace or near the King that way ..."

I stopped eating.

"What is it?" Father asked.

Lesson number one. *Trust no one.*

I shook my head. "No, sorry. It couldn't be."

"Elowen," Father said. "Tell me."

"Well, there is this one servant that has ... been kind to me." I winced a bit. "In the guest apartments. And he is there near you in the stands. He's here now."

"Which one?" Father asked.

"His name is Refa. He spoke to me earlier. Did you see?"

"Yes, I did." Father frowned. "It isn't unheard of for a palace servant to be assigned to the guest apartments and also here for the royal family. But it is odd."

"Is it so odd that he's nice to me? He could actually like me."

Father grinned. "He could. That's true. But I will watch him nonetheless."

The moment passed, and we sat in silence. I finished my food.

Father looked at me. "You did well today, Wen."

I met his eyes.

"Extremely well," he said.

"I was lucky to win."

"Maybe," he said. "The Ona has his ways. Much of it we don't understand. But even if you had lost, you gained the respect of every contestant today and the people of Jibryl. People around the world. Even the King."

"Even the King?"

"Yes," he said. "I was very proud."

The man I had just called a monster last night now said he was proud of me. That shouldn't mean anything. Logically, it should have insulted me.

But it didn't. My chest swelled, and my jaw tightened, suppressing the tear building in my eye.

"Well, now I get to fight the champion," I said after a few ticks of time. "The one who knows I was spying on him last night. He said he was looking forward to fighting me today."

Father shrugged. "You might beat him, too."

CHAPTER

25

M ia remained in the contestant dressing room while the others went to the stands. With only four of us fighting this afternoon, the other fourteen never entered this room after lunch. Odger had been quick in his preparation, wishing Mia and me iron luck on the way out to the field. Julius adjusted his padded armor in silence and left the both of us there.

I was done getting ready, but I sat and watched Mia while she finished. My eyes were drawn to her sword. What was it made of? How did she get it?

The woman sniffed and stood. "You have a question?"

"You spoke yesterday about fighting for yourself, for what you believe in."

"Something like that," Mia said.

I narrowed my eyes. "How did you know what it was you believed in? And how did you get free enough to fight for it once you knew?"

Mia put her hand on the hilt of her sword, that strange sword, and angled her head like she listened to something. "Freedom isn't something outside of yourself. Freedom is something that happens within, in your heart."

"You beat the evil in your heart."

"In a way." Mia took a step toward me and reached out her hand.

I frowned and took her hand. She pulled me to my feet and searched my gaze. I don't know what she saw. But her grin was sad.

"When this is over," she said. "You and I will talk. I will tell you everything I can. But there are some things I can't explain to you with words. If you want to know more, we'll have to spend some time together. I'll have to show you. You'd be welcome at my home."

I couldn't stop the cringe on my face. "To a human kingdom?"

Mia chuckled. "It isn't about the kingdom. Not my own of Veradis or even yours of Jibryl. But if you want to learn what I know, you must see how I live. Then you will understand what I mean. And you can make your choice."

"What choice?"

"Whether or not you want to fight the same battle as me," Mia said. "Make no mistake, it is the greatest battle, the most important, but it is difficult. And no one can be forced to fight it."

I bit my lip. "But I would be free?"

This time her smile was not sad. "Yes, Elowen. You will be free."

With a final squeeze of my hand, she walked into the tunnel.

It took me a few moments to follow.

Once out on the field, I sat in the stands with a space between myself and Conor, the human. Odger and Mia would be the first bout.

Then I would fight Julius.

As before, Mia stuck her personal sword in the dirt beside the platform. She paused with her hand on the hilt, her eyes closed. A prayer to her god? She stood and climbed up to the platform where Odger waited.

Father sat next to Aiken this time and near where Refa stood. A servant stood in each of the four corners of the royal seating area, and

Refa hovered in the top right. Four soldiers guarded the King, two on each side at the edge of the box, spears pointed up.

It couldn't be Refa, could it? It was difficult to believe that he had been kind to me for deceptive reasons. He seemed so genuine.

Trust no one. Rule number one.

I watched the platform but kept Refa and Aiken in my periphery. And Julius situated two rows below me.

The referee announced both contestants, checked if they were ready, and the bout began.

At this point, I had seen and examined their styles. For these two masters with more experience than me, there would be few surprises. Each had their own style, and the winner wouldn't be determined by the style but by the expertise in their style. There was no great gap between them. Rather, they were equal, as far as I could tell. The difference would be minuscule.

Odger barreled forward. Mia dodged and struck at the same time. He deflected and redirected to barrel forward again. This continued for a few minutes, the intensity rising with each exchange.

Mia slid to the side while Odger attacked and pushed forward; she placed her left hand on Odger's right shoulder and then leaped, using her hand to flip over the dwarf, her legs wide and up in the air. Mia struck down with her blunt sword. Odger blocked, turning to face her as she twisted mid-air and landed on the other side.

She batted away his next strike and swung back. The dwarf also recovered and stabbed forward. They both connected almost simultaneously, but Mia's blade hit his chest a split heartbeat before his.

The crowd cheered and whooped, smiling and entertained.

The two contestants stepped back, gasping, and looked to the referee. He looked between them, then came forward to take Mia's hand and lifted it.

"The victor, Mia D'Alor of Veradis!" the referee said.

Half the crowd cheered, and the other began to scream angrily at the referee, believing that Odger had won.

During the commotion, Mia and Odger smiled at each other and shook hands in the middle of the platform. They raised hands together, and most of the crowd joined together in applause. Even the King stood to show his appreciation of the bout.

Mia grabbed her sword from the dirt and brought both with her up to the stands. She smiled at me when our eyes met. I raised my hands and clapped.

She would fight Julius tomorrow.

Or me. If I won.

I caught his scent before Odger sat next to me. He laughed and nudged me. "Good fight, was it?"

"It was," I said. "Well fought. Sorry you lost."

"'Tis but a game, entertainment," Odger said. "Not a real battle. Everyone walks away from this one."

"Easy for you to say." I scoffed. "You don't have to face Julius."

"Bah," he said. "Still flesh and blood like the rest of us. Remember that and you'll be fine."

The referee called the names for the next bout.

"That's me, I guess," I said.

Odger slapped my back. "Have fun!"

Despite myself, I laughed and left to meet Julius down at the field. He was already on the platform when I arrived, standing to face me, his sword low at his side.

I didn't laugh anymore.

I went to the other side of the platform, opposite him, and the referee announced us, Julius first to applause.

"And Elowen, daughter of the Champion Natanel, of Jibryl!" he said with a passion that surprised me.

Not as surprising as when the crowd stood to their feet, roared, and called my name. "Elowen! Elowen!"

My eyebrows rose, and I looked at my father in the royal box. He grinned.

"Contestant, are you ready?" the referee said.

He's talking to me. I blinked and nodded back at him.

"Begin!" the referee said and backed to the edge of the platform.

Swallowing, I rolled my shoulders and strode toward the middle of the platform. Julius moved to meet me, calm and still like a quiet force.

Flesh and blood like the rest of us ...

I attacked, feinting with a stab forward. He blocked, and while our swords had contact, I spun and struck at his head. Julius ducked and countered at my midsection, which I blocked and stepped back.

Like a dance, Julius took his turn pushing forward, claiming space, swiping, and stabbing. He was fast and efficient. I retreated a few steps and changed angles to deflect and dodge.

Julius gave a nod and attacked again.

The strikes came faster. The feints were serious attacks on their own, all of them killing blows that took every bit of my energy and focus to keep the blade from my head or chest. Twice, his dull blade glanced at my body, left arm, and hip.

I circled, adjusting, and he moved with me. From the crowd, it might have been a beautiful thing, like art, but I was just trying to survive.

And I was surviving. I didn't think I would last this long. But I didn't lie to myself. If it hadn't been clear before, it was now.

He was better. Maybe even better than Father.

I backed away to get a breath and lifted my sword in a high guard. Julius turned, lowering his blade for a moment. I circled and faced him.

In my periphery, Father sat in the royal box and glanced back at my servant friend. Refa stood in his corner, watching me. Movement on the opposite side caught my attention. Another servant, an elfess, began to descend from her place.

I frowned and froze.

Julius' brows creased.

Everyone's attention was on us, on me, on the potential hero of Jibryl. Father watched me but sat near Lord Aiken and kept his eye on Refa.

A member of the Trust wouldn't act on his own and wouldn't attempt the assassination himself. But a servant might, one willing to give his life for the cause.

Or *her* life.

Our attention had been on Refa, the one that had befriended me and found his way into the royal box. But Aiken or another member could have slipped in a servant, someone other than Refa.

All these thoughts raced in my mind through the span of a heartbeat.

The elfess servant bowed to the guard. He bowed back. She had her hands in her sleeves. Movement under the cloth. She stopped at the King's row.

Two other figures from the crowd shuffled and jostled toward the royal box, their head coverings throwing faces into shadow in the afternoon sun. They wore long tunics. Both reached under the front fold of their clothes.

Crit. It was going down now. And Father looked the other way.

I lowered my blade, stood straight, and pointed at the servant. Julius cocked his head at me while I said, "Father!"

The elfess servant pulled two long daggers from her sleeves and spun, stabbing the guard with both in the chest. His eyes bulged, and he fell back, tumbling out of the box.

The servant turned with hate-filled eyes and lunged with the daggers at the King only a pace from her now.

Father reacted, rising and bounding over members of the Trust. He drew his sword in the air; he extended the blade and caught both daggers at once.

The crowd nearby saw it all and screamed.

Then the world became chaos.

Everything happened at once. People in the bleachers ran from the violence. Shaul grabbed the King with two hands and threw him away from the servant. The King's family and the Trust all scrambled in the same direction. The remaining guard on the right side rallied to protect the King.

The two elves from the crowd climbed and jumped up into the royal box, their hoods coming down and short swords emerging from their loose clothes. With the element of surprise, they slashed and killed the remaining three guards on the left side.

All within a split tick of time. In the next moment, Father would be alone to face three assassins.

I sprinted forward. Julius stepped out of the way. I launched myself from the platform, landing on the field with my feet running, the blunt sword still in my hand.

Father batted one dagger and then the other from the elfess. With a short and efficient strike, he ran her through the heart with Qatal.

The two with short swords attacked at the same time, coming from opposite sides, one from a step above Father and the second from a step below. Their short swords flashed in the sun. Father deflected the one above him and stepped over the strike from underneath. My mind registered they were better trained than any goblain we had faced in the past few days.

I reached the edge of the field and leaped onto the bleachers. The royal box was only two mitres away.

Father ducked a strike from above, turned and hacked at the goblain assassin below, taking off his head in a swift move. Father used the momentum of the sword to twist and step up to strike under the defense of the goblain above …

Then Father's knee buckled. His war injury. His limp. The one that always disappeared when we sparred and fought. It failed him now.

I made it to the front of the box, using my forward motion and left arm to swing up and in.

Father lost his balance. His strike went awry into the wood of the bench. The goblain assassin struck with the short sword. The assassin's blade sunk into my father's chest. To the hilt.

I screamed.

"No!"

Father fell to the ground, the bloody blade still in the goblain's hand. The assassin saw me coming, and after scanning around him – the King and his family and the Trust were gone; the bleachers were empty for ten or more mitres; the crowd still running away – he retreated up another row, raising his guard.

I hurdled by Father and attacked the goblain, coming from a low position, a disadvantage. And I held a blunt sword. It didn't matter. I was going to kill him.

My blade arced across his body, forcing him into a defense. Our swords connected with a clang, and I pressed forward, claiming the space aggressively. He tried to counter, but I was too fast. Batting away his blade, I came at his head. He ducked, cursed, and turned to run away.

With a breath, I followed him. He jumped from the royal box to the regular bleachers. The goblain looked down to the field where soldiers gathered, protecting the retreating royal family and the Trust.

Mia and Odger approached with their weapons in hand. Refa knelt over my father.

The goblain ran up the bleachers.

My legs pumped with all my effort, trying to catch him. We raced up the bleachers, row by row, bench by bench, until we reached the very top. Nowhere to go.

He turned to face me with his short sword up in a mid-guard. He bared his teeth at me.

We stood high over the city at the top of the massive arena. I could see over the roofs of buildings and the palace complex in the distance.

I wanted to kill him. With everything in me, I wanted to. But we would need to talk to him. Get answers. Even if we had to torture him. I'd torture him myself.

Approaching him, I took advantage of the blunt sword. We stood on even ground. My heart went cold and calm. I focused. I feinted once, kept contact with his blade, reversed it, and chopped down on his arm.

A sharpened blade would have sliced through his limb like a knife through delan sauce. The blunt blade snapped the bones instead.

He yelped and dropped his sword. He took a step back, holding his arm that was now bent the wrong way.

I advanced. Next, I would have to break a leg so he couldn't run anymore.

He grinned at me. A grin. "Daughter of Natanel."

I stopped at my father's name.

In that hesitation, he said, "For the Hateph! We will rise!" He spun on a heel and faced the end of the arena, the ground fifty mitres or more below.

No! I reached out for him. I tried to grab his tunic with my left hand. My fingers brushed against cloth, but I couldn't get a grip.

The goblain plunged from the top of the arena. I stood at the edge and looked down, my jaw open. I had to turn away when his body hit the ground.

I leaned over and put my hands on my knees. The energy drained from me.

Father.

I dropped the blunt sword. It clattered to the hard steps while I ran back down the bleachers. I climbed into the royal box. Refa knelt over my father, who now lay on his back, looking up at the sun. He shuddered when he breathed.

Mia and Odger stood a few steps down. The other contestants gathered at the edge of the field, Julius at the front, his head down.

I fell to my knees at his head. "Father," I said his name as a sob.

Blood covered the front of him. Refa was barechested, holding his servant tunic on the wound, just below the heart.

So much blood.

"Elowen," Father said, his voice tight. "My love ..."

"Oh, Father," I said. "The physicians, they're coming. Just hold on."

He licked his lips. "Forgive me. I should have told you. I should have ..."

"No, don't." I shook my head. "You should forgive me. I shouldn't have called you a monster. You're not a monster. You are a good father. The best. Please. Just hold on."

His eyes met mine. Tears flowed from them. He struggled for a breath. "Ran away. We should have. You and me."

"Not important now." I didn't realize I was crying until I spoke.

"Should not have come." He reached up. I took his hand. "You're all I have. Everything. Should have ..."

Then he stopped. Stopped talking. Stopped breathing. Stopped moving. The strength ebbed from his hand in mine. His eyes went empty. His jaw stuck open.

I gripped his hand tighter. "Father, please. We will leave. We will run away. I promise."

No answer. Refa sniffed.

"Please don't leave me, Father," I said. "I don't have anyone but you. Don't leave me all alone. I'm sorry. I take it all back. I'll do anything you say. Don't go. Don't go. Please don't go."

I pressed my forehead to his. My tears fell onto his face.

"Please. Don't go. Please."

But it didn't matter what I said. He was gone.

CHAPTER

26

I still had his blood on me.

They cleaned me up, bathed me, and gave me clean clothes. But a red drop remained on the back of my hand near my thumb. They missed one drop. His blood.

My father's body lay on a long slab in a room deep in the palace. I sat in a chair against the wall, facing him.

They had cleaned him, too. No more blood. New clothes. A Desert Corps uniform. Not his own. A new one, crisp and bright blue. Golden amulets covered his eyes to keep them closed.

My father's sword, Qatal, lay in my lap. The tempered steel was cold against the skin of my palms.

The large, rectangular room appeared designed for this moment. The slab in the middle for a body. Chairs around the side. Torches in the corners that gave a low, yellow light. Ancient symbols on the wall from Ona worship that communicated death and life and grief and gratitude. The ceiling was high. A raised platform and podium were situated at the end of the room, overlooking the body.

The King's Trust sat on the wall opposite from me – Fahim, Paavo, and Aiken. Mia sat on one side of me, two seats away. Odger filled a chair two away on the other side. His feet dangled.

If I had moved faster, left the match earlier, I could have saved him. I called him a monster.

I closed my eyes tight, trying to squeeze the thoughts from my brain. But they wouldn't go.

I failed. My father was dead. I was alone.

The King entered the room.

Shaul the Shield stepped in first, scanning the room for threats. Eight guard, with spears and shields clattering, followed the King into the room. The guard stayed at the door. Yacob and Shaul walked over and stood near Father's body.

Shaul gave me a stern look. Sighing, I stood and shuffled over to the King, Father's sword still in my hand.

I bowed. "My Lord."

Yacob continued to stare at Father's body. "Natanel was a hero. And a friend. A great elf of Jibryl. We will celebrate his life and loyalty when the Kaila Festival is over. The world will know of his great deeds."

"Thank you," I said.

"It is the least I can do," the King said. "He saved my life many times over the years. I'm sure there were more of which I was unaware."

Shaul frowned and nodded.

"That is all in addition to his many years in the Desert Corps as a leader and a general," Yacob said. "He protected our nation, did his duty, and became a champion. And died in my service."

"He was proud of his service in the Corps," I said.

You're a monster, I had told him.

"As he should have been." The King glanced over at me. "You impressed us all in the Tournament. He trained you well."

Not well enough. "Yes, he did."

"You also spotted the attempt on my life," he said. "You are your father's daughter. That is clear."

Not the daughter of a traitor?

I didn't know what to say, so I nodded.

"You don't have to decide now," Yacob said, "but I did speak with the organizers of the Tournament and with Julius of Kryus. All have agreed that there were … extenuating circumstances, and you would be able to fight again tomorrow at noon. The final would then be in the afternoon. If you still wish to continue."

I blinked and shook my head. "I … I don't know. I haven't really thought about it."

"That is understandable," the King said.

"When would I have to decide?" I said.

"Sometime before mid-day, I would expect." The King straightened his tunic. "Please. Let me know if you need anything. I must leave you. There is much to do."

Being dismissed, I bowed again. The King turned to leave. When he passed me, I reached over and grabbed Shaul's arm. He glared down.

"Wait." I leaned in, taking a few steps with him toward the door. "Have you found any information about the assassins? Who they were? Who was behind it?"

Shaul's glare deepened while he paused. "They were no one. It is over, child. The King was protected, and the attempt was thwarted. Your part in this is over. I must go and continue to protect the King."

My brow creased. "But …"

Shaul took a step closer, his eyes dark and his voice low and firm. "Your part in this is over." He gestured over toward my father's body. "You have other things to concern yourself with."

With a sniff, he turned and stepped out of the room in front of the King, his gaze like a hunter in the hall. The eight guard followed them out.

I took a deep breath, and upon catching the scent, I realized Odger stood behind me. I turned, and he took my hand in both of his.

"Oh, elflass," the dwarf said. "I must leave you now. I hope to see you again before the end of the Festival. You'll still be here, you will?"

I nodded. "Until the end of the Festival, yes."

His mustache contorted into a smile. "Very well. Good night."

Odger left, and I made my way back to my seat, Mia waiting there.

We sat together for a long time in quiet. The Trust left, one by one, each with their condolences. First Aiken. Did he know I saw him and Julius? Not important now, I guess. *Your part in this is over.* Next, Paavo made his exit.

Keeper Fahim stood the farthest distance from me when he spoke. "The loss of your father is tragic. Ona has blessed him to have a daughter that can take the time to finalize his affairs."

"Yes, Keeper," I said.

"And we thank Ona that you may live comfortably back at his estate," Fahim said. "To find a husband, raise a family. Carry on Natanel's legacy."

My jaw went tight. I didn't answer.

After the uncomfortable silence, Fahim placed his palms together and pressed the prayer to his lips. "May Ona give you peace."

"And you, First Keeper."

The priest turned and made his exit.

That left me alone with Mia.

"You don't have to stay," I said. "I know you have family."

Mia nodded. "I don't mind staying."

"The Keepers are just outside," I said. "They will stay until I leave."

"Okay." Mia straightened her long skirt and adjusted her sword. "Would you like for me to come and stay with you? In your room? I could sleep on a cot or something."

My eyes narrowed at her. *Trust no one.* "Why are you being nice to me? You don't know me."

"Ah." Mia glanced at the torches and then his body. "No one needs a reason to be kind. At least, that's what I believe. Beyond that …" She took a deep breath and lowered her eyes. "My father died a few years ago. I remember how lost and alone I felt. You're right. I don't know you very well." She lifted her head and looked over at me. The torchlight flickered in her eyes. "I thought that you might want someone to sit with you. Be with you. And I'm more than willing."

The breath caught in my throat. I cleared it with a cough. "That's okay. Thank you, but I'll be all right."

Mia nodded. "I understand. I'll see you soon." She stood and began to walk out of the room. She stopped at the door, and half turned to face me. With her hand on her sword. "You know, I meant what I said. When this is all over, you're more than welcome to come back with me. If you don't want to go home. Or if you don't know where to go. Even though we are human," she smirked, "you'd be safe. You're not alone, Elowen. You have friends. If you want them. Friends can become family, sometimes. Good night."

With a nod, she turned and left the room.

Time passed. Not sure how long, but my eyes began to close of their own accord. I didn't want to sleep here. I didn't want to sleep in my room, either.

I rose from the seat, said goodnight to the Keepers waiting outside, and took the hallway to the main area of the palace. From there, I went out through the courtyard to the stables.

Zaran and Laila waited in the spacious stall lined with fresh hay. They didn't growl. They whined at me. I had never heard them make that noise. They wept and cried. Did the war lizards know Father was dead?

I curled up in the hay. They both lay with me, one on either side.

What was I going to do? Fight Julius tomorrow? Take Father's body home and bury him there? Wait until the end of the Festival?

I had no idea. No motivation. Nothing made sense.

Your part in this is over.

I didn't have to decide tonight. Exhaustion overtook me. Other words echoed in my mind, however.

You're not alone, Elowen. You have friends. If you want them.

CHAPTER

I awoke after a fitful night of sleep, if I slept much at all. Rising, I brushed the straw from my clothes and rinsed them with water from a canteen in the stable.

Zaran and Laila both stared at me from the stall, their yellow eyes wondering, questioning. It crushed me. No one else felt this, however. Only me. I had never felt more alone in my entire life.

I straightened my tunic and trousers and glanced at the lizards. "What?"

Laila whined.

My shoulders slumped after fastening my father's sword to my waist. "I don't know what I'm going to do."

My things were up in my room. The saddles were here. In minutes, I could be packed and gone. Back to the house, the home where I grew up, the only home I'd known. Not this place of violence and death and secrets. Not the place where my world had been turned upside down. Not the place where my father had died at the hands of a common assassin.

My father.

If I packed, though, what would I do with his things? His clothes. The weapons. I would have to pack them, too, wouldn't I?

I didn't think I could do that. Not now. Maybe later.

There was nothing for me at home, though. Nothing for me here, either. What would my father do? What would he say? I chuckled at the irony of wanting advice from an elf I called a monster.

I could go to one place. The Temple. To see if they had answers.

"Oh, good morning," a voice said, waking me from my thoughts.

Blinking, I looked up. The young servant stood there a few paces from me with a canvas bag in his hand.

"Refa." I pulled the shawl around my shoulders over my head. "Hello."

The elf took a few steps toward me. He had stayed with me yesterday until the Trust and the Keepers called me to the internment room in the palace. They wouldn't let him enter, and he had disappeared.

He stopped only a miitre away. His dark eyes searched my face. He gave a tight grin and lifted the canvas bag in his hand. The bag bulged with items and smelled of pork and bread. "I heard you were leaving."

I sighed and shrugged with a glance at the sahala. Zaran bared his teeth at Refa. "I'm not sure."

"Hmm." He lowered the bag. "I skimmed this from the kitchens. Should be enough food for your journey. I mean, if you were leaving. I … didn't know if you ate last night."

Did I? I couldn't remember. My stomach felt empty, a deep pit of hunger, actually. But I didn't want to eat. Although I probably should.

I bit my lip. "Is there a flat biscuit in there?"

He nodded and rummaged through the bag. "A few." He pulled one out and handed it to me.

The warm biscuit felt like comfort in my hand. My stomach rumbled at the smell of fresh bread in my nostrils. Maybe I could eat, after all. "Thank you."

"Of course."

I took a bite of the bread and closed my eyes to savor it. I smiled back at him when our eyes met. "Could you do me a favor?"

Refa scoffed. "Anything, my lady."

I raised a brow at him.

He gave a short laugh. "I apologize. Anything, *Elowen*."

"Thank you," I said. "I have one place I'd like to go. Maybe I will walk the city to clear my head. Will you take the food to my room? I'll pack it with my things later."

Refa nodded and closed the bag again. "At once. Ona be with you."

"And with you."

Refa turned and walked out of the stables.

I tore off two pieces of the biscuit and gave one to each of the lizards. They stretched their necks and swallowed it down. Both gave me a nudge with their snouts, and I gave them each a bump with my forehead. "I'll be back soon."

The rest of the biscuit was gone by the time I walked from the stables to the front gate of the palace. The guard knew me and gave a slight bow when I passed. "My lady," they said.

I stumbled at the respect. *That's right. I'm the hero of the Kaila. The last chance for Jibryl to save their pride. Even if I am an elfdaughter. Did they think I would fight Julius again?*

Could I?

The vast square in front of the palace was rife with activity. The merchant booths had been removed, and others took their place – puppet shows, toy sellers, candied fruits. Elves from Jibryl raised tall poles and strung streamers of bright colors across the sky. Paper animals hung from the streamers and bobbed as the decorators adjusted the length and height.

The Children's Celebration ended the Kaila Festival tomorrow night. After the Tournament's final bout and other merchant events were done between foreign entities, the city and visitors had a night of singing, dancing, and children's entertainment.

Father took me once when I was four years old, one of the rare times we came to Jennah or traveled at all. The wonder and awe of the night still came clear to my mind when I saw their preparation. I felt like a princess in a world of royalty.

And Father had smiled that night, more than I had ever seen him before or since. He felt joy from my happiness. That was etched in my mind more than anything. It does something to a daughter when the father feels such joy because of you.

Because of me.

I wove my way through the booths and workers, supplies strewn about and waiting to be organized, used, and sold.

Once I arrived at the main street that led to the southern gate, I paused. Left would take me to the northern city. Where we had fought the goblain. Where I had met Bhelen, the old elfess. The one who had invited me back to be with her, to stay, like she was family.

Images from the battle in the northern city flashed in my mind. Assassins around me. More than once, they could have injured me, maybe killed me. But instead, they had tried to grab me. Why didn't they kill me?

Yesterday, looking into the eyes of the goblain that killed my father, that murdered him, there had been a hint of recognition. Had he been holding back? Had I imagined that? It had all happened so fast.

Your part in this is over, Shaul had said.

The assassination attempt had happened. My father had died to stop it. It was over. We had protected the King.

I sighed and turned right.

Many of the merchants had moved into the main thoroughfare now, crowding both sides of the street, leaving only a narrow strip to walk or ride a wagon through. The southern gate was near the wealthy region of the city with large homes and mansions. More elves wore silks and fine head coverings.

I put my head down and pushed through the throng of people, my hand on the hilt of Qatar.

Has your father told you how he got that sword? Bhelen had said. *Ask him.*

I shook my head to clear my thoughts.

The Great Temple of Ona stood before me, rising from the crowd of elves, humans, and a few dwarves. I stopped in the middle of the street and lifted my head, people avoiding me like I was a large stone in a river. The towers of the Temple stretched longingly for the heavens. The Keepers claimed to know the will of Ona. The Temple had been a beacon of faith, discipline, and education for twenty thousand years.

A respite in a sea of chaos. A place to pray and seek the god of my fathers.

Setting my body at an angle, I cut through the crowd to the long and wide steps of the Temple. Keepers stood at the open doors for morning prayers, one of the sacred times in Jibryl. Elves made their way into the Temple, and the Keepers greeted them in the name of Ona.

One of the Keepers scanned the crowd and locked eyes with me. He frowned. My brow creased, but I continued walking. The Keeper stepped from his station and intercepted me. The others in the crowd gave him room. He stopped right in front of me, and I stumbled to a halt, pulling my covering further over my head.

"Elowen," the Keeper said. "The daughter of Natanel."

"Yes," I said.

"May I help you?"

My shock at his statement froze me for a moment. I looked around me. A few elves went by. A few also stopped and watched.

"I'm here for morning prayers," I said.

A figure emerged from the Temple. Fahim. The First Keeper. He strode forward to stand next to the other Keeper, now both of them in my way. Fahim put his hand on the other's shoulder. "Thank you, Halif. I will handle this."

What the crit? Had he been waiting for me?

Halif nodded to Fahim and went to stand by the door. "Elowen," Fahim said. "What are you doing here?"

"I'm here to pray, like everyone else."

By this point, people had ceased going into the Temple, their attention on whatever was happening. What was happening?

"Well, that is noble of you," Fahim said. "I will pray that Ona will help you honor your father and see your place."

My eyes narrowed. "My place."

Fahim nodded.

"And where would that be?" I said through clenched teeth.

"You require me to say it?" Fahim said. "I heard you had been given a modicum of education. No matter. You can enter, but not armed with a sword."

Blinking quickly, I glanced down at Qatar. "You can't be serious."

"This is very serious, child," Fahim said. "We do not allow elf-daughters into a holy place armed."

My mouth hung open for a split second before I closed it again. "What about elfsons? Would you let them?"

"Officers in the Corps, yes," Fahim said.

"Only elfmen can be officers," I said.

"That is correct," Fahim said.

"What about champions?" I growled.

"Your father would have been allowed had he lived," Fahim said. "But not you."

"This is his sword. My father's sword. He just saved the life of the King. And I am a contestant in the Tournament. Representing this kingdom. My kingdom. Ona's people."

"You may not enter with the sword," he said.

I took a few breaths. Even people on the street grew quiet. How many had cheered for me in the arena yesterday? "What do you suggest I do with it? With my father's sword?"

The First Keeper spread his hands. "Take it back and leave it with his things. Give it to another warrior worthy of it."

Am I not worthy of it?

"You want me to give away my father's sword?" I said.

"To enter the Temple, it must be without the sword," Fahim said.

My shoulders slumped. Even if I beat Julius and won the championship, it wouldn't be good enough. Nothing would ever be good enough. I shook my head and forced my back to straighten.

"You say I should honor my father." My voice was low, but the silent tension allowed everyone within mitres to hear it. "But you are the one that dishonors him."

Fahim flinched like I poked him in the eye.

"He was a great general of the Corps," I said, "and your champion for decades, the greatest warrior in the world, the protector of your King, and you dishonor him."

Fahim recovered from his surprise. But I wasn't done.

"When the assassins struck yesterday, when they tried to kill the King, you ran. My father stood between the enemy and the nation, the duty he had done his whole life. He saved you and the rest of the Trust. He fought for his kingdom. And while you ran, while everyone ran from the fight ..." I lifted my head and surveyed the people surrounding me, my voice rising and echoing. I met Fahim's eyes again. "... I ran toward it. Like my father. Like he taught me."

I took a step toward the First Keeper, one of the most powerful elves in the kingdom. He recoiled.

"And you won't let me into the Temple because I carry his sword?" I said. "Shame on you." The crowd gasped. "Shame on you." I turned and left.

The people parted for me, quiet, staring with wide eyes.

I marched through them down the stairs, back to the street, and headed north.

CHAPTER

28

Like my father.

He ran toward the fight. He always did. And in that moment, so had I. When he was of age, he signed up for the Corps and distinguished himself as a soldier, rising in the ranks. He took the most demanding assignments, the most remote and dangerous, leading his corps-elves into battle and victory time after time.

And after becoming champion swordmaster of the world in the Tournament, his King had called upon him to be his Shield, to battle shadows themselves and even the elfess he loved, my mother, and Natanel had done it. And won. He had lost much. But he had survived.

At the height of his power, intimate friend of the King, he retired. For me.

He quit all of it to take me away, to try and keep me safe. He knew. That night before he left, he had begged me not to come. He didn't want me to come to a world where assassins waited around every corner, where elves in the King's Trust plotted betrayal, where those who were supposed to give access to Ona instead kept people away.

Where he had to be a monster to survive.

He left it all to keep me from it. I forced him to bring me anyway.

Walking with the crowd, I came to the southern square once more and the bustle of elves preparing for the Children's Celebration.

I called him a monster. He had become a monster to kill evil. Was there any other way?

He had gone into the shadows in the northern city, dangerous places, to root out rebellion. To people like Bhelen.

Bhelen knew more than she told us. The goblain had tried to grab me instead of killing me. After she called me family, she told me to come back and that I would be welcome.

Father and I had killed the assassins yesterday. Those elves had help, however, especially the servant in the royal box. Possibly someone in the Trust. Fahim? Aiken? What of Paavo? I knew so little of him.

Shaul had dismissed my help and told me it was over. I had gone with Father into the northern city. Shaul didn't even ask me what I knew, assumed he didn't need me anymore, that I was just an elf-daughter that couldn't help.

Your part in this is over.

But what if it wasn't? The people who organized and helped those assassins yesterday were still out there. Still dangerous.

And they had killed my father.

I didn't turn left to the palace, to my things, to pack and leave. Not yet. I kept walking forward. To the north.

I had been with Father when we went to Bhelen. I could find her shop again. And if she wasn't there, I could ask around, force people to tell me where she was. I had fought goblain. I had beaten a sword-master. I could be the monster to find the truth.

Like my father.

I approached the wall that separated the northern city. At the first gate, the guard both noticed me and shared a glance. They stood straighter.

I didn't recognize them, but the one on the right bowed and said, "Lady Elowen, good day."

"Ona be with you," I said when I stopped.

"And with you," the one on the right said. He stared at the sword at my hip.

"I have business in the northern city today," I said. "It has to do with the Tournament."

The guard's face twisted in confusion. "The Tournament?"

Part of me wished I had grabbed the missive my father used to gain easy entrance. But I would have to make do. "Yes. It is a matter of importance to our people," I noted the badge on his arm, "Sergeant. I'm carrying out a duty that had been given to my father."

"Do you need any assistance?" the guard on the left asked.

I shook my head. "I'll be fine. What are your names?"

"Rinal," said the one on the right, and the other identified himself as Carabay.

"Noted," I said. "I will tell the King how you have done your duty."

Rinal and Carabay shared another glance, both grinning.

"This won't take much time," I said. "But if I need any help, I'll be sure to send word."

"Yes, ma'am," Carabay said.

I nodded to them and walked through the gate into the northern city.

For a tick of time, I wondered if I would remember the way. I made sure that I entered through the same gate so I could retrace my steps. Eventually, I did, making the turns and winding through the streets.

There it was. Bhelen's book shop at the end of the street. I paused at the corner of a building, half in the alleyway, and scanned. The battle with more than two dozen goblain stayed in my mind. I looked over the roofs and into the shadows of the other alleyways. A little elfson played in a puddle across the way, using two sticks like they battled each other, oblivious to me. No one else.

It looked clear. Taking a breath, I stepped out into the sun once more. Bhelen's shop appeared vacant, pitch dark inside. The window coverings gave little insight into the rooms within. I hugged the buildings while I made my way down the street, light on the balls of my feet, making no noise.

The sun hung mid-morning, the air warmer. Getting closer to the shop, my head swiveled in a quick glance. The child was gone, the puddle still rippling in his absence.

I darted across the open area to the book shop, my hand on the hilt of the sword. Arriving at the door, I leaned on the building next to the opening and drew Qatar. With another deep breath, I twisted and kicked open the door, the old wood shattering in pieces, and jumped into the shop.

Landing in a crouch and the sword in a horizontal guard, I was plunged into darkness. My eyes adjusted from the brightness outside. Shadows coalesced into clearer shapes, contours into tables and books. I shuffled further into the shop.

Moments passed, dust swirling, disturbed from my entrance, and glittering when it caught the stray sunlight that penetrated the room. Bhelen's desk waited just in front of me. Looking over my shoulder and checking for anyone, I moved to the desk. Perhaps some clues there?

"You came back," Bhelen said.

I froze and searched the shadows in the corners. No movement.

Bhelen emerged from a narrow door, what seemed like a closet. The matted hair in braids made tinkling sounds.

Qatal lifted between us. "We need to talk."

"Ah, your father's sword," Bhelen said. "Did he tell you about it?"

She smelled of smoke and liquor. "I didn't get a chance to ask him."

"Perhaps I will tell you now that he is gone." She bared her teeth. "If you put that down."

"Not a chance. I know you had something to do with the attack at the arena yesterday."

Bhelen pursed her lips. "You do?"

"Or you know the people who did. You need to tell me everything."

"Everything?" She laughed. "That would take a while."

"You know what I mean. Tell me about the people who tried to kill the King. Who in the Trust is betraying him?"

Bhelen took a few steps forward, and I stiffened, ready for any violent move. She spoke softly. "What do you mean? We are only Ruchali. We are stupid. Less than elven, right? Savages. Animals. When we fight for our own rights, for our own survival, we are monsters, evil."

"You kill innocents," I said. "You want chaos and death."

"That's what your father told you," Bhelen said.

"Yes."

"And who did Natanel kill? Only criminals? And what happens when a tyrant calls people criminals?" Bhelen scoffed. "You can't be that naïve. You know what he did in defense of his King."

"To those who would rebel and destroy the kingdom."

"Do you believe the kingdom is worth saving?" Bhelen said.

I started to answer but then didn't. My mouth became a line.

"Is it so wrong to want chaos and death?" Bhelen said. "When all you've known is oppression, starvation, sickness, and watching your people waste away before your eyes, then chaos and death seem appropriate. Preferable, at least."

Two other shadows appeared from the narrow door. Elves dressed in black. Goblain.

The light behind me fluttered, and I glanced over my shoulder. Four more entered the room from the front door.

A snarl that would have made Zaran proud escaped me. "I knew you had something to do with the attack. You killed my father."

Bhelen stood still, her voice low and dangerous. "You know nothing."

The goblain around the room produced weapons, a few short swords, a few clubs, and one iron chain. It was my turn to scoff. "You think six of you will be enough? I've beaten swordmasters, killed dozens of you." I faced Bhelen. "I'm going to kill them all and then beat everything you know out of you."

"First of all, that would take a long time," Bhelen said. "I've lived for a thousand years. Secondly, no, you won't."

The goblain behind me moved forward slowly, all four at once. I flipped my blade and turned to face them, about to cut into them, when there was movement from Bhelen. I reacted but not fast enough.

A sharp pain erupted in my thigh, and I cried out. Looking down, a long needle with fletching at the end, like a small arrow, stuck in my leg. I glared at Bhelen, her hands held in front of her.

The goblain behind me kept approaching, and I twisted and swung Qatar at the first one, but too slow, like my arms were made of lead. So heavy. The leg with the dart in it folded under me when I twisted, and I went to my knees. The blade arced wide of my target. The goblain didn't even have to block it.

The room started to swim in my vision. I almost fell over. I closed my eyes. "Poison. You poison me?" It became difficult to talk. I had to force out the next word. "Cowards."

"Not poison," Bhelen said. "Just a drug to immobilize you, put you to sleep. Believe me, we have seen how good you are with that sword, both here in the northern city and in the arena. This way, fewer of our people have to die before I show you what you need to know."

I fell over on my side, slipping away from consciousness. "What?" The word was almost unintelligible.

"The truth, dear Elowen. The truth."

CHAPTER

The smell of damp, cool stone filled my nostrils before I could open my eyes. Shifting my weight, the hard and jagged surface underneath dug into my shoulder and side. I coughed and put my hands on the floor. Uneven rock. Heavy rope bound my wrists.

Opening my eyes, shadows surrounded me, a dim torch casting yellow light across the area. The blur in my sight cleared enough to make out the rounded edges of the wall and ceiling, curved marks like they had been dug from the stone and dirt.

The flame of the torch flickered from its stand near an oval opening, an exit from the cave-like area. I blinked to better get my bearings, using my hands together to push myself into a sitting position. Rope also tied my ankles, forcing me to rest my knees on the uncomfortable rock floor.

I shook my head and looked around the room, a cavern with a high ceiling, overall circular in shape, over fifty mitres in diameter, and I sat in the approximate middle next to a wooden crate. Something caught the light in my periphery, to my left. I turned my head to a figure, a shadow within a shadow. It held a long blade. A sword.

My father's sword.

"Qatar." A woman's voice echoed in the chamber, soft and even. Almost nostalgic. "I haven't seen this in years. A fine blade. A work of art, really. From what I hear, you never heard how he got it. Is that right?"

I lowered my head and squinted. It didn't help. She remained a shadow, sitting or crouching. Bhelen?

No, not Bhelen.

"Natanel did love his secrets," the shadow said. "He was still young, only a few hundred. And already a colonel in the Corps. Jibryl was in conflict with Faltiel over some piece of land. Elves, humans, dwarves, it doesn't matter. They draw imaginary lines on a map and then have to fight about it. The lines mean something important to them. More than anything. More than religion or morality. More than people. More than the innocent. It's almost always about land."

She sighed. "As I was saying, the Corps fought over a piece of land, and Natanel served under a general. A lazy general. At least, that's what Natanel thought. Not aggressive enough. They came across a village in the forest, one of the countless Faltiel villages. But that little town was particularly stubborn. Well organized. And a swordmaster led them."

The shadow stood, bringing the sword with her. "There were two battles, both hard fought and without a clear victor. Natanel blamed the general's conservative approach. Your father took it upon himself to infiltrate the enemy's camp, and he challenged the swordmaster. Killed him and took his sword."

Qatal turned slowly in her hands. "Faltiel does make the finest swords in all of Eres."

I leaned forward, straining to see her better. The shadow took a step toward me, her form becoming more defined.

"Natanel returned to the Corps camp and led them into battle," she said. "Razed the village to the ground. Elfmen, elfwomen, children, all of them dead. Imaginary lines on maps around the world moved. And Natanel became a general."

My eyes narrowed.

"He never told you that story?" she said. "Interesting. He did love to tell stories. But he was very good at being selective."

The shadow took a few more steps further into the dim yellow light. An elfess with darker skin, thin with sharp features. She wore a simple tunic and tight trousers. Her knee-high leather boots scraped the stone. Her head was bare, no covering, and her shorter hair was bunched in tight curls. The yellow light reflected in her eyes.

I swallowed and licked my lips. "Who are you?"

She cocked her head at me. "You don't know? Haven't you guessed yet?"

I glared at her.

"Perhaps it's the drugs." She continued to close the distance between us. "Or maybe you're not as smart as I'd hoped. That would be unfortunate. Especially considering what remains."

My brow creased.

"Oh, I'm sure you thought it was over," she said. "After the attempt on the King at the arena. After your father died, but that was a feint. They tell me you're quite proficient with a blade. You understand that. The real strike comes tomorrow."

"The real strike?"

She nodded. Now she stood a pace away. "I learned from the best, you know. The Knights of Truth have your father to thank."

"The goblain?" I said.

The elfess clicked her tongue. "Such a name. That's another tactic. Demonize the enemy. Make them creatures, animals, monsters. See them as less than. Then you can commit all manner of crimes in the name of your cause. Your father taught that well."

"*Who are you?*" I breathed out the words. But a part of me knew. The words wouldn't come forward. They hovered in the back of my mind like a ghost in the closet. Was it the lingering effects of the drugs?

She knelt before me, her face close, Qatar across her thigh.

"The last time I saw this sword, your father used it to strike me down," she said. "My lover. This blade found my chest, but when he took my child, he ripped my heart from my body."

The elfess reached out and touched my cheek with her knuckles. "My daughter. The one thing I loved in the world. You."

My vision swam, and my breathing went shallow. My features contorted. "Wait. You … you're my …?"

"Yes, Elowen," she said. "I'm your mother."

I sputtered for a moment before I could form actual words. "But you … father said he … that you …"

"Died," she said. "I'm sure he believed that. He had every reason to. I was dying. With a wound like that, I should have died."

"But then …?"

"Like all good legends, I rose again." She smiled. "A miracle, a sign that Ona is with me. Or the gods. Perhaps you could call it magic. It's all the same, isn't it?"

I frowned at her. I didn't know what to say. It couldn't be true. It couldn't.

I took a deep breath. She spoke of a feint, of deception. *Trust no one.* "You're lying."

She laughed. "I am?"

"You're one of his contacts," I said. "From years ago. He said there were a few that survived. You would know the story. You've used the story and claimed to be Talia. But she's dead."

She nodded. "It's a lot to take in, I'm sure. And there's more you have to see."

I clenched my teeth. "More lies."

200

"I am Talia of the Ruchali," she said. "Your mother."

I shook my head. "No."

"Think about it, Elowen," she said. "Why are you here? Why are you still alive? You've killed several of my friends. You came to Bhelen's store to, what, kill her? Get information out of her? Everyone else among the Knights of Truth wants you dead. Why would I keep you alive if I wasn't your mother?"

"I don't know. So you can turn me. Get me close to the King and kill him. Use me."

The side of her mouth curved up. "Sorry to disappoint you. But I'm already close to the King, as close as I could get. I could have killed him at any time I chose."

"You haven't been trying to kill the King?"

"Killing the King wouldn't do much good," she said. "He's one elf. Even if we killed his family, one of the Trust or a powerful general, or a royal cousin would take over. It might cause chaos for a time, even a civil war, but when the sands settled, the system would remain. The system is so powerful, all on its own, that there might never be any break in the line, barely a breath. No. We need to do something bigger than an assassination."

The real strike comes tomorrow. "All of it was misdirection?"

"Not exactly misdirection," she said. "More of a ... prologue. If we had killed the King? All the better."

"Was Father part of this plan?"

She paused and glanced down at Qatar. "Yes. We increased the attempts on the King. And I knew how much the King held Natanel in his confidence. Yacob had his doubts about Shaul."

"My father was a target," I said. "You brought him here so you could kill him."

"You don't understand now," she said. "But you will."

"And me? What was your plan for me?"

"Honestly?" She shrugged. "I didn't believe there was any way in the Four Hells that Natanel would bring you. I was sure he would leave you home or send you away to some secret hideaway. You made your way here, somehow. The one thing I didn't plan for."

My jaw tightened. She did know him. Well. But not me.

"When we heard you were here and then in the Tournament?" She threw her head back with a short laugh. "I couldn't believe it. Then you were in the northern city with Natanel. Amazing. The Knights tried to kidnap you yesterday but couldn't. I considered grabbing you earlier today, but that would have risked it all."

I cursed under my breath. "And I came right to you."

"More than I could have hoped for. To see you again. For years, I thought of ways to come and get you, fight for you, kill your father and bring you home. It could have exposed me, though, and kept me from my mission. I had more power dead. But I wanted to."

"Instead, you decided to help this Hateph kill elves and the King," I said. "You used your knowledge to concoct this plan with him. To help the rebellion. A traitor."

She stared at me for a long while, and time stretched. Her eyes softened. Her face went blank. I had to look away.

An elf appeared and stood at the entrance of the cavern. He didn't wear the usual black garb of the goblain but a sleeveless tunic and billowing trousers. Intricate black tattoos covered his arms and hands. Tall for an elf, his powerful presence emanated. The light in the cavern seemed to dim. My mouth went dry. This must be him. Hateph.

The muscles around her eyes tightened. "It is time."

The elf walked forward and stood behind the elfess that claimed to be Talia. My mother. His dark eyes looked through me somehow.

"Are they gathered?" she said.

"They are," he said.

"Good." She stood, stuck Qatar in a scabbard at her belt, and faced him. "Unbind her feet so she can walk. Then bring her."

She started to stride toward the round entrance to the chamber.

The elfman bowed to her as she left. "Yes, Hateph. As you command."

CHAPTER

Hateph? She's Hateph?

H He pulled a dagger from his belt and cut the rope around my ankles. His hand grabbed my arm and pulled me to my feet. I stumbled before I could stand. He led me to follow the elfess. To follow Hateph.

I pulled at the rope around my wrists, twisting them. The thick rope ground and moved, however.

The torch lit the area around us; the space behind fell into shadow. We came out of the cavern into a tunnel. Tunnels. Were we underneath the city? Underneath Jennah?

"How long was I out?" I said.

Hateph looked over her shoulder at me. "Only a few hours."

I pursed my lips. "We're still in Jennah? Or under it?"

She regarded the rounded top of the tunnel. "Under the northern city, yes."

"How long have these tunnels been here?" I said.

"Parts of them always existed," she said. "Other areas were extended and expanded long ago when the kingdom built a wall to keep us in the northern city."

"Secret from the King." If the King had known, he would have destroyed them, and filled these tunnels with dead bodies. I made slight movements with my wrists. "Did my father know about these?"

The Hateph chuckled. "These tunnels are the most closely guarded secret among the Ruchali. No. He never knew."

We took a few more steps in silence, our feet scraping on the dirt and rock beneath us. Oval openings to other caverns passed us on both sides, the rooms hidden in darkness. The torchlight cast a tick of light into those areas, but not enough to reveal anything. More secrets. Secrets under secrets.

"But I'm here," I said.

The elf at my arm glowered at me.

"You are my daughter," she said. "I'm hoping that if we show you what we're fighting for, you'll understand."

"Understand what?"

She didn't answer right away. "That the things we do are for our survival. For the survival of our people."

"What things?" I said.

"You would call it rebellion," she said. "But it is more."

The tunnel widened ahead and veered to the right, where a yellow glow appeared. Hateph turned to the right and angled her body to allow me to enter another massive cavern, even larger than the one where I awoke. The stench of urine and sweat hit me first.

I came to a complete stop, frozen, and my breath caught.

The cavern was filled with children.

Children of all shapes and sizes, most under the age of ten, barely clothed. They sat or lay on cots. Every child had a disability of some kind. White, blind eyes. Or one eye missing. Or a limb missing. One child had two stumps for legs.

Some faces turned to see me. Many didn't move.

An older elfess, ancient of age with long white hair, stood from feeding a child a morsel of bread. She left the rest of the small loaf with the child and brushed her hands on a stained robe that had once been white.

She bowed. "Hateph." When she rose from the bow, she nodded to the elf at my elbow. "Valez."

Valez, the elf with the tattoos, gave a curt nod.

"Wera," Hateph said. "This is my daughter, Elowen."

Wera's expression tightened. "Welcome." Wera turned and went to another child.

I barely looked at Wera. I couldn't tear my gaze from the children. I took a step forward. "W-who are they? Where did they come from?"

Hateph stood next to me. She also gazed over the room. Must have been three hundred. "They come from all over the city. The City Corps find the babies born with defects, the ones they say Ona has cursed. And they give them to the Keepers to kill them."

"They ..." My brow creased, and I shook my head. "They what?"

"The City Corps comb through Jennah, both the northern and southern cities," she said. "A regular culling. They call it mercy to kill them."

The Keeper in our village preached about the curses in the world. How humans, dwarves, and those with defects were cursed. I never paid much attention. Seemed like a breeze in the dunes, stirring up a bit of sand but not that important. Seemed important now.

"I didn't know," I said.

Hateph nodded. "Most don't want to know. The parents don't want to be labeled cursed with such a child. The kingdom doesn't advertise it."

I could only shake my head. Couldn't be true, could it?

Like she read my thoughts, Hateph continued. "Have you seen a child or adult with a defect in your village?"

I took a deep breath, taking a moment. Had I? "No." I swallowed hard. "But if that's true, where did these come from?"

Hateph crossed her arms. "A few parents hide their children when they are born with defects. We take them in. Hide them here, underground. With us, they have a reason to live. A purpose."

Tears began to blur my eyes. I sniffed. What could I say?

I turned and walked back into the tunnel, out of sight of the children. I couldn't take how they looked at me, the sadness and pain in their eyes. Lowering my head, I breathed slowly, my bound hands resting on my knee, the rope chafing my skin when I turned my wrists, although the knots were not as tight anymore.

Hateph and Valez followed to stand on either side of me.

"That is why we fight," Hateph said. "Why assassinating the King or even the royal family won't be enough. The system will adjust and move on. Continuing to kill and exile our people. We have to do something more."

I frowned. "Something more?"

"Something that breaks the system," Valez spoke for the first time. His voice echoed, deep and low.

My mind reeled around the cursed children hidden in tunnels. The pain and sorrow they must feel. I tried to process what Valez meant. "*Breaks* the system?"

"To the point it can't be remade," Hateph said.

I closed my eyes. Why had I never seen this? My father knew. He had to have known. But not just him. The King. The Trust. The Keepers. Those that spoke of the goodness of the Onamaker killing children in secret, erasing them from sight. How many knew?

Enough. If I had known, would I have questioned? Anger broiled within me, mostly because I didn't know what I would have done. Yet now I couldn't unsee those children in the room behind me.

The Ruchali were forced to hide. They were even hiding Jibrylan children. Here, underground.

Valez and Hateph waited in silence.

"How?" I opened my eyes.

"What do you mean?" Hateph said.

I stood straight and rolled my shoulders. "How will you break the system?"

"Ah," Hateph said. "That is not for you know. Not now."

Trust no one. Sounded like she knew that rule, too.

"Then why am I here?" I said.

Hateph sighed. "I told you. You're my daughter. I wanted to keep you safe, help you understand why I never risked coming for you, even though I wanted it more than anything."

"Not more than anything," I said.

The corners of her mouth turned down. "No. Not if I had to put more innocents at risk."

I snorted. "Not more than the cause."

She stiffened. "It's about people, Elowen. That's why I showed you those children. This is bigger than you and me. Sometimes we must make sacrifices."

Assassinating the King won't be enough. Break the system. Bigger than you and me. I wanted to keep you safe ...

"Keep me safe," I said. "That's why you brought me down here. You're going to do something big. In the city."

"Hateph ..." Valez's voice carried a warning.

After a glance at Valez, she forced a grin. "You will have to wait and see."

Bigger. Bigger than killing the King. Creating chaos and destruction makes sense.

"The real strike comes tomorrow," I mumbled.

Valez raised a brow at me.

Tomorrow. *Tomorrow ...*

I gasped and turned back to look into the room at the children. The children the kingdom declared cursed.

"No," I said. "You wouldn't ..."

Neither answered me, their faces going blank.

I looked at Hateph in horror. "The Children's Celebration. You're going to attack the close of the Kaila Festival."

"Talia." Valez's fists clenched, all but confirming what I said.

Hateph glared at him. "Quiet."

My breathing came short. "You're going to attack the Children's Celebration to expose the kingdom and embarrass us in front of the world."

They remained quiet.

"But those are innocent children, too." My horror twisted to confusion. "You're going to kill innocent children to show that it's wrong … to kill innocent children?"

Hateph gestured to Valez. "Take her away and tie her ankles."

"Wait," I said while Valez grabbed my elbow. "There will be children from all over the world, from the other elven kingdoms." My voice rose. "You'll start wars! Other nations will blame Jibryl. Those kingdoms will all attack at once."

Hateph skidded over in front of me, to face me, and Valez had to stop pulling me away. She snarled. "We will do what we must to break the system."

"You and Father are the same," I said. "He justified it, too. Justified killing the innocent to save the kingdom. Just like you."

"We were the same," Hateph said. "Now he's dead. I won."

"You *won*?" My mouth gaped for a moment. "This is a game to you?"

"He had to die," she said. "I know you loved him, but he had to be removed. He knew me too well."

I lowered my head and shook it. "I called him a monster."

"Oh, Elowen." Hateph's voice dripped with pity. "We are all monsters. You'll see. The only question is which monsters will survive."

I groaned.

"Now take her," Hateph said to Valez.

He started to pull again, but I resisted. "One more thing, *Mother*."

I spat the word, used it like a weapon, and she froze like she'd been slapped. There were only the three of us in the tunnel.

"Whoever tied me up didn't do it very well," I said.

My wrists came free from the rope, and in one motion, I turned and struck Valez under the chin with the palm of my right hand. His teeth clapped, and his head snapped back, the rest of his body leaning and falling away.

In the next heartbeat, I kicked out with my left foot, a simple straight kick that slammed into Hateph's abdomen. She let out her breath in a whoosh and bent over with her eyes bulging. Hateph stumbled back, and I started to run past her.

The direction was a total guess. I didn't want to go back the way we came, though, and the next logical choice was forward. There had to be a way out.

I was two steps into a sprint when my body locked. Pain filled my whole body, beginning with my heart, which spasmed, and drowned the rest of me in agony. I couldn't even cry out. I just fell to the ground, my face bouncing off of the dirt.

But I didn't feel that. Other pain overwhelmed me. My vision narrowed. My eyes reeled back in my head. I managed to roll over, and while the circle of my sight grew smaller, Valez stood over me, his hand outstretched, his fingers curled. His face was one of fury.

"Valez!" Hateph screamed from far away. How far away was she? "That's enough!"

In the next tick of time, it stopped. The pain was gone. But the echo remained. I could finally make a noise, and it was one of sobbing. My own.

"She knows too much, Hateph," Valez said. "And she was getting away."

He stood straight now; my vision blurred. He had been doing something to me without touching me, like it was magic.

Magic.

"Where could she have gone?" Hateph said. "She would have been lost without a guide in these tunnels."

I coughed and spit, my sobbing beginning to subside. "Magic. He's a … a *solona* wizard."

"Yes, he is." Hateph rubbed her stomach.

Each *solona* wizard had their own power, their own way of manipulating the physical world. Some could take the life from beings, from animals, from people. From me. The power of Yor.

"*Solonayor*," I said. The gods of death.

Valez shook his head with a glower across at Hateph.

"Take her and tie her up better this time," she said. "And don't harm her. We have work to do."

CHAPTER

31

Valez found rope from somewhere and tied my hands and feet. I don't know if I could have walked, but it didn't matter. Bound, I could barely sit up. Valez picked me up a little too easily. Was he always that strong, or did some of my life force increase his power? Not sure I wanted to know.

Hateph disappeared, and Valez carried me down the tunnel. The same direction I was going to try and escape. I focused despite my exhaustion, attempting to pay attention to the turns he took. The tunnel rose a bit and lowered at times. Regular torches lit the way. Valez took a left and then a right to other tunnels.

After a few minutes of travel, he entered a dark room that smelled of sour water. A large boulder sat in the far corner. Valez took a few steps into the dark and set me against the wall. His shadow knelt before me in the faint light from the tunnel outside. He didn't move for a long time, too long.

I fought the urge to cringe, to withdraw as much as I could into myself. With a thought, he could drain the life out of me. And he wanted to. He had made that clear. I shivered, suddenly very cold.

Valez snorted, stood, and left the room.

My shoulders slumped, and I breathed a sigh. I leaned the back of my head against the wall, closing my eyes. I could fall asleep. When had I eaten last? Taken a drink? It had been hours. My throat was parched. I coughed and licked my lips.

Chains rattled in the far corner.

I opened my eyes, sat up straight, and narrowed my eyes at the large boulder in the corner.

The boulder moved. Chains rattled again.

That wasn't a boulder.

Cloth scraped against stone, and a shape rose from the boulder. Not a shape. A head on shoulders. Its breath combined with a half snore. A trodall? Had these goblain really put me in a room with a trodall?

Pushing with both feet, bound at the ankles, I tried to move away but couldn't get farther into the stone, and my hands came up to my chest.

I had never seen a trodall. Only heard stories. But didn't they have horns? I squinted, trying to see better in the dark. My eyes adjusted. No horns. Maybe tufts of hair. No elf could be that big.

Leaning forward, I said, "What are you?"

Its eyes opened, reflecting the tunnel's light, and they fixed on me. The form shifted with more iron clatter.

"No one." The voice was low and booming, even though he didn't project.

Too big to be an elf or even a human. Although ...

I grunted. "You're a Gedai."

He didn't say anything to confirm or deny. Didn't need to. My eyes adjusted a bit more, and there were human features and forms, although shaded in the lack of light.

A Gedai. A giant. I had only seen one years ago in Jennah, not at the Festival but another visit to the city with Father. That giant had been chained, as well, serving as a slave of sorts in a construction project. His steps had been slow, plodding, his eyes empty. A handful of elves guarded him with spears like he'd been a constant threat. As a small child, I pitied him. Until I saw him lift a stone as tall as an elf and put it into place. A stone that had to weigh even more than he did.

Then I had clung to my father and hurried him away.

Giants. They were considered human. A human could get to two mitres, maybe two and a half. A short Gedai began at three mitres, most closer to four. A few thought the Gedai were a separate race altogether, even though they were in every way similar to humans, only bigger.

They had once thrived among the humans, but at some point, the humans began hunting them, enslaving them. So had the elves and dwarves. I never learned why. Now very few existed.

The Keepers also considered them cursed, along with those with disabilities or the seriously infirm. Many didn't even use the word Gedai anymore, called them *gedders*, a derogatory term.

I shifted my weight. "How did you get here?"

He cocked his head at me. "How does a gedder get anywhere?" His voice didn't carry any harm or offense. "Sold."

"Okay. But what about the tunnels? How did you fit?"

The boulder shoulders shrugged. "Not easy."

"What about in the city," I said. "Did they sneak you in?"

"A tunnel began outside the wall."

Made sense. The goblain had extended the tunnels. They would have done so under the southern city, whether to sneak assassins in or cursed children out and outside the walls to get people in and out apart from the City Corps security.

"Do you know why?" I said. "Why you're here? They must have a reason."

The Gedai shook his head.

I nodded. "What is your name?"

His head rose, and he peered at me. "My name?"

"Yeah. You have one, right?"

"Yes," he said.

"My name is Elowen."

His breathing deepened; his shoulders straightened. "My people once had a tradition. A belief."

When he didn't continue, I said, "What belief?"

"They believed that names have power. And to ask a name was to ask to be a friend, for only a friend or family should have that power."

"Oh. Sorry. I was just making conversation."

"Yes, I know," he said. "Brone is the name my first master gave me."

"Brone. Peace to you."

Footfalls sounded outside in the tunnel, and an elfess entered the room. One with long braids.

I bared my teeth at her. "Bhelen."

Carrying a bottle, a small leather bag, and a torch, she turned to me. "Elowen." Bhelen walked over and set the bag and bottle down in front of me. I curled my lip at them. "Water and food. Your mother thought you might be hungry and thirsty."

"My mother," I growled. "Is it really her? The elfess you knew?"

Bhelen knelt in front of me. "Of course. What are you saying?"

"As far as I know, she could be anyone."

She smiled at me. "Believe what you will. But that is your mother. I thought she had died. We all did." Her smile vanished. "Thought your father killed her. Then she appeared, she and Valez. It had been ten years. But make no mistake. It wasn't long enough to make me forget my friend. It was Talia."

"Then she is the Hateph? The one unifying the Ruchali? They accept an elfess as a leader?"

"Most don't know who she is, not really," Bhelen said. "The same rules apply – separate cells independent from each other. Her legend grew, though. Death to life. And no one could deny her results. She knows how the kingdom tries to divide and conquer us."

"Things my father taught her."

"He is a good teacher," she said. "You should know. You fought well in the Tournament."

I scoffed. "Not well enough."

"You're young and beat swordmasters." She grinned. "That's pretty good."

I shook my head.

"Ah, you mean you didn't save your father." Bhelen sighed. "There are forces here beyond your control or mine. Forces at work for centuries, maybe longer. Before anyone here became part of it. You were never going to save your father. All you can do now is save yourself."

Maybe they had other ways, but Bhelen had told them of Father's visit, had helped them know what contact he would have made next, helped send those goblain that we fought that day. She was part of it all. My father's death.

The only question is which monsters will survive.

"Survive what?" I said. "What is she planning?"

Bhelen gave a short laugh. "Child, even I don't know all that she's planning."

"You know she's going to attack the Children's Celebration? She's going to kill innocent children."

She frowned. "She's going to break the system."

"Now you're just repeating what you've heard, what she says. Break the system by killing children? Innocents?"

Bhelen's frown became a glare. "If that's what it takes, then yes. Who do you think you are? What do you know? We've tried everything. Petitions, rebellions, negotiations, all of it. Nothing has changed. Maybe this. Maybe this will change."

She was right. They'd been fighting this war for so long. What did I know? "I know this. If Jibryl killing children is wrong, even the cursed, then what she has planned is no better. Even if you win, even if the whole system falls, what will take its place?"

"Anything," Bhelen said.

I lowered my head and caught sight of Brone, the giant. He stared at me. He only wore a loincloth. The thick iron chains were now visible, driven into the stone, clasped to his wrists and feet. Another chain hung around his neck, like a necklace, with a large, smooth red gem at the end.

I turned back to Bhelen. "Did you know that Velez is a *solonayor*?"

"Of course," she said. "That's how she survived your father."

My mother? "Heresy."

"That's your belief," Bhelen spat. "Not ours. The Ruchali see value in the gifts of Ona."

"Gifts in the gods of death," I said. "What is his part in this?"

"To protect your mother, the Hateph," Bhelen said.

"He has the power to take and give life. And he's a bodyguard?"

She shrugged. "I told you. I don't know any more than that. Only a few do."

I nodded over at the giant. "And what does he have to do with it?"

Her mouth became a line. "Again. Only Hateph knows."

"What is that around his neck?"

Bhelen turned and shone the torch over at him. "A gem of some kind."

"Why does he have it?"

"Something to do with the *solonayor*, the magic," she said. "You don't understand, Elowen. I've only seen Velez a handful of times. Few have. My place is as a contact above."

I met her gaze. "You own a shop with books."

"What does that mean?" she said.

"You read them, right?"

Her eyes narrowed. She nodded.

I leaned in, lowering my volume. "You know as well as anyone how Valez gets power. The power to give life, he has to take it from someone. Whose life did he have to take to save my mother?"

Bhelen said, "With all that she's done, unifying us, helping us, that doesn't matter."

"Doesn't matter?" I sniffed. "You say you don't know the plan, but I would be interested. He seems like more than a bodyguard. And the Hateph talked about something big. Taking life, giving life, that sounds pretty huge to me. A major weapon. If he's giving life, using that power somehow, he'll be taking it from someone. Who will that be?"

Bhelen turned from the giant back to me and stared.

"I would want to find out," I said. "Then again, like you said, what do I know?"

She glanced at the Gedai once more and then stood. "Keep trying to manipulate me if you want. All you're proving is that you're just like your father."

I chuckled. "Maybe. But if I get free, then you should pray that's not true. You should pray that I'm not like him at all."

Her nostrils flared. "Eat, drink. You'll need it." Then she left.

After she was gone, the room plunged back into a dim shadow, and I lowered my head. So much death, hate. Hopelessness. What could I do to stop it? Nothing. Who was I to think I could do anything?

"Elowen," the giant said.

Breathing in through my nose, I took a moment to respond. "Yes, Brone?"

"Brone is the name my first master gave me."

My brow creased. I lifted my head. "Your first master?"

"Yes."

First master gave him a name. A slave name. "But that's not your real name."

He shook his head.

I smirked. "What is your real name?"

"My real name, the name my mother gave me, is as ancient as the forest and deeper than the sea," he said. "Gomundur."

I repeated it. "Gomundur."

He bowed his head. "Elowen."

"Thank you. I will guard it well."

"As will I, yours," he said.

I looked down at the bottle of water and the bag of food.

Bhelen was right about one thing. I picked up the bottle, took a drink, and began to eat.

CHAPTER

G iants snore.

Leaning back against stone and tied at my wrists and ankles was uncomfortable enough. Add to that, thoughts and questions raced through my mind – what was my mother going to do with the magic of death? How was she going to attack the Children's Celebration? Horrific visions filled my brain. My imagination conjured up things worse than reality.

At least, I hoped.

Whatever happened, I had to escape. Twisting and pulling the knots didn't do anything this time. I tried for what seemed like hours. But I couldn't measure time here, underground. In the end, I only chafed my wrists to bleeding.

That didn't help.

The food and water refreshed me, settled me, and exhaustion pulled me under. I couldn't hold my eyes open. I rested my head back, surrendering to the fatigue.

At that point, the giant started snoring.

I cursed under my breath and tried to ignore it. Didn't work. The more I tried to ignore the sounds like avalanches reverberating in the room, the more they annoyed me.

Restless, I shifted my position over and over, hips and elbows and shoulders sore from constant contact with the hard rock and dirt.

The exhaustion overcame my exasperation at some point, and I did sleep.

I didn't know how many hours had passed when the noises in the room woke me, the movement of chains scraping the floor. I snorted and lifted my head from the wall. The room had brightened with another torch. Someone stood in front of me, holding it.

Hateph. Talia. My mother. Which name did I use? Qatar hung from her hip.

Valez stood close to Gomundur, and the elf continued to unlock the chains from the giant's hands and feet. Once done, Valez raised his hand, fingers splayed, toward the gem around his neck.

The red stone began to glow, faint at first, then intensely, throwing more light over the room. Gomundur's eyes closed, and when they opened, they also glowed crimson. The giant stood. Valez backed out of the cavern, past Hateph, who gave him a wide berth.

Gomundur marched forward, one plodding step after another, his red eyes unmoving. Valez walked into the tunnel, and the giant followed, having to crawl on hands and knees to get through the mouth of the cavern.

The gem controlled the giant somehow, connected to the life within.

Hateph turned to follow and paused. "You ate. I'm glad. This will be over soon. Then we can talk."

"Talk about what? How you killed children? The innocent?"

She frowned. "If you wish. But more importantly, what you want to be in the new world we're about to create."

"Create? You're only going to send our country into further darkness."

"No," she said. "I'm exposing the darkness that already exists. There's a difference."

I shook my head. "You know, when I was young, I dreamed about you. Father wouldn't tell me anything. I was left to my imagination. You were beautiful or ugly. Smart or stupid. A hero like Selina the Brave. Or timid and quiet. Lots of things. I even thought you might be alive, that Father was wrong somehow, that you would come to our town and explain how much you had done to get to me. You would have fought through armies of trodall. Or I would see you in another city, maybe Jennah, and we would embrace. You would hold me and tell me you missed me. I longed for that. Different versions of that."

I lifted my bound hands to her. "But not this. Never this."

Hateph stared at me for another moment. My mother then strode out of the room, taking the torch with her.

Back in a room with little light, I lowered my head in the new quiet. What were they going to do with the giant? Nothing good. Giants were already slaves, forced to comply. Why would Valez need more control? What would he force Gomundur to do? What would he *need* to force him to do?

I missed the steady rumble of the giant's snore.

Time passed, possibly hours. I might have slept for a few minutes. Then noises of movement in the tunnel, feet running and walking, larger groups. Something was happening, and I uttered foul words at being in the dark, unable to move.

Silence reigned in the tunnels. I pulled my knees against my chest and lowered my forehead to rest on them.

A scream broke the silence, distant and faint. I lifted my head with bulging eyes. Another shrill shriek followed, all the more chilling from the echoes, and one last before returning to the quiet.

They sounded like children.

I strained against the ropes that bound me once more, not caring about the pain and the blood on my wrists, accepting the pain, letting it fuel me, motivate me. All I accomplished was more blood on the coils. My shoulders slumped.

The light in the tunnel grew, and I looked up at a figure in the doorway. Bhelen held a torch and a short sword. The flame flickered near her face, tears falling from dark eyes.

She shuffled to me, a pace away. The sour scent of her oils and drugs mixed with smoke wafted over me.

"Hateph sent me home," Bhelen said.

I raised a brow at her.

"I asked her." She blinked and cleared her eyes of tears, although they only filled once more. "What you said. I asked her what Valez was going to do with that gem and the giant."

"And?"

"She sent me home," Bhelen said. "It wasn't for me to know. I had done my part. Told me to go back to my shop and stay safe tonight. Wait for the end. She would call on me then."

I stared at her.

"There are books at my shop, though, like you said." Her grin didn't touch the sadness in her gaze. "I always loved books. Was good at them. Reading." Her grin faltered. "Finding information."

I waited.

She took a deep breath. "The books sat there. I tried to busy myself with other things. To sleep. But I knew they were there. I knew where to find the information, and knew that if I read, I would find out. The books would tell me. I went to bed, telling myself I didn't need to know. I should trust my friend. She's done so much …"

She lowered her eyes, lost.

"Bhelen," I said.

She met my stare. "I needed to know. I couldn't help myself."

"What did you find?" I whispered.

Bhelen knelt before me and looked at the cords on my ankles. "That gem is called a Bloodstone. You can find it in the mountains, north of the Firestone Fields, where the *solona* used to train in their magic before Jibryl hunted and killed most of them."

"Valez used it to control the Gedai," I said.

"Yes, controls. And gives life to the wearer. But it does more than that. In the hands of a *solonayor* like him, it can ... transform them."

I narrowed my eyes. "Transforms who?"

"Elves, dwarves, humans, Gedai," she said. "Anyone who wears the stone. It acts as a ... repository of power, of magic. Then Valez can use it as he wishes, when he wishes."

"Transforms them how?"

Bhelen shrugged. "The books said into something, but I didn't understand it, an ancient word I never read or heard before."

Into what? Could be anything. What was he going to turn the Gedai into?

"You said a repository," I said. "Like it stores the power?"

She nodded. "That's why I came back. I had to know."

I swallowed. "Had to know what?"

"What you asked before. Where he would get the power."

"Where is he getting it from?" I said.

Bhelen winced like the question hurt her. "You'll have to come and see. I can't ..."

"Okay," I said.

She lifted the short sword over my ankles. I scrambled to extend and part them as much as possible, especially since the blade shook and wobbled in her hand. Bhelen brought it down and the sword cut through the ropes in one strike. I released my breath when she missed my skin and didn't chop off a foot.

The sword shifted from her right hand to the left, now holding the blade and the torch together. Bhelen stood, extended her free hand, grabbed the ropes around my wrists, and pulled me to my feet.

I gritted my teeth at the pain and stretched my back once upright. With the sword back in her right hand, she gestured for me to enter the tunnels. I did. She pointed to the right with the blade when she joined me. "That way."

We walked with me in the front. The tunnel rose a bit as we traveled and came to a junction. Bhelen directed me to the left, which led us to a descending and dark path. Fewer torches lit the way, and the path became darker.

The air also became stale, and my lungs had to work harder to breathe. I glanced over my shoulder, and Bhelen eyed something ahead. I followed her stare to the mouth of a cavern. My steps slowed.

I stopped at the doorway. Bhelen handed me the torch. She wasn't going in. I had to go in alone.

Carrying the torch in both hands, I stepped into the room.

The flame lit the vast room. It took a moment for my brain to process the shapes before me. They were bodies. Small bodies. Skeletons? No, whitened skin. Tattered clothes on them.

I groaned.

They were scattered throughout the room, their skin once dark tan now white and shrunken, husks of something once alive, once elven.

The children. The cursed children. Dead.

But more than dead, worse than dead. Drained of their whole essence. I thought of the pain when Valez drew the life from me yesterday – had it been yesterday? That had only been a few ticks of time. How long did it take to empty a child of life? I couldn't imagine.

I turned from the room back into the tunnel, dropped the torch, bent over, and vomited what little had been left in my stomach on the dirt floor.

"Ona help me," I cried.

"I thought I was working for peace," Bhelen said with a moan in her voice. "I worked with your father, thinking that if I kept the worst of the violence from happening, then it would change. But it didn't. The Ruchali kept dying. Jibryl kept destroying the innocent among us. Then Talia told me it would be different. She would break the whole system. And we would protect the children Jibryl had cursed. But she wasn't protecting them."

They will have a purpose ... sacrifices must be made.

I stood straight and wiped my lips with my sleeve. "She was saving them for Valez."

Bhelen nodded and took a step closer to me. "Are you like him?"

"Like who?"

"Your father. Natanel. Can you stop this?"

"Can I stop this?" I shrugged. "I don't know. But I will do my best. On that, you have my word." I lifted my hands so she could cut the ropes.

She took a deep breath. "Remember, most of those in the northern city are just trying to survive, make it to tomorrow, feed their children. They know nothing of all this. Nothing." Her gaze softened. "I know you grew up with your father as a Jibrylan. But we are your people, too."

"I understand."

"I'm not sure you do," she said. "Either way, you have to swear to keep these tunnels secret. No matter what."

How could I swear that? My face went blank. Even tied up like this, I could take her down and get that short sword. But could I find my own way out of the tunnels? I didn't know how many elves I might have to fight through and still get lost.

"Fine," I said. "I swear."

With a glance at the dark room full of dead children, Bhelen lifted the blade and cut the ropes from my wrists.

CHAPTER

Bhelen ran through the tunnels. Sore and tired, I pushed myself to follow. She took random turns, and it seemed we went in circles more than once. Several times, Bhelen slowed and waited at a junction, hiding the torch and making sure that no one waited around the bend.

I was glad I didn't knock her out and try to find my way out alone.

We approached the end of one tunnel where a ladder rose overhead and to the surface. Bhelen stopped and faced me, both of us panting.

"This will take you to an alley near the southern square, across from the palace," she said in a quiet voice. "Make sure no one sees you. Then do what you can to stop what's coming."

"I will." I grabbed the rung of the ladder. "Thank you."

Bhelen handed me the short sword in her hand. I started to take it but hesitated.

"You might need that." I placed both hands on the ladder. "Get out and be safe."

Bhelen scoffed and lowered the sword. "I think I left safe behind me long ago."

"Me too."

"I heard someone say that the attack would begin at the wall," Bhelen said. "And move from there into the city."

"Okay," I said. "Thanks."

"Remember. You swore."

My brow creased. "I remember."

I climbed up the ladder into the dark and met a wooden hatch with the top of my head. Feeling around with my fingers, I found a metal ring and pushed upward. Dirt fell into my face. I spat and coughed before lifting with my shoulder, and the hatch door came free and opened to a crate with light coming through the lid.

Keeping as silent as I could, I crawled into the box and closed the door under me gently. I pressed against the lid with a palm and peeked out. An alley, just as Bhelen had said. And empty.

The lid scraped on the edges of the crate when I twisted it to the side, enough to slip out. I dropped to the ground in a crouch, glancing up and down the alley once more. No one. I had to squint in the light, even though the alley was in shadow.

I straightened and walked to the end of the alley, blocked in the other direction. I brought the hood of my tunic up and over my head before stepping out into the street, a side street just off of the main southern square. The late afternoon sunlight bore down on me, and I used my hand to shade my eyes.

The Children's Celebration would begin in a few hours. What to do first?

Go to the palace and warn the King. Or maybe Shaul the Shield would help me. I couldn't do this alone. We needed the army, at least.

The side street was busy but not crowded, most of them elves of Jibryl, although many were elves from other kingdoms and dwarves and a few humans. I walked along the street and breathed deep the city scents of food. A breeze brushed my face.

Turning to the left at the next smaller street, it took me to the southern square filled with people. The decorations finished with streamers and different colored booths, everything bright and welcoming. I lowered my head and made for the palace.

Once I arrived at the main gate of the outer palace, the guard there frowned at me, my clothes ragged and streaked with red and black dirt, and my chafed and bloodied wrists. But when I got closer, they recognized me.

"Lady Elowen," the lead guard said, a Captain. I didn't remember his name.

I nodded at him, and the rest of the guard, a dozen at the gate, relaxed.

"People have been looking for you," he said. "The report said you left yesterday morning and didn't return. Some thought you had left."

"I didn't," I said.

"Are you well?" he said.

My appearance more than suggested I wasn't. "I will be. I need to get to my room, my things. Clean up."

The Captain got the hint and moved out of the way. I thanked him while I walked through the guard and passed the formidable statues of former kings and heroes of Jibryl. Looking up at the vast stairs and the main entrance, I didn't want another confrontation with the guard, at least not another dozen.

I swerved right and took the path to the courtyard between the palace and the stables. Those guard knew me better, used to seeing me pass and walk freely. They greeted me with confused faces but let me pass without incident to the side entrance into the palace.

Inside, I hurried to the main hallway. Where to go? I started to climb the stairwell, and a voice called from behind me.

"Lady Elowen?"

I turned and could have sobbed. "Refa."

Refa was dressed in his usual servant uniform. His brow creased, and he approached. "What happened?" He took in the dirty garb and my bloody wrists. "Are you hurt?"

"I'll be okay."

"I expected you yesterday, and you never returned," he said. "What happened?"

His tone carried such innocent concern I could have kissed him on the cheek. "I can't tell you right now. I need to see the King. And Shaul, the Shield. To warn them."

His brow unfolded and shot up his forehead. "Warn them?"

"Refa. Please. There's no time. Do you know where they are? Can you take me to them?"

His face returned to a frown. "I believe they are together in a meeting room on the top floor."

I grabbed his hand. "Can you show me?"

Refa nodded and clasped my hand in both of his before releasing me and passing me when he ascended the stairs.

We rushed up to the next level and then across to another set of stairs along the southern side of the palace. Soon we arrived at a long passageway with one wide set of doors to our right. I followed Refa, and halfway down, he paused at those doors.

"I believe the King is here." He cringed.

I nodded and opened both doors to a round room twenty mitres in diameter with couches and lush chairs in a circle. Directly in front of us, a high window the length of the room gave a view to the west – over the palace wall and into the city.

Two guard waited at the doors and faced me with spears in their hand. The King and Shaul stood at the window, the sun beginning to set behind them.

Walking past the guard, taking advantage of their shock, I strode through the middle of the room toward the King. Shaul spun on me, his hand on his sword. The iron shield was on his back. The Shield of the King.

"Your Majesty," I said. "I need to talk to you."

Shaul slid over between me and King Yacob, who stared at me with wide eyes. Shaul surveyed my appearance, first with disgust. Then he flinched. I saw fear in his eyes for a tick of time, returning to his visage of anger.

"Elowen," he spat.

"Talk to me?" the King said.

A presence came up behind me, the guard gripping their spears. I looked over my shoulder. Refa waited by the door, his hands clasped in front of him, looking down.

"There's going to be an attack tonight," I said.

"I told you," Shaul said. "That your part in this is over. You need to leave."

I glared at him. My fists clenched. "Will you shut up and listen! You might think I don't have anything to do with this anymore, or maybe you think I never did, but I'm telling you this isn't over. There will be another attack tonight."

The King frowned. He reached out and put his hand on Shaul, pushing him to the side to step closer to me. "Another attack. You mean an assassination attempt?"

"No," I said. "Those attempts were just distractions."

"Distractions?" the King said.

"Yes. Distracting you from the real plan. The goblain are going to attack the Children's Celebration tonight. You have to send the Corps to the wall around the northern city. You have to stop them."

"How?" The King narrowed his eyes. "How will they do this?"

I sighed. "I don't know. But they have a wizard with them. A *solonayor*. They're going to use him somehow."

The King shook his head. "I don't understand. How will they get past the wall? A wizard? They've been heresy for a century."

"I know, sir, but …"

The King continued, "And how do *you* know all this?"

I blinked slowly. "One of my father's contacts. I went to confront her yesterday, and she told me what she knew."

"You got this from a single contact?" the King said. "You want me to send armed men through the streets during one of the busiest nights of the Festival? Based on the word of a single contact?"

I groaned. "It's more than that. The goblain, they captured me, and I escaped. That's where I learned about the *solonayor*, that they're planning something tonight." I waved at the sun, beginning to dip behind the walls of Jennah. "Soon! You have to believe me."

"King Yacob," Shaul said. "One contact? That contact could be playing us. Bringing our army through the streets during the Children's Celebration would be an embarrassment, and possibly trying to weaken the defenses around the palace for another attempt. This child doesn't know how to vet these tangled situations."

"I'm telling you the truth," I said. "How much more embarrassing will it be for goblain to cut down children tonight? Stop dismissing me because I'm too young or an elfdaughter and listen."

Shaul drew his sword and bared his teeth. He grabbed my arm with his other hand and pulled me away from Yacob. "These are the ravings of a mad elf, my King. Her grief at her father's death has driven her delusional. I will take her to her rooms and place her under guard."

"No!" I struggled against him, trying to get free, but his grip tightened. Pain shot up my arm, and I cried out. I looked up at Shaul. "Stop! You're the Shield. You have to protect the King. Just because you didn't want my father here, don't let that stop you from listening to me."

The guard both pointed their spears at me, backing toward the open doors. Like I was some criminal.

"Not want him here?" Shaul said. "Child, I was the one that told the King to send for him."

"What did you say?" I breathed.

"Yes," he said. "It was me."

Someone from the Trust. Father believed someone from the Trust had to be involved to replace the Courier. To get a servant assassin in the royal box. That had to be someone in the Trust.

I had been looking at the others, the ones with power like Paavo, Aiken, and Fahim. But the Shield was in the Trust, as well. And closest to the King.

But I'm already close to the King, Mother had said, *as close as I could get. I could have killed him at any time I chose.*

Any time I chose ... as close as I could get.

Maybe he wasn't dismissing me because I was young or an elf-daughter. Maybe there was a bigger reason ...

I gasped and stared up at him. "It's you. You're the traitor in the Trust."

Shaul froze. His nostrils flared.

"When were you going to kill him?" I said. "The King? Before or after dead children from around the world piled up in the square?"

The guard before me shared a glance and wide eyes.

"Shaul?" the King said from the window. "What is she talking about?"

"Tell him," I said. "Tell the King who the Hateph is. Tell him who *she* is."

Shaul's face went blank, the calm look of a warrior. I knew that look. That's what my father looked like when he went into that place inside himself, that place where he could be the cold warrior.

"She?" the King said.

Shaul looked from the guard and back to me. "Not how I would have chosen to do it. But now is as good a time as any."

The Shield of the King lifted and threw me to the floor. With his left hand, he reached down to his belt and grabbed a dagger, pulling it and spinning it at once.

"My King! Duck!" I managed to scream.

The King's eyes bulged for a moment and began to dive to the side.

Holding the hilt, Shaul hurled the dagger sidearm. Just before it left his hand, I kicked out with both feet at his lower legs, throwing him off balance, but the dagger still spun toward the King.

The dagger blade sunk into the King's shoulder, and Yacob landed with a thud.

I turned over and scrambled away on all fours. Shaul cursed and swiped down with his sword, missing me by a milimitre.

The guard were moving by now, thrusting at Shaul with their spears. Shaul took a step back, swatted one spear away with his sword, and caught the second with a hand. He yanked that guard off his feet and stabbed him through the middle. While the second guard brought his spear back to slash, Shaul surged into the elf's body and pulled the blade from the dying guard to strike the second up and through the neck.

Both guard were on the ground, bleeding and dying, and I had made it out of range to a nearby couch, tumbling over for cover. Refa found a separate one to do the same.

All had happened within a couple of heartbeats.

Shaul turned around and started for the King, who was wounded and crawling away, trying to get as much distance as he could. The Shield took measured steps.

I needed a sword. Or a weapon of some sort. Both guard had a spear and a scimitar on their hips. I hurtled the couch, and Refa was already up and running toward the King. And he was closer.

"No!" I said.

Refa passed the dying guard and bent over to wrench a spear from one of them. He held it straight and in front of him and sprinted toward Shaul's back, leaning forward and yelling like a fool. "Ahhhh!"

I reached the guard in their own blood, leaned down, and grabbed both swords, barely slowing in my run.

Shaul pivoted mid-step and brought his sword around while he dodged. In such close quarters, however, Refa was able to slash across Shaul's back with the blade of the spear, but it glanced off the ancient iron shield. Shaul hacked at the shaft of the spear and cut it in two with his fine sword.

Shaul brought his sword up high and moved toward Refa for a killing blow. Refa froze with the broken spear in his hand.

I bounded between them with both scimitars in hand, landed, and took the full blow of Shaul's blade on mine. Shaul's sword bounced off, and he separated to get a better angle. In the split moment, I kicked and connected with Refa's chest. He tumbled backward.

"Get the King out of here!" I said.

Shaul recovered and attacked, his sword a blur.

I gritted my teeth and met his attack, deflecting, retreating. It took both scimitars spinning to keep his sword from skewering me or removing my head from my body. He was good. Too good. And I was too tired.

Just survive until the King can get away. Maybe he'll believe me now and get the Corps to the wall.

I stumbled over one of the guard bodies, and I fell.

Shaul's sword arced in a horizontal swipe, and I went with the momentum of my fall – the tip of his blade came within a finger's width of my throat. I arced backward, extending my arms and using my hands, holding the swords, to flip over.

My feet kicked out at Shaul, one of them striking his face. He gave another grunt and paused enough for me to turn completely over and land in a crouch, holding both scimitars.

Blood trickled from his nose. He wiped it with the back of his hand.

Refa helped the King in my periphery, lifting Yacob to walk toward the door.

Shaul stepped calmly over one of the guard, no longer gurgling or bleeding, dead. "This isn't a tournament."

He swung his sword. I deflected with one of my blades and struck forward with the other. He slipped to the side, and I missed. I backed to the left and back, trying to pull him away from the door.

Shaul glanced behind him, seeing the King and Refa crawling to the door to escape, and said, "That's enough."

Shaul swept aside both my scimitars with one strike and kicked out low, which I blocked with a knee. He followed with a backhand, his left fist connecting with my cheek. My head snapped to the side, and I lost my balance. Before I could catch my feet and recover, Shaul kicked with his other foot, slamming into my stomach. All the air left me in one forced exhale, and my feet left the floor. I went airborne for a moment and landed on my back, both swords clattering from my hands.

"You are good, Elowen." Shaul took a step toward me. "I'm impressed."

I couldn't catch my breath but reached out for the hilt of one of the scimitars, anything, to fight back. My fingers brushed the blade.

"Your father taught you well," he said. "But not well enough."

His stance shifted, angling the sword to run me through and pin me to the ground. My vision began to narrow from the lack of oxygen, the room fading.

"Ahh!" Refa's voice sounded from the right. I blinked over to see Refa fly at Shaul, a dagger flashing in the servant's hand, blood on the blade – the dagger that had been in the King's shoulder.

Shaul was good but not fast enough. He tried to turn to block with the sword but only managed to open his side to the dagger being plunged into his ribs.

The Shield of the King yelled in pain and frustration. He lifted his elbow and caught Refa under the chin. The servant yelped and tumbled away.

I rose enough to grab his sword hand with my left, pushing it up and away, and I punched him between the eyes with the heel of my right hand. He froze for a moment, then blubbered the next.

Which gave me time to yank out the dagger sticking in his ribs and shove the blade into his temple.

His face held only shock for a moment before falling over into the wall. I didn't have the strength to hang on to the dagger, releasing it when his body went limp.

I rolled over on my hands and knees, finally gasping and getting some air. Tears fell from my closed eyes. I groaned my breaths.

"Lady Elowen," Refa said, his own voice weak. "Are you all right?"

After a few more breaths, I could speak. "I … am … okay." I moved to a sitting position, my own shoulder against the wall. Refa knelt before me. The King slumped next to the door, blood down his side. "You?" I licked my lips. Blood on them. "I'm sorry I kicked you."

Blood trickled from Refa's mouth. He chuckled and rubbed his abdomen, wincing. "Might have a broken rib or two." He glanced at the dead Shield of the King. "But I believe I can forgive that."

I smiled back at him and sat up. I kissed him on the cheek. I had to wipe the blood from his face when I pulled away.

"What was that for?" he said, his face darkening.

"I wanted to do that earlier. Don't know if I'll get another chance. Thank you. I owe you one."

"I think we owe you," the King said from the door. He stood now but still leaned against the doorway. The blood down his arm and side didn't look good.

I turned to Refa. "You need to get the King to a physician. I'm sure there's one here in the palace?"

Both Refa and the King nodded.

The sun was barely peeking over the western wall of Jennah.

"Good," I said. "And get word to General Paavo or someone. Evacuate the Celebration. And get help to the northern city wall."

I willed myself to stand up. I swayed a bit, my jaw tightened, and I took a deep breath.

Refa stood with me. "What are you going to do?"

I bent down and pulled the old, ancient iron shield from Shaul's back. It wasn't as heavy as it appeared. I put my arms through the handles and slung them on my shoulders. I breathed easier now and walked over to the two dead guard. I knelt and took one of their helmets, a helmet from a dead elf, and after pushing back the hood of my covering, put it on my head.

I turned to face the King and Refa. "I promised I would stop this if I could. And someone has to be the Shield of the King. We seem to need a new one."

Refa frowned at me. "You're going alone?"

"I will do what I must." I grinned. "And I won't be alone."

With a final bow to the King, I walked out of the room.

CHAPTER

34

I ran back down the stairs and through the levels of the palace, exiting out the side again. In the courtyard, I jogged into the guest building. Passing through the lobby, I saw many of the other contestants sitting at tables. The woman, Mia, and Odger, the dwarf in a booth together. Julius from Kryus lounged in the corner, sipping wine.

All eyes turned to me, brows raising, and a few called my name.

I didn't answer and took the stairs up to the third floor, to my room.

I needed my sword.

I burst into my room and started to go back to where I kept it when I noticed my father's things sitting in near the door. In the last day and a half, someone had gathered his clothes and bags and brought them to my room. And his weapons.

There was a note on parchment.

I thought you would want these before you left. It was signed, Refa.

I could have kissed him all over again.

I rummaged through Father's bag and found long strips of cloth, part of our supplies for dressing wounds. Using the washbasin near my bed, I rinsed my wrists and face, removing the helmet of a dead elf for a moment to flatten my hair. I wrapped my chafed wrists with the strips of cloth. And drank some water from the pitcher.

Two daggers went into the leather belt. The throwing knives we had left, only five, went into different pockets on my tunic. I wore my sword, the one my father had made for me, and the scabbard. Grabbing one of the spears, I walked from the room and bounded down the stairs.

Claudim, the swordmaster and contestant in the Tournament from Jibryl, hovered at the door to the courtyard and glared at me. Others stood and watched me pass. Claudim slid over to block my way, so I paused at the door.

"That is the Shield of the King," he spat like an accusation.

I don't know what he saw in my eyes, but the glare softened.

Odger's voice spoke from behind me. "I would move out of her way if I were you, my friend."

Julius stood to my left and watched me, his face unreadable.

Claudim looked from the dwarf to me. My eyes narrowed.

He moved.

I walked through the courtyard and toward the stables. For a moment, I had the frightening thought that they wouldn't be there. I had been missing for more than a day. Would someone have moved them?

Their growls and whine met me before I saw them. I leaned the spear against the outside of the stall. Their snouts extended over the door.

"Zaran," I said. "Laila." I reached up and stroked each one across their cheeks. "I need you. Will you come with me?"

The war lizards snarled and bared their teeth. I took that as a yes.

I opened the wooden door and began putting the saddle on Laila. Zaran could run free.

"I missed you yesterday," his voice came from outside the stall.

I straightened and looked over Laila's shoulder.

Julius stood with his hands held behind his back. His sword was at his side. "We didn't get to finish our match. We were rudely interrupted."

I snorted. "You'll have to wait a little longer, I guess."

"When you didn't show, they assumed you forfeited," Julius said.

I began fitting the reins to Laila's head. "You fought Mia for the championship?"

"Correct," he said.

"And who won?"

"Mia is a master swordswoman."

I rolled my eyes. "But you won."

Julius inclined his head in a slight bow. He was champion once again. "Are you leaving the city?"

I finished with the strap on Laila's saddle. "No."

"Interesting," he said. "May I ask where you are going?"

"You need to get out of my way." I took Laila's reins and led her forward. Zaran snapped at Julius.

Julius glided to the side. "Of course."

Once out of the stall, I grabbed the spear and climbed up on Laila's back. The sahala shifted under my weight.

I sighed and looked down at Julius. "This has nothing to do with you. This is Jibryl. This is our problem."

"Ah," he said, moving to block me from leaving. Laila snarled at him. He didn't react. "And yet, this is the Kaila Festival, when Jibryl invites people from all over the world. There are people here from every nation. Every race. If it has to do with your rebellion, and that surfaces with the world at your doorstep, it becomes our problem, does it not?"

"And you care?" I asked. "About the children from all the other kingdoms and races? You? From Kryus?"

Julius' unreadable face broke into a grin that didn't touch his eyes. "Since I am here as a soldier, an officer, and a representative from Kryus, and from your urgency, it doesn't seem like I'll have time to filter out my people from the rest, then perhaps. We are not monsters, after all."

We're all monsters. You'll see.

"No, there isn't time," I said. "Yes, our rebellion will put all those children and the whole city in danger, and I'm going to the northern city wall to stop it. Me and a couple of war lizards. Hopefully, we can slow it down enough for the Corps to get there and protect everyone. Happy?"

His grin faltered.

I glowered at him. "Now, seriously, I've had a really critty day, and it doesn't look like it's getting better, so get out of my way, or I'll have Zaran tear your intestines from your body."

Zaran hopped back and forth like he understood what I said and would be overjoyed to comply.

Julius, the champion of the Kaila Tournament, hesitated and stepped aside, and extended his hand. Like I needed permission.

I wasn't asking. Grut-sucker.

I kicked Laila forward, and she raced out of the stables with Zaran right behind us.

We made our way out to the courtyard, yelling and voices behind us. I didn't slow or care. The guard scurried out of our way along the path to the front of the compound. The war lizards had a few days of rest, and the wind whipped my face while I rode Laila between the golden statues of the old Jibrylan heroes.

We approached the main gate. "Move! Make way!" I called, and my voice echoed in the vast courtyard.

The guard who gathered at the gate turned their heads and froze at the sight of two war lizards and me barreling toward them. I lowered my head, bared my own teeth along with the sahala, like I was one of them, and kicked Laila forward. I lowered the spear in my hand and pointed it in front of me.

The guard scattered and made way, screaming and yelling.

We exited the palace grounds and plunged into the Children's Celebration.

Music played to my right, children and parents dancing, noise and light and activity all around. Kids played games and laughed.

I pointed the spear up. Zaran and Laila roared, a horrifying sound that rose above the din.

People stopped dancing and singing, music screeched to a stop, and the people in the southern square began to run. While the war lizards were an advantage – along with their ferocity, I couldn't have made it this far this fast on my own exhausted feet – the chaos that ensued made it difficult to maneuver without injuring the very children I was trying to protect. Not and keep speed.

I pulled on the reins to more of a jog, directing us to the left, angling north, and we swerved back and forth, parents and children scurrying. Did some try to get in our way? I prayed to Ona to keep everyone safe.

We hugged the row of booths on the northern edge of the square, giving people some predictability in our movement, which worked. Customers and merchants gave us a wide berth. I kicked Laila back to speed.

Soon, we reached the main street and veered further left and north. With a glance to my right, the sun was now below the city wall, throwing the city into twilight and shadow.

The streets had already been sparsely populated, most congregating in the square, but those that remained had obviously heard or seen the chaos around me. They pressed themselves up against buildings or dove into doors and alleyways.

"Evacuate!" I yelled, waving the spear in my hand. "Get away from the northern wall!"

A few heard and began running south. Others stayed frozen. I hoped they listened. But why would they listen to some crazy elf-daughter with war lizards? They might have been running away from me more than anything else.

I came to the space between the city buildings and the wall, the brick street perpendicular to the main one through Jennah. I slowed Laila and pulled her to a stop thirty mitres from the wall.

It was quiet. I didn't see anyone. Scanning back and forth, no guard stood at the main gate. Zaran walked to stand next to us. He growled a low warning. To what, I don't know.

"Easy there," I said to him. His nostrils flared, and he shifted on taloned feet. "What do you smell?"

After patting Laila's neck, I swung my leg over and dropped to the street. Faint echoes of the remnants of the Children's Celebration carried from the square. I walked to stand in front of the sahala. Should I go through the gate? Where were the guard? Is this the right part of the wall? Bhelen could have been wrong. She could have misheard.

Or Shaul had been right. She misled me on purpose. There could be hundreds of secret ways into the city, hundreds of goblain armed in the city. And here I am like a fool. But then why would they need a giant? Or ...

The cobblestones vibrated underneath me. Just a single tremor.

Laila and Zaran both growled together.

Another tremor followed it, slightly stronger.

Then a noise traveled over the top of the wall, muffled. A cry. A low-toned sob. The cry grew louder and clearer, a sound of pain that made the war lizards flinch. I winced. The cry of pain changed into something else. More animalistic. More primal. A twisted scream became a bellow in the next heartbeat. The bellow sent a chill down my neck.

"What the crit is happening?" I breathed.

The next tremor shook the ground. Another came after, then another, like running, like a gallop.

The whole wall in front of us shuddered with a boom and moved toward us a bit, stones and dust falling from the top. With another sound of impact, the rock wall convulsed, and fractures like stone lightning wound their way up and down the grey masonry. But that was in a different place, a few mitres from the last one.

"Oh, great Ona," I said. "They're going to knock it down."

Break the system. Break it down. Starting here with the symbol of division and oppression, the wall. The instrument of segregation.

The wall buckled in a third place, still further down, with more cracks, stones, and bricks coming loose. Whatever waited on the other side bellowed again and sounded angry.

Once more, something hit the wall, and the old structure couldn't take anymore. Like a long scream of thunder, the wall exploded out toward me near the gate, thick stones arcing out in the air, and because other areas of the wall had been weakened, much of it crumbled down like an avalanche that had waited for a long time.

I brought my arm over my eyes to protect them and took a few steps back. Only small shards of stone made it to me. If I had been closer to the wall, however, the rain of bricks would have crushed the war lizards and me.

Turning back, a hundred-mitre section of the wall was gone, rubble.

A beast bounded through the cloud of dust and powder, five mitres tall with grey skin, a nose that extended into a thick trunk, and curved horns out of the forehead.

It looked like a hornoth, a giant creature from the plains to the north, but it lumbered forward like a human on two back feet, not all fours as usual. The tusks on either side of the trunk were shorter. It wore a loincloth, too, but I had never heard of a hornoth wearing clothes.

The eyes were not animal eyes. Intelligent eyes that glowed red. A chain hung around its neck, a red stone at the end of it, which also shone.

I gasped. The size. The stone. A bloodstone. "Gomondur."

The creature climbed over the rubble and stood between me and what was left of the wall, twenty mitres away or more.

Elves emerged from the dust cloud, as well, and I recognized the first one.

She hopped down from a pile of stones and met my stare. She shook her head. "Elowen." She wore my father's sword.

"Mother." I rested the butt end of the spear on the street with my left hand and drew my sword with my right.

Valez walked forward to stand next to the creature, the giant hornoth. He wore a sword, as well. His glare shot death at me. Other goblain dressed in only short trousers, perversely bare to the waist and barefoot, climbed through the rubble and began to form a line on either side of Valez and the hornoth creature. None wore a weapon. A bloodstone hung from each neck, smaller than the giant's.

Mother craned her neck and pointed at the shield on my back. "Is that what I think it is?"

"The Shield of the King," I said.

Her brows rose. "You had to kill him to get that."

I shrugged. "I had help."

"I'm sure," she said, her face now a frown. Did she know or guess of Bhelen's betrayal? "You've been busy."

I pointed at the were-hornoth with my sword. "As have you. What evil is this? Is that what you wanted with the giant? Is that what the bloodstone does?"

"It does many things," Mother said. "And much you don't know."

"I know you killed those children. The ones you said you saved? You used them to give these stones power. What have you done?"

"Fighting for my people," Mother said. "They are your people, too. If you fight us, you're fighting for a corrupt regime. You saved an evil king. He would do the same as us."

"Maybe," I said. "But you're not the one in a position to judge. Not now."

"And you are? You don't know all Jibryl has done. Natanel sheltered you. You know nothing."

"I was sheltered," I said. "But I know enough. Please. No one else needs to die. They're evacuating the Children's Celebration even now. The Corps is on its way. You can do this another way."

"There is no other way," she said. "It has to be like this."

I took a step closer. The war lizards snarled but stayed with me. "I just saved the King. Maybe he'll listen to me. You're right. I'm both. Jibrylan and Ruchali. I'll help you."

A hundred goblain now stood in a line, fifty on either side of Valez, Mother, and the were-hornoth. A hundred bloodstones.

"Things have gone too far, Elowen," she said. "If the Children's Celebration is evacuated, we'll move into the wealthy southern part of the city. We will have vengeance and blood tonight."

"Don't do this, Mother," I said. "Please."

Valez glanced from mother to me. "Hateph! We must begin."

The wizard lifted his hands waist high, his palms up, his fingers curled like claws. He closed his eyes.

The bloodstones began to glow red. All hundred of them.

"Get out of the way," Mother said. "You can't stop this."

I flourished my sword and twirled the spear. "I have to try. Or else innocent blood will be on my hands. I can't allow that. Even if it is alone, I will fight."

My mother's brow furrowed. Valez's eyes shifted and widened, looking beyond me.

"I told you before, Elowen," came the voice from behind me. "You're not alone."

My mouth dropped, and I looked over my shoulder. Mia walked up, her sword in her hand. That simple yet strange sword. Others emerged from the shadows to stand with me.

Odger winked at me and carried a round shield and a broad, thick sword. Claudim walked around me with his blade across his back. Julius followed him.

"What … what are you doing here?" I said.

We stood in a line against the goblain and the others.

"Julius said you might need some help," Mia said.

Julius shrugged and lifted his sword. "We were bored."

Odger scoffed. "Is that a giant? How lucky can we get?"

I met Claudim's eyes. He nodded at me.

"Are those … bloodstones?" Mia said.

My brows rose. "How did you know?"

Mia's face set, her eyes hard. "Long story."

"You seem to have a lot of those," I said. "Watch out for the wizard in the middle. He's a *solonayor*."

"Of course," Julius said. "We wouldn't be here if it were easy."

"Don't get too close to him," I said. "He can kill you with a thought."

"This is why I'm here." Mia gripped her sword tight.

"I've got the giant!" Odger said.

"Don't kill him," I said. "He's a Gedai, a slave, held against his will."

"*Don't* kill him?" the dwarf squealed. "How do you propose I do that?"

I shrugged.

"I make no promises," he said.

"Elowen …" Mia said like a warning.

Turning back to Valez and the goblain, the bloodstones all glowed bright crimson, the hundred goblain with red eyes now. My mother drew Qatar.

The elves arrayed against us began to contort, their bodies twisting, and they cried out in agony, a chorus of voices in pain. Limbs bent one way and then the other, like possessed by something unseen. Their skin began to change and grow fur. Spots appeared. Mouths and noses extended, becoming snouts like canines. Ears traveled up and expanded, hairy.

"Hyenas," Claudim said. "They're becoming hyenas."

He was right. Hands lengthened and fingers grew claws. But they didn't become full hyenas – half elf, half hyenas like the giant hornoth. Were-creatures.

"Were-hyenas," Mia said. "Can you taste the death in the air?"

I licked my lips. The air had become stale. Like the air in the cavern where they killed those children, sucked the life out of them.

"We only have to keep them busy until the Corps gets here," I said. "They're on their way."

The hyena-elves opened their snouts showed us sharp teeth.

"You sure?" Julius said.

I wasn't, and the look we shared told him. "Either way, I'm ending this now."

"*We're* ending this." Claudim crouched into a stance.

"Leave the wizard to me." Mia raised her sword in a front guard. It almost … hummed.

"Lady's choice," Odger said.

"Let's do it, then," I said through a clenched jaw.

Valez opened his eyes and smiled.

The giant hornoth roared and charged us. The hyena-elves followed.

CHAPTER

O dger raced forward with a war cry, his shield up, and straight at the giant hornoth.

"Zaran, Laila, go," I said, and like the trained battle lizards they were, they bounded away in different directions – Zaran to the right and Laila to the left – aiming for the wave of creatures coming at us.

"Circle up," Julius said. "Back to back. Four of us, one for each direction."

We moved without comment or argument. I stayed facing the north and what remained of the wall. Julius took one side, Mia the other, Claudim at my back.

Odger neared the giant hornoth, and the beast roared, reared, and lifted its arms, the stubby gray hands as fists, ready to crush the dwarf. Odger turned at the last possible second, the hornoth lowering his fists to slam on the cobblestones. The dwarf circled around to the side, changed directions, and rammed into the back hip of the hornoth, throwing the beast off balance.

Zaran flung himself into the hyena-elves. A handful went down in a tumble of claws, teeth, and screeches. Laila sprung high and landed on the chest of a were-creature, her back legs crushing and her teeth ripping when they fell together. Three others turned to attack her. She swung her tail around, knocking two away, and then bit into the third.

"Get ready," Mia said.

The hyena-elves reached us.

If we had an advantage, it was that the hyena-elves exhibited no organization beyond the feral, animalistic nature of their attack. They possessed the numbers and could have surrounded and arrived at once, but either they didn't understand or didn't care.

The creatures came in twos or threes, randomly and with clawed hands as strikes. I lowered into a firm stance and swept wide with the spear in my left hand, knocking one aside with the shaft and slicing another with the blade at the end. The sword slashed back and forth in my right hand at another that came close, cutting deep through the chest.

When the hyena-elves died, their red eyes went dark.

The swordmasters with me didn't talk. They wasted no effort. Julius danced back and forth in my periphery, carving through each one like a harvester with a scythe. The battle was chaos, no strategy but pure reaction and response, but Mia flowed from form to form, changing pace and rhythm in a symphony of death.

My body protested. I was already exhausted from the capture, my confrontation with Valez, my escape, and fighting the Shield of the King. Within a few seconds, my reactions slowed, and I had to will my arms to move, and my hands to grip the weapons. Tired. That would cause me to make mistakes and be vulnerable.

One were-hyena got past my defenses and raked claws across my left forearm. Another scraped my thigh. I scowled in concentration, forcing myself to focus, to watch for every detail from every angle.

The creatures were scattered around us, and the sahala roamed about, picking off one at a time like the hunters they were. Father would have been proud.

Odger continued to dodge and sprint; the giant hornoth twisted at the waist, spread its forelegs – arms? – and aimed its head at the dwarf. Odger spun out of the way and darted in, using his sword to open a deep gash on one of the beast's back legs. The giant hornoth rammed the ground with its forehead and horns, twisting and bellowing in pain.

I twirled the spear from one side to the other, smacking one were-hyena under the chin, slashing across the abdomen of a second. I stabbed another through the chest with my blade.

Dead and bleeding bodies sprawled around us. We had to be dwindling their numbers. Unless Claudim had fallen – and that wasn't likely; Julius or Mia would have adjusted to close the circle – we all still stood, fighting. We might make it out of this, maybe even alive.

Then one of the dead hyena-elves stood, blood pouring from the open wound in its chest. Its eyes, which had been dark a moment before, began to glow red again. The bloodstone shone brightly. Another creature resurrected and joined the first. And another.

Were they coming back to life? "What in the name of El?" Mia screeched.

"I see it, too," I said. Beyond the battle around us, Valez stood there, legs apart and shoulders slumped like he carried a heavy load, his hands like he gripped stone. He kept that creepy smile. I wanted to cut that smile from his head.

The bloodstones. They did more than I understood, Mother had said.

The once-dead were-hyenas joined the battle. The sound of ripped cloth came from beside me, and Mia grunted.

"Take their legs," Julius said. "They can't get very far without legs."

That was one solution, but there was more at work here. Valez transformed them and kept them alive with those stones.

Two leaped at me, one without an arm, and swiped at me with their claws. Lowering my head, I knocked the one-armed creature aside with the spear and cut through the neck of the other with my sword. While the latter bled out, I swung my sword back and hooked the chain on the creature's neck with the tip of my blade. With a swift jerk, the chain broke, and the bloodstone dropped to the ground and shattered in a burst of red light.

The hyena-elf spasmed, dropped to the ground, curled up, and began to transform again. The fur and claws disappeared. Within another few heartbeats, it was an elf again.

I batted away another were-hyena and removed the arm of a second before yelling, "The bloodstones! That's the secret. Remove the bloodstones."

The creature I had batted away came again, and I used the spear's edge like a surgeon and cut the chain from its neck.

"Odger," I cried out. "Cut the bloodstone from the neck!"

He glanced over his shoulder, frowned, and nodded.

While I cut back and forth, looking for opportunities to remove the stones and chains and even severing the leg from one hyena-elf, Odger sped toward and then around behind the giant hornoth. As the beast turned, the dwarf cut the back of its leg. The were-hornoth reared in pain. Without a sturdy leg, it began to fall backward.

Odger gave a burst of speed, coming all the way around to the front again. He hefted his shield, tucked it under his arm, and tossed it at the beast. The shield whistled, spun, and slammed between its eyes. The head snapped back; the beast fell over and landed. The ground shuddered.

The dwarf never stopped moving. He angled and jumped higher than I would have guessed he could and arced in the air to alight on the giant's stomach. Odger took a few steps and sliced the chain that held the bloodstone. The crimson stone went dark and flew in the air to clatter and spin away.

The giant hornoth began to quiver and shake, squealing in pain. Odger toppled from the giant and rolled over and down to the street. The were-hornoth's skin began to turn from gray to tan; the horns, wide floppy ears, trunk, and tusks shrunk within moments. Soon, the half-naked form of Goromund lay on the cobblestones, the gashes on his legs still bleeding.

The giant turned on his side and sobbed.

"Claudim's down," Mia said. "Form up."

I retreated a step, slashed down at a were-hyena, and now we were a circle of three around a wounded Claudim. Even with the giant out of the fight and a way to keep the were-hyenas from resurrecting, we were tiring and lost a swordmaster.

Odger stood alone without a shield, hacking at attacking creatures. Zaran and Laila were covered in scrapes and bleeding.

I could fall over at any time. I was so exhausted.

We had to finish this soon. Now.

Valez's smile had morphed into a grimace of effort and concentration. My mother stood beside him, Qatar in her hand, watching the death and chaos.

There were opportunities in the chaos.

"Julius," I said.

He glanced over his shoulder. In one move, I tossed the spear to him and then reached back and grabbed the shield on my shoulders, bringing it over my head, running my forearm through the straps, then smacking a hyena-elf in the head with it.

Julius snagged the spear in mid-air with his left hand, spun it, and brought it down on a creature, splitting its head with the blade at the end.

"I'm ending it," I said and ran forward, using the shield to protect against claws raking at me and slashing wildly with my sword.

"Elowen! Wait!" Mia's voice was weak behind me.

But it was too late. I was gone.

I passed Odger. "Help Julius and Mia," I told him.

The dwarf cut the leg off a creature at the knee and nodded, his legs propelling him back behind me.

"Zaran! Laila!" I cried out, and the sahala roared in response. They sounded so far away, but a second later, they approached at a run, one on either side of me, their snouts leaning forward.

Maybe if we rushed him, distracted him, gave him too much to concentrate on, I could kill him. I could end this.

I closed within ten mitres of the wizard, who glared at me. I sheathed the sword and grabbed one of the daggers, pulling it from my belt and throwing it in one motion. The dagger tumbled in the air, end over end, straight to Valez's heart.

The blade of Qatar stretched out and intercepted the dagger. My mother stood between the wizard and me. Now within five mitres, I grabbed and threw the other dagger with everything I had, stumbling and recovering in the attempt. Mother slapped that one away, as well, with my father's sword.

Zaran barreled in from the left, Laila from the right.

I removed my arm from the straps of the shield, gripped it with both hands, and hurled it at both Valez and my mother. The Shield of the King whirled through the air at my mother's face. Her eyes widened, and she raised Qatal.

The shield took her down, and she fell into Valez. He staggered to avoid her body.

This was my chance. He was distracted. I was close. Maybe I could strike him, kill him, wound him, stop him, or something. The sahala appeared on either side of me. With all the strength I had left, so little of it, I reached down to draw my sword.

My fingers grabbed the hilt, and I had the sword out when pain wrecked me, every milimitre of my skin, joints, and bones. My heart constricted in my chest. I spun on a heel, my sword spinning away, clanging among the stones, and I crashed to the ground in front of him. A step away.

So close.

Perhaps my attack had taken his attention and energy away, enough that the war lizards could get to him. But while I sobbed, a desperate choking sound, I turned enough to look. Zaran and Laila were also on the ground, writhing, and whining. He was sucking the life from them, too.

So close.

"Valez, stop it!" my mother screamed. Rolling my eyes in my head, she stood next to him, her sword at his throat.

He snarled at her, but the pain stopped. I could breathe, coughing and groaning. Zaran and Laila, however, still twitched.

Valez screamed at my mother. "Your weakness has cost us everything! Years of planning, gone, a failure."

"Weakness?" my mother said.

"Your love for your daughter, yes," Valez said. "Weakness. You should have killed her in the tunnels. Even better, you should have slit her throat the moment she emerged from the womb."

"Shut up!" Mother said.

"I should have never saved you," Valez said. "All those years ago, you promised that you would help us, that you would break the kingdom for good and lead us to something better. But you lied. I should have let you die."

"I am the Hateph!" Mother said. "I united the Knights of Truth when no one else could."

"And now, what will we have?" he said. "Nothing."

The skin of the sahala turned a lighter shade of green, their eyes sinking into their skulls. I stopped coughing and could move. Just a little.

"No," Mother said. "We will go and hide. It will take time, but we will return. Even stronger than before. Come with me."

"Your daughter knows all our secrets," Valez said. "We kill her. That's your price for failure."

"You don't have to," Mother said. "We can take her with us. Now!"

Valez scoffed. "I should have known better than to let an elfess lead us. Elfwomen are weak. I should have known …"

Someone yelled from the other side, away from Valez and Mother. "Elowen!" A woman's voice. Mia?

Mother twirled on a heel, swinging the sword. A figure vaulted me, half in shadow, and two blades met with a clang.

Mia's sword flashed when she attacked with smooth and efficient strikes. My mother had to retreat from the barrage, barely deflecting the human's aggressive moves. Mia's clothes were torn – scratches and claw marks along her shoulder, arm, and upper thigh. None of it seemed to phase her. Mia battled like the master she was.

Don't kill her, I tried to say. Only my lips moved. But who was I talking about? I didn't want either to die.

Valez turned and extended his hands toward Mia, his claws raking like he would tear the flesh from the body of my friend.

Nothing happened. Mia continued to attack Mother, unaffected. I heard that humming again. From the sword?

The wizard's face went blank. His mouth went slack for a tick of time, and he tried again. His hands, arms, and body shook.

Nothing.

Except … I swore the humming of Mia's sword grew louder.

Mia dove forward at Mother, slapping the blade of Qatar up, exposing Mother's chest.

I rolled to my side, reaching out.

Mia plunged her sword in between Mother's breasts, to the hilt, and jerked it back, blood sprouting from the new wound.

"No," I breathed.

Mother's eyes went glassy, and she crumpled to the ground.

Mia used her momentum to spin and leap toward the wizard, her sword raised high.

Valez blinked and drew his own sword, taking a step back to give space and divert Mia's first strike. Mia's face was relaxed but determined. She never slowed. Within two more moves, it was obvious. She was too good. Valez couldn't beat her.

In my periphery, Mother rose to her feet.

She was alive? How? I squinted at her. Something red shone from beneath her tunic, something that hung around her neck. A bloodstone.

Mother lifted Qatar, took three silent steps and drove the blade through Mia's back. Mia's body went straight and stiff, her head craning back. The blade of Qatar protruded from her stomach.

Mia gurgled something, and Valez rocked back and then toward her, stabbing her in the chest with his own scimitar, a look of glee in his eyes.

Both Valez and Mother pulled their blades from Mia's body.

Mia bent over, clutching her chest, the sword in her hand but hanging down. She staggered back, wavered, and fell. Right next to me.

Valez continued walking forward. Toward me.

"Valez!" Mother's eyes glowed red. "Come. Let's go!"

He growled and shoved her away with one hand on her chest. Her arms whirled, and she tripped over a stone at her feet and dropped.

Mia's eyes were empty. She stared at nothing. But the sword hummed. It vibrated through Mia to me. It called to me. Not with words, but a call nonetheless.

"We will leave," Valez said. "After I kill your daughter."

Mother screamed at him. But I couldn't understand the words. All I could hear now was the humming, a constant tone from Mia's blade, a singing note. I raised to my hands and knees.

Valez stood over Mia and me. My fingers crept over Mia's body and gripped the hilt.

Less pain in my body. More energy. A sudden burst of strength. My eyes bulged. I gasped.

Valez lifted his sword for a killing blow.

I raised to my knees in a flash, the sword almost pulling me up and toward the wizard, and I leaned forward. Mia's blade entered the wizard's body.

Time stopped. No sound. Even the humming and singing of the sword was gone. Like it had finished its mission.

Time began again. Valez dropped his scimitar. His face was a look of absolute horror. I fell to the ground, Mia's sword rolling from my hand. Light leaked from the fresh wound on Valez's abdomen.

I turned over and covered my face with my arms.

Something exploded. Everything went white. Then black.

CHAPTER

My shoulder shook. But not of its own accord. A hand. A child's hand? A fat child? The body odor filled my nostrils. I coughed and turned away. Not a child. A dwarf.

"Elowen," he was saying to me.

I opened my eyes. "Odger. What …?"

"It's over." He sighed. "You're alive. I wasn't so sure there for a second."

I started to sit up. Julius stood over me with his sword in one hand and the spear in the other. No tears on his clothes. And the blood on his face wasn't his.

"Easy now," Odger said.

"My mother," I said. "Where …?"

Odger's brow creased. "Mother?"

I pushed his hand away. A weak move, but he acquiesced. I started to stand. Odger helped me up, his strong hands at my waist and back. I swayed, he steadied me, and I turned around toward where the northern wall used to be.

I blinked the blur from my eyes. There she was. Lying still. The explosion had thrown her body, as well.

I trudged over, each step an effort, and I dropped to my knees next to her. I removed the soldier's helmet from my head and put my hand on her arm. "Mother," I whined.

A chain hung around her neck, but the stone at the end was no longer red and shiny. It was now a grey rock. Underneath, the wound in her chest poured blood and life on the cobblestones.

Her eyes fluttered open. "Elowen."

I killed her. When I killed Valez. I killed my mother. Tears dripped from my cheeks. "I'm sorry."

Mother grabbed my hand. "For what?"

I licked my lips. They tasted of blood and salt. "I don't know."

"Sounds like you have your answer." She coughed up blood. "You know. I dreamt about it, too."

"What?"

"Meeting you," she said. "What it would be like. The last time I saw you, you were a baby, my whole heart. I died that day. Twice over. I imagined what you would look like, what you would say. That you would run into my arms. Or maybe you wouldn't know me at first. We could become friends, and then I would tell you."

"Mother ..."

Blood pooled in her mouth, and she spit it to the side. "I did fight for you in those dreams. I fought your father, the one who ripped you from me and stole you away. I fought him over and over. Just to be with you. I imagined it a million different ways. And every time, I lived again. That part of me that was dead lived again.

"But I didn't imagine this," she said. "Never this."

I leaned over, the sobs coming from somewhere deep inside of me.

"Elowen." Her voice was weak now. "You were right. Your father and I, we were the same. But different, too. Both monsters. But not when it came to you. He wasn't a monster when he loved you, taught you, cared for you."

"No," I said. "He wasn't."

"And in the end, neither was I," she said. "Not with you. I should have killed you. That was the best strategy. We could have won. We could have broken the system. The one that never made room for us. The one that never protected us. We could have burned it all down. But I would have had to kill you. I couldn't do that. I couldn't be that monster."

Mother closed her eyes for a moment, and her breaths became ragged and short. Then she opened them one more time.

"No one planned for you, yet you're the best of us," she said. "The best of two monsters, two people, two nations. Whatever good we were, that's what you are. Remember that, Wen. My daughter. My love. Remember that."

Her breathing stopped. Her eyes stayed open but looked beyond me to the dark sky, to nothing. Her life was gone. Dead. This time for good. No magic to save her this time.

My shoulders slumped, and I closed my eyes.

I didn't know how much time had passed, but the sound of feet echoed in my ears. Boots slapping on the street. Lots of them. In a rhythm.

My eyes opened, and I sat up enough to gaze to the south. The Corps. Not the City Corps, the proper Desert army with shields, armor, spears, and scimitars. The High Marshall of the Corps, General Paavo, sat atop a horse at the front of the procession, high plumes of blue and red spouting from his helmet. A legion, a thousand soldiers organized by company and platoon and officers. The company commanders rode horses, too. Their armor, shields, and the blades of their spears glistened clean in the light of the three moons.

No wonder it took them so long to get here. Did they polish their swords, too?

Paavo stopped five mitres from the blood and carnage, and he raised a fist in the air. The Corps took position across the street, several rows deep, and halted behind him.

"Legion," Paavo called. His eyes marked the giant, sitting up now, and then the destroyed wall. He glared at the northern city beyond. "Prepare arms."

The front row of Corps troops pointed their spears forward to skewer something. Every soldier raised their shield.

Julius and Odger looked at me and back at the legion.

I sighed and placed the soldier's helmet back on my head. I lifted my knee to use it as leverage to stand. I bit my lip, straining to stand. The world spun and then righted itself. I plodded over to the sword on the ground. My father's sword. Qatal. I bent down, groaning from the pain in my side. What had injured my side? I didn't know. I held the sword.

After a few more stumbling steps, I found the shield. The Shield of the King. I cursed while bending down and grabbing it by the straps. I stood, stretching my back.

I turned on my heel, which took me some time, and walked forward, past the dead husks of the war lizards, past the body of Mia, past the sitting and crying Goromond, past the nervous Odger, past Julius with one brow raised, past Claudim on the ground with cloth bandages around his knee and leg, past the dead bodies and severed limbs. I never took my gaze from General Paavo.

I finally stopped ten paces in front of the High Marshall.

"What are you doing?" I managed to say.

Paavo frowned before answering. "We are entering the northern city."

"To do what?" I grunted.

"We will burn it down," he said. "The rebellion ends tonight."

I shook my head. "You're not going anywhere."

His frown deepened. "Says who?"

"Me," I said. "Elowen, daughter of Natanel, killer of assassins and wizards, protector of the King."

General Paavo glanced from me to the remnants of the wall and back. "The barrier is down. Look at what they've done with their perverse magic. We must root out every drop of rebellion from the northern city."

Julius appeared at my right. Odger at my left. Both of them held their swords in front of them.

"Are these the orders from the King?" I said. "To burn down the northern city?"

Paavo's lips became a line. "He did not say those words."

"Well, pray tell," I said, "what words did he use? What were his orders?"

"He ordered me to come and assist you, stop the rebellion, and protect the city," the High Marshall said.

I managed to glance over my shoulder at the carnage and death. Without falling over, which was a win. "Does it look like I need assistance?"

"Do you really want me to answer that?" Paavo said. "You can barely stand."

"I'll ask it another way," I said. "Do you see any rebels? Any still alive?"

He hesitated. "No."

"No," I agreed. "I don't need assistance, at least not with the rebellion. And if your orders are to protect the city, isn't the northern city part of Jennah?"

"I don't think that's ..." Paavo began.

I spoke through clenched teeth. "Answer the question. Is the northern city part of Jennah?"

The General's nostrils flared. "Yes."

"Are those people citizens of Jibryl?" I said.

His brows hooded his eyes. "Technically, yes."

"Not technically. Yes, they are." I lifted the shield in front of my chest. I bent in a crouch with Qatar in a low guard. "This is the Shield of the King. Those people are his subjects, too."

Claudim appeared on the other side of Odger, using the spear I had given Julius as a crutch. He held his sword out, as well. When our eyes met, he gave me a nod. I would have smiled if I had the energy.

"You are going to fight us?" Paavo shook his head. "A legion? The four of you?"

I swallowed. He was right. I could barely stand. A toddler could knock me over easily.

"I will protect the King's subjects," I said. "And the innocent among my people."

"I'm with her," Odger said.

Julius grinned. "Four against a legion? They'll write about this in history books. Children will read about it all over the world. Yes. Let's do it."

The General looked at Claudim. "You too?"

"I serve the King." Claudim gestured over at me. "And the one that carries his shield."

"But the barrier is down," Paavo said.

"Post your elves here," I said. "They can make sure no more rebels come into the rest of the city. After tonight, I don't think you'll have much of a problem."

General Paavo stared at me. "You would die for them? For the Ruchali?"

"You would kill the elfdaughter that just saved the King to burn them down?" I scoffed. "But yes. I will protect the King's subjects. *All of them.*"

Sometimes you have to repeat things.

Paavo took a deep breath and blew it out. "Very well. Officers, post two companies here, in front of the opening in the wall. Do not enter the northern city until I speak with the King. The rest of you take position along the main street between here and the palace. And Lieutenant Pincas?"

Lt. Pincas, the officer that showed us to the palace a few days ago, rode forward through the legion on his horse. "Yes, General?"

"Take these four back to the palace." Paavo dismounted from his own horse. "Take my horse and your own and get Elowen and Claudim to the physician."

"Sir?" Pincas said.

"You heard me."

"Yes, sir."

At that point, I fell to my knees, dropped my father's sword and the Shield of the King, and closed my eyes.

CHAPTER

T he next time I opened my eyes, light peeked through a slit in curtains at a window. Pillows and blankets surrounded me, along with a faint scent of soap. My mouth was parched.

"Thirsty?" said a voice from my left. I turned my head. That hurt.

"Odger," I said, my throat hoarse.

The dwarf held a mug in front of my face. I strained to lift my head; he put a hand on my neck and helped. After a few sips of strong herbal tea, he gently laid me down on the soft, silken pillow. Then he sat in the corner near the bed, his feet dangling over the floor.

Qatar, my father's sword, sat in the corner. Polished. That blade seemed to follow me. I was glad.

"How long?" I said.

"How long what?"

"How long have I been asleep?"

"Ah, yes. Just a day, two nights, and a day. It is morning now. You had no major injuries, so the physicians prescribed rest and fluids, they did."

"Where am I?"

"The palace," Odger said. "Guest rooms. You hungry?"

Was I? "Yes, but no. No food for now."

He nodded.

I focused on breathing for a few moments. "My mother? The Hateph? Is she … ?"

"Dead, she is." His gaze lowered, and he whispered. "And Mia."

The image of her fighting, attacking my mother, flashed in my mind. Mia and her sword.

"Laila? Zaran?"

The dwarf's brow creased. "Who?"

I had to wait a moment, gathering strength. "The sahala. War lizards."

"Ah." Odger nodded. "Yes, also dead."

"Go – the Gedai," I said. "What happened to him?"

Odger averted his gaze. "Well …"

"They killed him?" I started to get up.

He sat forward and put out his hands to stop me. "No, that's not it."

I rested on the pillow. "Then what?"

"They took him back into custody, or captivity or whatever," Odger said. "The Corps-elves were going to kill him, tainted goods and all, to their words, but then when the physicians said he could walk – and work – again, they decided to sell him. I felt so sorry for the gedder, when the King asked me what he could give me as a reward, I couldn't help it. I couldn't. The first thing that came out."

"You asked for the giant?"

"It just came out!" he said.

"Now he's your slave."

Odger clicked his tongue, leaning forward, speaking softly like someone might be listening. "I'm going to take him home, set him free, I will."

I smirked. "I thought you were called the Giantbreaker."

"I was!" he said. "I mean, that was my nickname. And proud of it, I was."

"You're gonna need a new name," I said. "The Giant-saver? The Lover of Giants?"

"Please stop," he said.

"Just giving some ideas." We chuckled for a moment. Chuckling brought pain. Then we were silent.

"Claudim?" I said.

"The physicians said he'll walk again, but with a slight limp," he said.

"Hmm." I took a deep breath through my nose. "I knew a great elf with a limp."

"You did, at that," he said. "Actually, Claudim has been active, even with that injury."

"He has?"

Odger shrugged. "Claudim told everyone about your speech to Paavo."

"I didn't have a speech." I glared at him.

"It was close enough. Even the Ruchali have begun calling you the Hero of Jennah."

"What?"

"Some must have seen you the other night," Odger said. "Seen you protect them from the legion."

I grunted. What to say?

"Claudim has kept Paavo and the Corps at their word," the dwarf continued. "They have kept position outside the northern wall. Or what was left of it. There hasn't been any more violence. Been pretty quiet, it has."

"Best we could hope for," I said. "And Julius?"

"I see him around, lurking. Even though he is trying to seem uninterested, I think he's waiting for you to wake up. But who knows?"

"Who knows," I agreed. "You'll tell him that I'm awake?"

"I will," he said. "Would you like me to right now?"

"Not now. Thank you."

"Okay. You want me to go? So you can rest?"

"Not unless you want to," I said. "You can stay. It's nice to have someone here. A friend."

He gave me a short nod and smiled at me through his bushy beard.

We rested in silence. But together. Friends.

* * * *

Later that afternoon, Odger left to check on the giant. I sat up in bed and ate. After a flatbread, fruits, and jerky, I started to feel better. Less aches.

A knock sounded at my door.

I adjusted the covers around my waist. "Enter."

The door cracked enough for Julius to stick his head in. "Am I disturbing you?"

I shook my head. "Please come in."

Julius made his way into the room, closing the door behind him. He sat in the chair Odger had used earlier. Julius' feet reached the floor.

"You're eating," he said. "I'm glad to see it. You're looking better."

I placed the half-eaten plate of food on the table beside the bed. "I'm ... feeling better."

Julius cocked his head at me. "Are you?"

"Well, physically."

"I understand." Julius straightened his robe around his thighs. "Much has happened. You lost your mother and your father within days. I can only imagine."

"Yeah," was all I could say.

"I'm very sorry," he said. "Truly."

"Thank you."

He gave a bow. "I came to tell you that Mia's son, Lucas, and the nurse, are leaving after the ceremony for your father in the morning. At least, I think that woman is a nurse."

"She's an aunt. Even I know that." I frowned. "I thought you were some sort of intelligence operative or something."

"I didn't ask," he said. "Not of national importance."

"But important enough to tell me," I said.

"I thought you would want to know." He set his hands on the arms of the chair. "The King is giving them quite the escort to the port in Dicash."

"Well, thank you for the information," I said. "And what about you?"

"What about me?"

"When will you leave? I'm surprised you're not gone already."

His face went blank. "I will also be leaving tomorrow. This has been quite interesting. More than I thought before I made the trek. To think I almost didn't come this year to the Tournament."

"You weren't going to come? You're the champion."

"True," he said. "I didn't think there would be much of a challenge, to be honest."

"And was there?"

"Was there what?"

I rolled my eyes. "A challenge, grut-sucker."

Julius paused and looked away before meeting my gaze. "At the Tournament, no."

"Wow," I said. "You're so kind."

"I mean no disrespect," he said. "Mia was very good. A master, assuredly, especially for a human. Of course, I didn't get to finish my match with my most compelling opponent."

I gave a short laugh. "You think I would have been able to beat you?"

"Not beat me, necessarily, but you have a certain knack for finding great trouble. Or for creating it. I'm not quite sure which. I would have been interested to see how that match went."

"And outside of the Tournament? Was there a challenge?"

"I fought against a rebellion of monsters and wizards and giants," he said. "Well worth the trip."

"I'm glad we could entertain you. Anything of national importance?"

"Definitely, much to put in a report." He smirked. "Also, I got to see you in action. You have great potential. More than anyone I've seen in centuries."

I took a moment before speaking. "No one here believes that. They never have."

"Because you're an elfess?" He dismissed the idea with a wave. "The thinking of your priests and leaders is ludicrous in the extreme."

I raised a brow at him.

"You know it's true," he said. "To exclude half the population from access to leadership and other positions of value is like cutting off your own leg and being proud of how you hop around. Ludicrous."

I laughed. Then shut my mouth and covered my lips with my hand.

"At any rate, your father didn't believe those things. Or else he wouldn't have trained you."

My smile faltered. "That's true."

"I saw him fight in a match years ago. In his prime, *he* would have given me a challenge."

I had to muster the courage to say, "Maybe even after his prime."

"Possibly." Julius nodded. "At any rate, I mean to say you have learned much. But you are still young and have much to learn if you will continue your training with another master."

I paused. "What are you saying?"

He frowned. "Only that you have immense potential. You beat masters while but an elfdaughter. There may be … others that could continue your training."

"I don't know," I said. "I … don't know what to do now. Where to go."

Julius stared at me a moment. "The good news is this," Julius said. "You don't have to know today. Just rest. Get better."

He stood and walked toward the door.

"Oh, and I'm not worried too much about what you will do," he said. "No one has been able to stop you from finding trouble. I don't believe they will in the future, either."

"You really believe that?" I said.

Julius shrugged. "I've only been around you a day or two. What do I know?" He opened the door. "Be well." Then he left, closing the door behind him.

CHAPTER

"It was a pleasure to meet you, it was," Odger said. "And fight with you."

I leaned over and took both of his hands in mine. "Me, as well. May Ona bless you."

The ceremony for my father earlier that morning had been small and simple in the palace. I had said my goodbyes. But they had transported his body to the military tombs outside the city with a parade of Desert Corps. The city had been quiet and somber.

Now, we stood at the main gate to the palace, a contingent of Desert Corps waiting out in the southern square. The square was empty of booths or merchants. The gray morning light lay over the city. I wore a simple tunic, trousers, sandals, and a shawl over my head. Qatar hung from my hip.

Odger's head swiveled, scanning the area, and drew closer to me. He whispered, "If you ever have the need, call on me. Jurgen is difficult to find, and dwarves are very suspicious people, they are. It can be very dangerous to visit, you understand." He frowned and rubbed his beard. "Just surrender to the first dwarf you see."

"Surrender?"

"Yes. Definitely. And offer to clean their boots and do housework for a time." He looked up at my glare. "On second thought, that last part's not necessary. But do make an official appeal to King Tollusk. He will know how to find me, he does. Most of the time." His teeth showed in a wide smile.

I grinned. "I will."

With a last shake of my hands, he turned away.

A shadow fell over me, and I straightened to look up. At the giant. "Brone."

The Gedai bowed. He didn't wear any chains, only simple clothes. Large clothes. "Lady Elowen. This is our goodbye."

"It is," I said. "Ona's blessings on your journey with the dwarf."

"Thank you," his voice rumbled.

It was my turn to speak softly. "Will you tell him your name? Your real name?"

"If he asks," the giant said. "And if he keeps his word."

"I believe he will."

"We shall see," the giant said. "Farewell."

I inclined my head to him.

Odger and Goromund left the palace complex.

I turned and froze. Mia's son, Lucas, and his aunt Shallam. Ten Corps-elves stood in a line behind them, and several of them held bags and cases. A small cart with two horses waited behind the soldiers. A body-sized wooden box lay on the small cart.

Lucas held one item, long and thin and wrapped in white cloth. The shape was unmistakable. A sword. Mia's sword. It didn't hum now. At least, if it did, I couldn't hear it.

The boy glowered at me, his light brown eyes piercing. Shallam scowled.

I bent low at the waist. "Lucas. I know you hear this all the time, but your mother was a great woman. A hero. Many would have died if she hadn't come to the wall." I took a deep breath. "I'm so sorry. She was my friend. At least, I think we were friends."

Lucas hugged the wrapped sword to his chest. A lock of his black hair fell into his face.

Shallam stood behind the boy and put an arm on his shoulder. "Mia spoke highly of you. We are … proud she fought the battle against the wizard."

I nodded and turned to Lucas. "Is that your mother's sword?"

When Lucas didn't answer for a few moments, Shallum said, "It is."

"It is a special sword," I said. "It made all the difference. I'm glad you have it."

Lucas sniffed. "I'm taking her sword back, but I'm not keeping it. My da and I will take it to the Tree and back to the Creator."

"Oh." Something about their religion? I didn't know humanity very well. "Okay." I peered at Lucas. "You know, your mom invited me to your home. I'd love to learn more about her. She said she had lots of stories."

The boy's eyes narrowed. He might have been ten or twelve, but in that moment, he seemed like an elf with the age. "I don't want you to come. Ma fought for El, for what she believed. That was her right. And one day, it will be mine." He bared his teeth. I flinched. "But don't come to my home. Don't come to Veradis. I don't ever want to see you again."

Lucas, the son of Mia D'Alor, pulled from Shallam's arm and walked forward to follow Odger and Goromund out of the palace gate.

I stood straight.

Shallam watched the boy go and sighed. "We have a long road ahead of us. I wish you well, Lady Elowen. I will pray that El gives you peace one day."

I didn't respond. She grinned, sadly, and strode forward, the soldiers following. The cart with Mia's body on it passed me.

I stared after it. Alone.

Someone cleared their throat behind me.

I turned and relaxed. Refa stood there, but his servant garb had changed, more formal.

"Good morning, Lady Elowen," he said.

"Good morning." I pointed at the uniform. "What is this?"

"I have been promoted," he said. "I am now one of the Royal Master Servants."

"Is that good?"

He chuckled. "Very good. Better food, at least."

I smiled. "I'm glad. You deserve it. I missed you."

Refa's smile faded. "Been busy. The King has been busy, so …"

"So that means you've been busy."

"That is correct," he said. "I would have come if I could, I swear to you, but I knew Odger and Julius were keeping you company."

"Odger, at least," I said. Where was Julius? Why wasn't he here to say his farewells to Odger and Mia's family?

"Speaking of my new duties, I have been sent for you."

"You have?"

"Yes," he said. "Once you are done here, the King commands your presence."

"Commands?"

"Those were his words," Refa said.

I looked over my shoulder at the people leaving the palace, Goromund's head and shoulders bobbing high over everyone else's. "I think I'm done here." I faced Refa. "Let's go."

Refa turned and led the way back to the palace proper, past the golden statues, taller than the Gedai, up the broad steps into the entryway. He didn't lead me to the stairway up to any of the meeting rooms but continued forward.

Other servants passed us. They came to a complete stop and bowed while I passed. What was happening?

I followed Refa to the throne room, where twelve guard stood outside the door, six on each side. Refa halted outside, as well.

"This is as far as I go," he said. "The King and the Trust are waiting for you."

"The Trust?" I squeaked.

"Yes."

I grunted when my stomach clenched. I took a deep breath through my nose and walked forward. Two guard opened the door to the throne room.

I entered.

It was as I remembered from only a couple of days before, although it might have been another lifetime.

The King sat on his throne up on the dais. The Trust stood on the floor below him – Paavo on one side, Fahim and Aiken on the other, making room for someone to approach the King.

For me.

I put my hand on Qatar's hilt and strode forward. When I reached the King, the Trust next to me, I knelt before him. "Your Majesty. I'm glad to see you are well."

Yacob's left arm was bent and in a sling across his body. "Thanks to you, I am alive and well. Rise and stand before me, Elowen."

I stood, making sure I kept my shoulders back. Paavo's face was blank as usual. Fahim glowered at me like I had burned down his house. Aiken's lips curved in a slight grin.

"The kingdom owes you a debt," the King said. "You and Natanel. You exposed an assassin here, among my Trust, and defeated him. You protected our sacred city from abominations and rebellion."

"I had help," I said.

"Yes," King Yacob said. "You did. And we have honored those heroes as much as we are able. We all need help, Elowen. That is the purpose of this Trust. Even the King can't run the kingdom without assistance."

"Yes, sir," I said.

"You have done much, suffered much," Yacob continued. "More than anyone could have expected, especially from one such as you."

"Such as me, your majesty?"

"An elfess. The daughter of a traitor," the King said.

I lowered my head. "I understand."

"You have proved yourself superior, and performed impressively," the King said. "Endured such grief. But for the good of the kingdom, at a moment of great crisis, I must ask of you one more service."

I frowned. "Service?"

The King nodded at Paavo. The General walked up the dais to the side of the throne. He bent down and lifted something.

The Shield of the King.

Paavo stepped down from the dais and stood before me with the shield in both hands.

"Elowen," the King said. "I admit, we were skeptical when your father brought you. But at every turn, you proved yourself worthy. You fought well in the Tournament. You protected the Royal Family in the Arena. You escaped capture by the goblain. You protected me once again here in the palace. Then you stood against the monsters and rebels at the wall, even your own mother, to protect the city during the last night of the Kaila."

I was also ready to fight a legion of Desert Corps. He didn't mention that one.

"At every moment, you could have run," the King said. "You could have quit. But you didn't. You fought for Jibryl, for the children of other nations, risking your life."

The King leaned forward and squared his shoulders. "Elowen, daughter of Natanel, I call upon you to be the Shield of the King like your father before you."

Paavo raised the shield and offered it to me.

I frowned and looked from Aiken to Paavo to Fahim, the only one who showed his displeasure.

"You're serious?" I said.

King Yacob smiled. "I am."

"Everyone agreed to this?" I said.

"There has been consent from every member of the Trust," the King said. Even Fahim? The elf didn't make a sound.

Like my father before me. A Shield of the King. A hero of the kingdom.

"But why me?" I said.

"I told you." The King's smile weakened. "Your actions over the last few days have proven your value to our kingdom."

"My value?"

The King paused before continuing. "You've been in contact with the goblain, seen their secrets. That is power. More power than a sword. We can root out the goblain rebellion once and for all."

"And find the other wizards," Keeper Fahim spat. "There must be more. We will find them."

"While we rebuild the wall," Aiken said. "I have the construction crews already hired. Once the King releases the gold from the treasury."

My chin dropped for a tick before I spoke. "Rebuild the wall?"

Paavo said, "You can't expect us to station a legion indefinitely to protect the citizens of Jennah from those people."

"I told you before, General," I said. "*Those people* are citizens of this city, too."

"We must maintain order," General Paavo said. "Keep the people safe."

"With your help, Elowen," the King said. "We can end this rebellion. Then all will be safe. Everyone."

I stared at the shield again.

"Do I have to point out the unprecedented moment you are in?" the King said. "You are the first elfess appointed as Shield of the King in the history of Jibryl. And the youngest elf to have the honor. Take the shield, Elowen."

This was the dream. My father had tried to push me to education, but my dream was to be a warrior for my home, for the kingdom, to be a great hero like Selina the Brave. I forced my way to Jennah. I lost my father, my mother, Laila, and Zaran, a new friend in Mia. All for this. All to be that hero, that elf I imagined – a warrior like my father.

As Shield of the King, I would have power. Real power. Power to change things, to help people, to do what my mother dreamed. To transform the system from the throne in the name of the King. I could learn to play the game of politics, the strikes and forms of manipulation, and national power, all for the good of others.

I could be my father and my mother. I just had to take the shield.

I glanced over at Fahim, then Aiken. Paavo held the shield, arms outstretched, waiting. I stared up at the King. Elves that were masters at the game. I had beaten masters before.

We are all monsters, Elowen. You'll see.

Be the best of us. Don't waste this, Elowen.

I bowed to the King. "I am sorry, your majesty. I cannot accept."

Every elf went still, their faces in shock. Even Fahim, the priest. My words hung in the air like an enraged war lizard no one would touch.

The King finally spoke. "You misunderstand. This is not a request. This is a command. From your King." His quiet voice carried threat and danger.

"Has no one rejected the offer before?" I said.

"No," the King said. "Not in thousands of years. Not since the First King Muhid created the position."

"Then I don't need to point out what an unprecedented position we are in," I said.

King Yacob's scowl mirrored Fahim's.

Aiken shifted his weight from one foot to another. "Are you actually saying you won't be Shield?"

I put my hands behind my back. "I am."

Paavo lowered the shield, bringing it close to his chest. "Can you tell us why?"

I scanned the elves around me, the most powerful elves in the kingdom. "I would take the Shield with every intention of changing things, to see the Ruchali treated with dignity. To tear down the rest of that stupid wall. To save the children you take from their mothers and kill, the ones you call cursed."

King Yacob narrowed his eyes at me. The others looked away.

"But none of you want those changes," I said. "You would fight to keep a system that treats elves like animals and kills children. Because it gives you power or makes you money. Or it makes you feel superior. Or perhaps you actually feel you are right. Either way, I would have to fight you.

"And like the Tournament, I'd have to fight by your rules. This means that to do what is right and make changes, I'd have to learn to fight like you. I'd have to become you. And if I became you, nothing would really change at all, would it?"

All four elves, the King and his Trust, glared at me like they would kill me if they could.

"My father warned me before we left. He begged me not to come. Because he knew this was not my path. He wanted to keep me from it. That was why he retired when I was born. And in his memory, to honor him, I must refuse to be the Shield of the King. I don't know what consequences there are, but that is my decision."

I lowered my head.

Paavo stepped aside, holding the shield at his side. "You will join the rebellion? The Ruchali like your mother?"

I shook my head. "No. That is not my path, either."

"Then what will you do?" Aiken said.

I shrugged. "Not sure. Find my path."

"And what is your path?" the King said.

"Don't know," I said. "I'll know it when I find it. Maybe I'm already on it. Maybe this is the first step."

Paavo shook his head. "The question is – what will we do? Execute her?"

"Put her in the dungeons?" Aiken said.

"Flog her openly for her heresy," Fahim said.

The King raised his hand, the one not in a sling, and the Trust fell quiet. "She is right about one thing. This hasn't happened before. There is no precedence."

"I have a possible solution if it pleases the King," I said.

Yacob sighed and waved at me. "If you must."

"Who knows you tried to appoint me as Shield?" I said.

The elves exchanged glances.

"No one," Aiken offered.

"Then no one needs to know," I said. "I won't tell anyone. And if you're looking for someone to honor, someone with more experience, I would suggest Claudim."

The elves pondered, rubbing beards and frowning.

"I did suggest that earlier," Aiken said.

"You would keep that secret?" the King said.

I nodded. "You could tell people that you brought me in to commend me. Then I will disappear. You have my word."

"Your word?" Fahim said.

"Yes," I said. "You punish me, the elfess that saved the city from the rebellion, you might have a bigger crisis than you have now. Some are calling me a hero, I hear."

Paavo frowned at me. "You say you don't want to play the game, but you play it well."

That would be the problem. "Thank you," I said.

"Very well," the King said. "We will consider Claudim. And you will keep this meeting quiet. This conversation doesn't leave this room."

I put a hand on my father's sword and bowed low. "Yes, your majesty. Thank you."

"If you go back on your word," the King said. "Then you will be a traitor. Like your mother. You will be an enemy of the kingdom."

"I understand."

I bowed once more, turned on my heel, and walked from the throne room.

Refa still stood outside of the throne room.

"Walk with me." Once we were out of earshot of the guard, I said, "I need you to do some things for me."

"Yes, Lady Elowen. Anything."

CHAPTER

The guest quarters were empty. All of the contestants had left, the last of them today, and the quiet struck me strange the first time I returned since the battle at the wall.

I gathered some things from my room. Not everything. Only a bag with clean clothes, my personal effects, and a short bow with a quiver. Qatar hung from my belt.

Refa waited for me just outside the guest quarters. He held the reins of a horse. Leather satchels were attached to the saddle. Refa's eyes were red.

It was goodbye.

My shoulders slumped and something caught in my throat. I walked over to tie the canvas bag and quiver on the saddle, and I hooked the bow over the pommel.

Then I turned to Refa, extended my arms, and embraced him.

It was a scandalous act, an elfess hugging an elfson, a lady with a servant. Fahim would have called it heresy or something. I didn't care.

Refa embraced me back.

I pulled away and smiled at him. "Thank you."

"My pleasure to serve, my lady."

"No, not as a servant. As a friend. You are my friend."

His jaw clenched. "I am. Always."

"Good."

I touched his arms once more and turned to the horse.

"Where will you go?" he asked.

"I have an idea," I said. "I need to get stronger if I'm to stand for what is right. And I don't think I can do that here."

Refa nodded. "And will you return?"

"I don't know," I said. "I hope so."

I climbed into the saddle.

"But if I do return." I looked over at the palace. "I don't think they'll like it when I do."

"They may or may not," he said. "But I will be glad to see you again."

"As will I. Ona's peace to you."

Refa bowed. "And to you."

I spun the horse around and rode away toward the main palace gate.

I didn't know what time he had left, only that he was gone, as was his horse from the stables. I would get out of the city and possibly catch him on the road north, assuming he was going home. Refa was supposed to give me a map.

I started to open the satchel on my right, twisting in the saddle, and ...

"You rejected their offer?" he said.

I jumped, almost out of the saddle. "Julius."

The elf smiled at me. He sat on his own horse, a tall and majestic black animal. He inclined his head to me.

"What offer?" I said. "I don't know what you're talking about."

"That's fine. You don't have to answer. They would be fools if they didn't. Well, more foolish than they already are. And, of course, you rejected them. You are gifted at causing trouble, after all."

I didn't answer. I just stared at him.

"Enough trouble that you need to leave," he said. "They may have promised many things, but it is not safe for you here. You may be the hero of Jennah, but that won't protect you from a dagger in the shadows."

I still didn't say anything.

Julius adjusted the reins of his horse. "I must warn you, however. If you come with me, what's ahead might be even more dangerous than staying here."

"But you will train me?" I said.

"If that is what you want."

"You said I have potential but that I had a lot to learn." I walked my horse closer to him. "I want to continue my training. Get better."

"Why? Why do you want to get better?"

I thought of Mia, of her sacrifice at the wall. "So I can always be free to fight for what I believe in."

Julius barked a laugh. "In this world, that is the most dangerous path of all."

"You asked me why."

"I did."

I leaned toward him in the saddle. "What about you?"

"Me?"

"You said I'm good at finding trouble."

"Or creating it," he added.

"You want me to ride with you? A troublemaker?"

His eyes sparkled. "Definitely."

"Then it's settled," I said. "Which way will we go?"

"Back to Kryus," he said. "I have already begun to gather others there with the potential to be great warriors, maybe even something greater still. That is where we will train. And possibly finish our match."

"I would like that," I said. "So we'll be going through the Firestone Fields to the northern mountains?"

"And the Remana Pass."

I raised an eyebrow. "There might be bandits and trouble on the way."

He placed his hand on the hilt of his sword. He smiled wide, his eyes fierce. "We can only hope."

THE END

Acknowledgements

To my Becca: My wife, my friend, my adventure partner. As always, your support has been invaluable.

To my three amazing kids: Thanks for being sounding boards and giving input. Blessings on all your creative endeavors.

To Word Weavers and Serious Writer organizations: Both groups have shared invaluable information and continued to be friends and family to a goofy author like me.

To Kent and Yorkshire Publishing: It's been such a pleasure to work with a great company and better people.

To God, without whom nothing good is possible.

For more information on MB Mooney, check out his website www.mbmooney.com and his YouTube channel, Great Stories Change the World.

MB Mooney believes Great Stories Change the World, and he loves to live and tell great stories. In the 2nd grade, Mooney was bored and getting in trouble, so his teacher said, "Why don't you write me a story?" He's been writing science fiction and fantasy stories ever since. Check out his YouTube channel, Great Stories Change the World, for reviews and tips on writing. MB Mooney lives in the Atlanta, GA area with his amazing wife, three creative kids, and a mischievous dog. You will often find him fueled by coffee and rocking out to heavy metal when he writes.